Courting
an Unexpected Desire . . .

"Why nothing, Charles. You know how young men are—"

His frown grew. Of course he knew.

Arabella informed him that the gentlemen came regularly to tea at Hedgwick Hall; or, rather, they came to visit and stayed to tea.

"Oh, they do, do they?" Charles snorted.

"Yes." Miss Ansley giggled. "Grandmama says if they came any more frequently, she would have to build a wing on the house for them!"

"What?"

Arabella glanced at him sideways and smiled. "She is just joking, Charles," she said.

"Well, I don't think it's very funny!" He was staring straight ahead, glaring at the road.

Arabella looked at him in surprise.

"Why, Charles!" There was a teasing grin on Miss Ansley's face. "If I did not know you better, I would almost believe you are jealous!"

D1153805

Books by Judith Nelson
from The Berkley Publishing Group

BEAU GUEST
LADY'S CHOICE
PATIENCE IS A VIRTUE

Instructing Arabella

Judith Nelson

JOVE BOOKS, NEW YORK

This book is for Roberta,
who introduced me to Max and Yoda,
and for Michele,
who first made the works
of Georgette Heyer
known to me.

INSTRUCTING ARABELLA

A Jove Book / published by arrangement with
the author

PRINTING HISTORY
Jove edition / May 1992

All rights reserved.
Copyright © 1992 by Judith Nelson.
This book may not be reproduced in whole or in part,
by mimeograph or any other means, without permission.
For information address: The Berkley Publishing Group,
200 Madison Avenue, New York, New York 10016.

ISBN: 0-515-10847-2

Jove Books are published by The Berkley Publishing Group,
200 Madison Avenue, New York, New York 10016.
The name ''JOVE'' and the ''J'' logo
are trademarks belonging to Jove Publications, Inc.

PRINTED IN THE UNITED STATES OF AMERICA

10 9 8 7 6 5 4 3 2 1

❧ 1 ❧

"Sir Rupert!

"Sir Rupert, stop that!

"Stop that, sir, this instant! These are not the actions of a gentleman, sir, and I demand that you—

"SIR RUPERT!"

Charles Carlesworth, brought suddenly awake by the rising shrillness of an obviously nearby—and obviously upset—female voice, sat up abruptly. He shook his head, trying to orient himself following this rude awakening. One hand automatically brushed leaves from his coat while the other smoothed back the auburn locks his vigorous head shaking had draped across his forehead. For a moment he could not place where he was, or why he was lying on the ground on this warm summer day. Above him piled-high clouds drifted across a deep blue sky; at his head was one of the tall, thick hedges used as fences in this part of the country; near at hand a book and the remains of his luncheon provided his answer. He'd eaten, grown sleepy, and given in to the urge to laze, closing his eyes and drifting off to the gentle rumblings of a rambling bee. It was so seldom he took the opportunity to do nothing in this pleasant way; looking after his grandfather's lands and pursuing his interest in the ancient Greeks usually fully occupied his time.

When he'd left High Point, his grandfather's chief and favorite estate, early this morning he'd chosen the path along the cliffs because so few people usually came that way. Charles had thought he could depend on the isolated area to grant him an entire day without interruption. The angry voice on the other side of the hedge proved him wrong.

"Sir Rupert!" It was evident the voice belonged to a young lady; the energetic and vociferous way in which she berated her

1

companion suggested she was a young lady with excellent lungs. "You despicable cur! You should be ashamed of yourself, sir! Ashamed!"

Not one to shirk his duty, Charles heard her words with no more than one regretful glance toward his book and a soft sigh for the loss of his solitude before springing to his feet. Listening once more for the lady's voice, he allowed it to guide him as he sought a weakened spot in the thick hedge that separated them, determined to rescue her and do battle on her behalf. With heroic disregard for the new coat that had arrived just that week from London, and with only an occasional *"Ow! Ow! Ow!"* to mark the prickly hedge's heroic attempt to bar his passage, Charles barreled through the branches.

By the time he had pushed his way to the other side he was sucking a particularly nasty cut on his thumb made by one of the hedge barbs, and he had acquired a certain speed. Emerging from the hedge with what to the uninitiated might have looked more like a suspicious stagger than a hero's swagger, Charles was not able to stop as quickly as he would have liked, and he ran headlong into the lady he had come to rescue.

"Oof!" said the lady, bouncing off him onto her backside, where she lay, her body supported by her elbows, blinking bemusedly up at him. She was a rather small lady, he saw, and one who looked quite startled at both his sudden appearance and her current position.

"I say—" Charles, appalled, stopped sucking his bleeding thumb and hurried forward to pick her up, glancing about to see if he might locate the despicable Sir Rupert.

Unfortunately, the lady misunderstood his good intentions. Before he could reach a hand down to her Miss Arabella Ansley, knowing the attack of a lunatic when she was the object of it, jumped to her feet and began beating her assailant with her parasol, all the time berating him in a way that made Charles, astonished by the blows raining upon his back and the arms he now held protectively in front of his face, wonder if perhaps it was the missing Sir Rupert, and not the virago before him, who was to be pitied in whatever had passed between the two moments earlier.

"How dare you!" Arabella hissed, wishing she held a sword in her hand, and not this little piece of wood and lace that even now was showing the worse for wear for having been brought rapidly down no more than a dozen times on her attacker's slim shoulders.

Arabella's father had taught her to fence one winter in Spain, when she was thirteen. He had said rather enigmatically at the time that it was a skill he thought she might have use for—later. He had, as he so often did, proved right.

Because of that, and because she enjoyed the sport so, her father had continued to fence with her over the years. But when he had deposited her in her grandmama's care three weeks ago in London, he had most straightly adjured her not to lift a sword—or even the neat little walking stick that held a blade that he had given her on her fourteenth birthday—while she was in England.

People would not understand, he had told her, and then, seeing that something in her eyes that he always read when no one else could, he had thoughtfully removed the walking stick from her luggage before sending her off with her grandmama.

"Just removing temptation, my dear," he had said, that mocking light in his eyes that made many people dislike him, but made her like him well. If he were here now . . .

Arabella redoubled her attack on her attacker. If her father were here, he'd cut the sniveling wretch into little pieces; he'd make minced meat of him; he'd—he'd—

"Knock *me* down," Arabella panted, adding a kick to her well-aimed parasol blows. "Running around the countryside like a madman, attacking defenseless females—it isn't to be borne! In the king's England, too! It is outrageous! Villainous! Shame on you, sir! Shame! Shame! Shame!"

Since each "shame" was accompanied by a sound whack upon his person, Charles was busy defending himself and could not for several moments even begin to make it clear to the small fury before, behind, and beside him that he wished her no harm; that he had, in fact, been coming to her rescue; and that he was not in the habit of attacking young ladies, or in being mistaken for such an attacker, thank you.

It was only when Miss Ansley's parasol, to her obvious disgust, broke in two that he was able to grab the pieces and talk to her. Holding the much-maligned configuration of silk, wood and lace in front of him as he backed warily, Charles said, "No, no!" watching her carefully for any signs of sudden attack.

For the moment she seemed content to glare at him, her small fists balled, her jaw jutted forward, and he breathed a sigh of relief. "You misunderstand! I thought—I heard—I mean—"

Carlesworth stopped, took a deep breath, and began again. "Where," Charles asked, trying to keep one eye on the young lady and with the other scan the countryside for evidence of her earlier companion, "is Sir Rupert?"

Miss Ansley continued to glare. If he meant to throw her off guard with that or any other ridiculous question, he would not find her so easily taken in. Sir Rupert, indeed!

Stifling the ungentlemanly realization that he wished he'd stayed at High Point to work that day and had never heard her cries for help or met the young lady, Charles tried to decipher the thoughts behind the frowning countenance so resolutely turned toward him. It was clear from looking at her that she was young; he would guess about seventeen. Happily for him he did not guess aloud, for a highly indignant Miss Ansley would have made it clear that she was *nineteen*—almost. In six months. And not to be treated like a child.

In height, he saw, she did not reach quite to his chin. Her skin was creamy, and Charles thought that if her lips ever turned up into a smile instead of down into the fierce and forbidding frown directed at him, she might look very well indeed.

Several errant curls of soft brown hair peeped from the sides of the silken bonnet sitting sadly askew atop her head. Charles had a momentary memory of a feather tickling his chin as he'd broken through the hedge, and he colored as he realized he must be responsible for the sorry state of her hat.

She had a neat figure, and it was clear her clothes were styled by a first-rate modiste. Her particularly expressive brown eyes were flashing fire as the lady continued to survey him, and it occurred to Charles belatedly that she might resent what had become, he realized now, his rather studied assessment of her physical appearance.

The lady frowned further as the ridiculous man turned pink up to his ears.

"What?" she snapped. Something in her expression made it clear she had said the word before, when he wasn't attending, and Charles flushed further.

He gulped. "Sir Rupert," he said. "I was on the other side of the hedge. Sleeping. I heard—I thought—it sounded as if—"

Much sooner than he'd expected Charles had the opportunity

to see the lady's brown eyes warm with humor. She began to smile, then grin.

"Do you always sleep under hedges?"

Her tone was milder than any he had heard heretofore today, and the words were laced with amusement. Charles shook his head, confused further by this change of face.

"No." One hand ran through his hair, raking it forward. "I was reading and grew sleepy—" As the amusement in her eyes deepened it occurred to him that he owed this impertinent chit no explanation, and he frowned in what he hoped was a perfect imitation of his grandfather when the old man was most displeased.

Her grin grew.

"You should not be out walking alone," Charles told her, his tone as severe as even the strictest chaperon might wish. The lady giggled.

"I was not alone," she said. "Sir Rupert was with me."

"Yes, well—" He allowed himself one small derisive snort, he who never snorted, being much too polite to employ that tactic used to such advantage by his older brother Jack. The snort did not affect her in any way, and Charles's brow darkened. "I heard how you addressed your Sir Rupert, and can only guess as to his abysmal behavior. And as I asked you before, where is he now, your fine companion?"

If he thought to discompose her with the question he was disappointed. The lady folded her hands in front of her and, pursing her lips, said Sir Rupert had run away.

"Well, I don't blame him!" Charles spoke his thoughts aloud, a habit that almost always got him into trouble. "If you bashed him with your parasol half as much as you bashed me—"

"Well, it's your own fault," the lady said, taking offense at his first sentence, but focusing on his second. "Bumbling through hedges, knocking the wind and scaring the life out of innocent young women! And I did *not* bash Sir Rupert. As if I would!"

Charles frowned at that but let it go. In a somewhat acid voice he suggested that the quick application of her parasol to his head and shoulders implied the life had been *far* from scared out of her.

Far from taking umbrage, the lady smiled. "I take it, sir," she said, her chin raised in the manner of a grande dame, "that in

your original way you are telling me you were only coming to
my rescue when you so rudely knocked me down."

Charles nodded, his forehead wrinkling. He made an inartic-
ulate protest at her reference to rudeness, but his focus was on
the jut of her chin. There was something about it that was
familiar, and spoke to him of danger.

"I, of course, could only think I was being attacked when you
pushed your way so violently through the hedge—" Arabella
continued.

No, Charles said, no. In point of fact, she might have thought
any *number* of other things. Especially, he said, as she was being
attacked when he rushed to her rescue.

Once again Charles looked in vain for the errant Sir Rupert.
The lady laughed.

"But no, sir, you misunderstood," she said. "Sir Rupert was
not attacking me—at least, he was not attacking my person. My
reticule, alack—" One hand went artistically to her forehead,
and for the first time Charles realized a knot of ribbons dangled
from her wrist, and that the small silk bag that once must have
hung from them was there no more.

"Robbed!" Charles was astounded. "The cur! The scoundrel!
No gentleman worthy of being addressed as *sir* would ever do
such a thing!"

The lady made a gurgling sound, turning it into a cough as
Charles peered more closely at her. His training from early
childhood took over, and a solicitous Carlesworth said, "You
have taken a chill." He glanced worriedly at the light pink shawl
she wore over an equally light muslin gown of white trimmed
with pink ribbons and small flowers of a deeper rose. "No doubt
the excitement and shock—"

With what she considered remarkable forbearance the lady
refrained from commenting on the warmth and sunniness of the
day, and her firm belief that only a nodcock would think anyone
could grow chilled in such weather. Instead she shook her head.

"No, I am quite fine," she told him. "Really. It is just
that—that—"

Charles was never to hear her put into words what it was
"that," for she was looking beyond him with a most peculiar
expression. Sensing they were no longer alone, Carlesworth
tensed and half turned as a brown streak hurtled into him.
Charles staggered backward as two dark eyes bored into his. A

hairy chin was pressed close to Carlesworth's own, and hot, malodorous breath fanned his cheek.

Two brown paws rested on his shoulders. One brown nose sniffed Charles inquiringly, and one brown tail wagged in recognition before the newest player on their stage, one of the larger descendants of a favorite of French royalty, dropped to all fours and approached the young lady, tail wagging. Letting a much-chewed object fall from his mouth, the dog whuffed and sat back on his haunches, regarding them both with approval as the lady scratched his ears affectionately.

"Kind sir," she said, her eyes brimming with laughter as she made Charles a slight curtsy, "let me make you known to my walking companion—Sir Rupert."

⚹2⚹

"But—but—" Charles stared openmouthed at the poodle, who stared back just as openmouthed, and with a great deal more humor. "That's a dog!"

The lady agreed.

"Lady Hedgwick's dog!"

Again she nodded, this time with more interest. If the man knew Lady Hedgwick's dog, he must certainly know Lady Hedgwick.

"Clorimonde, His Excellency and Rightful Ruler of All Upper and Lower Dogdom!"

By now Charles's voice was almost a yelp, and Arabella regarded him with awe.

"You actually remember that horrible name!" she said.

"Well—I—" Charles continued to goggle at Clorimonde who, having heard himself so addressed, now sat on his back legs, waving his front paws rather regally in front of him. The dog's tongue hung out, and his head was tilted inquiringly to one side.

"Oh, look!" The lady clapped her hands in delight. "He knows you! He likes you! He wants to shake hands with you!"

"Well, I don't want to shake hands—paws—whatever!—with him!"

Charles snapped the words, and both the dog and the lady looked at him inquiringly. It occurred to him that they were both in fine fettle, as if the happenings of the past half hour were part of their everyday lives.

Well, such happenings were definitely not part of Charles Carlesworth's well-ordered life, nor did he want them to be. Charles Carlesworth did not appreciate being either bashed or bemused. He did not appreciate it at all.

"I thought—you said—" Carlesworth frowned at his own incoherence and took a deep breath, collecting his thoughts. With a start he realized he still held the lady's broken parasol. Holding it out toward her, he felt his world was almost as atilt as the one small bow that hung crazily from a thread near the parasol's tip.

The lady reached for her property but before she could reclaim it, Clorimonde, ready for a new game, snatched the frilly item and raced away. Arabella, alternately cajoling the dog to come back and calling insults after him, seemed to enjoy the exercise quite as much as her four-legged friend.

"Why do you call him Sir Rupert?"

Charles was almost as surprised as she that of all the questions bubbling in his head, that was the one that rose to the surface first.

Miss Ansley giggled. "He reminds me of a Sir Rupert I knew once," she said. "In Belgium. Sir Rupert the man had just that sort of vacuous grin Sir Rupert the dog gets when he is sitting by the fire at night watching me."

"I take it," Carlesworth said, his tone dry, "that that is not a compliment either to man or dog."

"Oh, no!" She opened her eyes very wide. "I did not in any way mean to insult my doggie friend!"

Carlesworth smiled in spite of himself, and Arabella's dimples deepened as she peeped up at him.

"He wanted to marry me, you know," she offered.

"The dog?"

"No!" She paused a moment to right the bonnet that had fallen farther forward on her forehead with the rapid shake of her head. "Sir Rupert the man! Silly creature! As if I would!"

When Carlesworth made no answer she grew reflective, her eyes fixed on the poodle happily romping over the hill in front of them. "I don't know why he wished to do so. He was always irritating me, you see, and when people irritate me I sometimes say such awful things—"

"I can believe that!"

It was apparent Carlesworth's words had been a bit too heartfelt for the lady's taste, and she frowned.

"I am not that often irritated," she informed him, nose in the air. "Although now—" She looked him over, top to bottom, speculation in her eyes. In spite of himself, Charles grinned again.

"Who *are* you?" he asked.

Arabella reached out a hand, and there was again something of the grande dame in the gesture that rang illusive bells in his head. He had seen the gesture before. . . .

"I know we should be properly introduced," she said, with her most regal smile, "but since our mutual acquaintance"—a nod of her head indicated the frolicking poodle—"has chosen to ignore his social duties, let me make myself known. I am Arabella Ansley. And you?"

Charles, taking the hand because it was so very clearly expected of him, made a punctilious bow and raised it to his lips in the manner he had often seen his brother Jack use. Miss Ansley watched approvingly.

"Charles Carlesworth," he said.

It was then, in an afternoon of surprises, that the lady did the most surprising thing of all. Astonishment vied with delight in her expressive face as she heard his name. Clapping her hands together, she beamed at him.

"Are you really?" she breathed. "*Really?* By all that's famous! This is wonderful! I have been quite longing to meet you, Mr. Carlesworth! You are to teach me to dance!"

After staring at her for several moments, his eyes wide, his mouth at half-mast, Charles berated himself soundly for his foolishness. How could he have missed it? Obviously she was deranged—or, at the very least, completely overset by the day's events. It was understandable. Charles was feeling more than a bit overset himself.

Speaking soothingly, as he was sure one was supposed to do when dealing with mentally unbalanced people, Charles asked her where she was staying.

Arabella regarded him critically.

"Why are you speaking to me like that?" she demanded.

"Like—what?" He made each word clear and slow, so as not to agitate her.

The lady's frown deepened. "Like that," she said. "As if you've stopped for tea between each word!"

"Miss Ansley." Without thinking Charles bent to retrieve the remains of her reticule from the spot where Clorimonde had dropped it, then took her arm. "I believe you have had—a shock. . . ."

"A shock?" She seemed surprised. "Well, yes, it was a shock when you came whirling into me, but I believe I am made of sterner stuff than to be overturned by such a trifling—" Something in his expression made her stop and peer more closely at him, her brow furrowed. Then she laughed in sheer disbelief.

"You think I'm an escaped bedlamite!" she said.

"No, no!" Hurriedly Charles strove to reassure her. "Not at all! Just—confused, perhaps! Overtired—"

Her eyes were mischievous. "Because I said you're to teach me to dance?"

Charles thought it appropriate to note, in the kindest manner possible, that he was not, nor had he ever been, nor did he ever plan to be, a dancing master.

"You're also to teach me to ride—like a lady." The last was clearly an afterthought, and just as clearly conjured up a meaning Charles did not care to dwell on. He had no doubt the creature before him was quite capable of riding astride, but he was not—thank goodness!—responsible for breaking her of that habit.

"I should also tell you that I am not a riding master," he said, this time perhaps not quite as kindly.

"And—" Her eyes were brimming with laughter, as if she enjoyed a private joke. "You're to teach me to go on in society. I am told you are a high stickler when it comes to proper conduct!"

"Nor," Charles's tone grew colder as hers took on added warmth, "am I a governess." He glanced around, hoping that by now someone would have found her missing and come looking for her, but there was no one to be seen; even Clorimonde had disappeared.

"Well, I should hope not!" Arabella said decidedly. "I have had more than enough of governesses to last a lifetime! Not," she eyed him speculatively, and it occurred to Charles that whoever had had charge of her had had their hands full indeed, "that they ever lasted long."

"Or had any success in instilling even a modicum of ladylike behavior in you!" Charles retorted, stung by the feeling that she was laughing at him. Why, he wondered, when she was so clearly the one who was mad, did he feel so off balance?

He was immediately sorry for his words as Miss Ansley's face fell, and her mouth took on a definite droop.

"How ungentlemanly of you to say so," she mourned, looking away. With one hand she fumbled in the remains of her poor reticule. Charles, appalled that she was right, pulled his handkerchief from his pocket and handed it to her, watching in dismay as she buried her face in it.

Why, he asked himself, did he never remember he must mind his tongue with young ladies? Why did he not have Jack's way of saying precisely what it was they most wanted to hear, or his grandfather's ability to discern when he was steering himself into treacherous waters in time to steer himself safely out again?

Young ladies, Charles had unfortunately found, always seemed likely to take a pet just when he most needed them to be sensible—which was one of the reasons he avoided young ladies whenever possible.

"Here," Carlesworth began. "I say, I didn't mean—that is—it was most wrong of me to say that! Please, forgive me!" He patted her shoulder awkwardly, and after a moment one appraising eye appeared from a corner of the handkerchief.

"Oh!" she said. "All right, then!"

Folding the handkerchief, she stuffed it briskly into her reticule, and turned such a calm face to him that he was certain she had not cried a single tear. Charles goggled at her.

"Of all the—" he started, indignantly.

Miss Ansley gave her most engaging grin. "Don't be angry!" she coaxed. "I did want to show you I have learned *some* useful arts! And I am a very quick study!"

She said the words so cheerfully that Charles, once again running a distracted hand through his hair, could only stare at her, eyes wide. "But," he asked at last, "I don't—that is—*who are you?*"

"But I told you!" Arabella gazed at him in some surprise. "Arabella—"

"Yes, yes!" He waved her name impatiently away. "Arabella Ansley. But *who* is Arabella Ansley, and *what*"—here his eyes fell on Clorimonde, once again bounding toward them—"is she doing with Lady Hedgwick's dog?"

❧ 3 ❧

"Sir Rupert and I," she informed Charles as the dog returned to her, tail wagging, "are out walking."

Something in her voice suggested that anyone with half a brain might have gathered that, but if Mr. Carlesworth could not ascertain such a simple fact from the evidence before him, she would make it clear.

Charles, flushing at her tone, watched her reach for the parasol Sir Rupert—*Clorimonde!* Drat the girl, the dog's name was *Clorimonde!*—still carried in his mouth. The poodle, sensing that her persistent pulling could signal an invigorating game of tug-of-war, growled happily and backed, pulling the determined lady with him as she clung to the handle of her much-the-worse-for-wear parasol.

"Do give over, Sir Rupert," Carlesworth heard her coax as she tugged harder and harder on the parasol. "I shall see that you have a nice meaty bone for supper if you do. Wouldn't you prefer that to this silly old thing?"

Sir Rupert exhibited no such preference. Everything from his determined stance to his expectant expression made it clear that he found a parasol in the afternoon much preferable to the promise of a bone at night. Growling again and bracing his back legs, Sir Rupert shook his head, and the lady's arm, in the process.

"Bad dog!" said Miss Ansley.

"Grrrr," said Sir Rupert.

"Enough!" said Mr. Carlesworth.

Two heads turned toward him inquiringly as Charles, in a voice that brooked no nonsense, said, "Clorimonde, enough!"

Reaching out his own hand, Carlesworth took firm hold of the parasol. Clorimonde, to Miss Ansley's private disgust, let go of

15

it immediately. The dog further enraged her by dropping to its stomach and licking first one paw and then another, acting for all the world as if this was one poodle who did not have, never had had, and never would have, any interest at all in such mundane things as little pink silk parasols with pink ribbon bows all over them. Nor, his expression said, did he have a clue as to what all the fuss was about.

The dog might have appeared even more innocent if one of said bows had not come off in their struggles and twined itself into the heavy brown curls above his left eye.

"Traitor!" said Miss Ansley.

Carlesworth frowned at her. "If you wish the dog to mind, you must not play with him as you do."

"Play with him!"

Arabella's mutterings and outraged expression made it clear that, far from playing with the dog, she was considering having him shot. Since she absently stroked the nose Sir Rupert turned to her with one hand as she gestured with the other, Charles did not think the poodle in imminent danger of demise.

Miss Ansley informed the world at large and one male member of it in particular that said dog had ruined both her reticule and her parasol—well, she amended consideringly as she fixed Charles with a less-than-friendly eye, someone *else* had actually ruined her parasol by being beaten with it—but Sir Rupert had more than done his part to contribute to its dilapidated condition, and she was far from happy with him.

Miss Ansley ended her diatribe with *"Beast!"* and since she was looking at the poodle at the time, Charles chose to interpret the remark as aimed at the dog. Clorimonde, however, took it another way. He ceased his washings and cocked his head in Charles's direction. Then he growled.

"Don't you growl at me," Charles snapped.

The dog growled again.

"Quiet, sir!"

The tone of command was quite spoiled by the poodle's response. Clorimonde barked. Repeatedly.

Miss Ansley giggled.

"Yes?" Keeping an eye on the dog who, at Miss Ansley's laughter, had quieted to consider her, Carlesworth turned his attention to the lady. His icily civil tone only broadened her grin.

"It does my heart good," Arabella informed him, "to see how well he minds you."

"At least he gave me the parasol!"

Miss Ansley shrugged, and seemed to stifle a yawn as she gazed off toward the horizon. "He was tired of it, I would imagine."

"No such thing!"

"He was just getting ready to give it to me when—"

"Ha!"

Belatedly it occurred to Charles that to be standing in the middle of nowhere arguing with a young woman he did not know about a dog's intentions was almost as ridiculous as the lady's earlier assertions that the dog had grown tired of the parasol game.

And what was she talking about with these ridiculous statements that Charles, of all people, was to teach her to dance?! And ride. And go on like a lady . . .

Resisting the strong urge to shudder, Charles turned his attention to the situation before him. Favoring Miss Ansley with an even more authoritative stare than he had turned upon the poodle, Carlesworth said, or rather, demanded, "What are you doing with Lady Hedgwick's dog?"

Arabella's expression fluctuated between aggrieved and resigned. "I told you," she said. "Weren't you listening?"

"You told me you were out walking with Clorimonde." She nodded agreeably, and his jaw tightened. "That tells me nothing at all!"

"It tells you what I was doing," she began.

Charles frowned. "And *how* did you come to be walking with Clorimonde?"

"We do so every day."

"Nonsense!" Charles snapped the word and the lady's chin came up, her lips tightening. People who pronounced Arabella's statements "nonsense" did so at their own risk.

"Lady Hedgwick has not been in residence for more than a week, at most," Charles continued, ignoring the growing storm signals in the lady's eyes. "I myself just heard of her arrival home yesterday."

Arabella nodded. "Yes," she said, her words as clipped as his own. "Sir Rupert and I walk every day. We have done so—for a week."

The emphasis on the last three words, coupled with the lady's challenging stare, made Carlesworth's color heighten. Usually the most amiable of young men, it was not like him to so wish to—well, *throttle!*—a young lady.

"I take it," Charles said, one hand absently ruffling Clorimonde's topknot as the dog shuffled to his side and sat leaning against this longtime friend, "that you are a guest of Lady Hedgwick's?"

Arabella nodded, her forehead puckering at the picture the two presented. For all she berated him, she had thought Sir Rupert had better taste.

"I cannot understand," she said, frowning at them both, "what makes that dog like you so."

Charles's color increased as he suggested it might be because he was a very likable person. "Animals sense such things, you know."

Although she said not a word, the lady's eyes made it clear she did not believe that could be the reason. Charles's teeth clenched further.

"How long," he asked, continuing to stroke Clorimonde's head as the dog snuffed and whuffed in appreciation, "will our humble countryside be graced with your presence?"

Arabella flushed, and so perverse did Charles find himself that as soon as it was obvious she had taken his meaning, he wished he could unsay the words. Instead he asked, in a milder tone, "Lady Hedgwick is a friend of your family? You are bearing her company for a few days?"

His look was inquiring and grew even more so as Arabella considered him, her head tilted slightly to the left. Looking down, Carlesworth found Clorimonde watching the young lady, *his* head tilted to the left. The mirrored action made him smile, and the softening of his features brought a reluctant softening of Miss Ansley's own.

"You really ought to do that more often," she said approvingly. "It improves you vastly."

"I beg your pardon?" Charles looked up, startled, and Arabella's smile was encouraging.

"You ought to smile more often," she said. "It makes you much more—more—"

"I shall remember that." The dry note with which his words were uttered diminished Arabella's smile. She shrugged.

"I just thought that if you are to help me learn how to go on, I might help you, too."

Carlesworth shook his head, unwilling to further dignify her assertions that he was to aid her as she'd said. Instead he said, "Miss Ansley, I was inquiring as to how long you are to be a guest of Lady Hedgwick's."

"Oh!" Arabella's eyes crinkled, and once again she smiled. "Of course! You think I am a guest!"

"If you walk daily with Clorimonde, it would suggest that you are staying with Lady Hedgwick."

"But yes!" Arabella clapped her hands, and at the sound Clorimonde left Carlesworth's side to approach the lady, settling comfortably in front of her as Arabella took up patting him where Charles had left off. "I am staying with Lady Hedgwick and Sir Rupert here, and we are having the grandest time together!"

"Yes." Patiently Charles kept working toward his goal. "I am sure you are. And how long will you *be* having this grand time with Lady Hedgwick?"

He had expected the answer to be a week. He might even have been prepared for a month.

If the chit was an old friend's granddaughter who had made some sort of social faux pas—which he could readily believe!— and who had been sent on holiday until the *ton* forgot her error in favor of a fresh scandal, he might even expect to hear several months.

What he was *not* prepared to hear was the lady's sunny, "Why, forever, of course! Or at least"—this was added conscientiously—"until I find a husband. Which is why you must teach me to dance!"

❧ 4 ❧

Charles stood staring at her for several moments before he realized his jaw hung slightly agape, and his eyes seemed in danger of popping from his head. Miss Ansley was watching this reaction with much more approval than he deemed appropriate, and it occurred to Charles that Miss Ansley liked to shock people.

"You're not going to tell me, are you?" he asked, a heavy frown once again descending on his forehead. Charles did not like shocking young women.

"Tell you?"

It did not seem fair, Charles thought, that someone so exasperating should have such a musical voice and such an innocent expression.

"What you are doing here." As he snapped the words Charles could not help noticing that the more irritated he became, the more Miss Ansley's mood improved.

She smiled. "But I *have* told you," she protested.

"Very well." Charles made his most icily civil bow; as he rose and extended his arm toward her she said he did it very well.

"What?" His heavy frown increased at her words.

"You show your disgust in such a civil way. I imagine if I had greater sensibility, I would be quite mortified—crushed, even!—by your evident disapproval."

"Greater sensibility!" Carlesworth snorted the words. Perhaps, he decided, he was not quite as polite as he had once thought. "First you'd have to have *some,* before it could be *greater!*"

"Oh."

It was that mournful tone he'd heard earlier, and Charles regarded her downcast head with suspicion. "Here now!" he

21

protested, half-angry, half-beseeching. "You're not going to cry again, are you?"

Miss Ansley giggled. Quite distinctly, she giggled.

"Here now!" he said again.

The young lady turned a laughing face toward him, and Charles, torn between relief and further exasperation, could not help returning her grin.

"No, no," she assured him. "I never waste my tears."

"Waste—" Once again Charles goggled at her. "You really *don't* have any sensibility, do you?" he asked.

Only after the words were out did it occur to him that that was not a question a gentleman with sensibility would ask a lady. He blushed.

Miss Ansley did not seem to mind. "Not a whit," she answered cheerfully. "It was a great trial to my second governess, Miss Whitcomb, but Gervase, my father, always says sensibilities are a great bore, and I am better off without them."

Charles, sure it was not a sentiment shared by any of the fathers he knew, blinked and said, "He does, does he?"

Miss Ansley gave an emphatic nod. "And great bores are not to be tolerated, you know. At least, not by Gervase."

"I see." Charles put one hand to his head in an effort to clear it. He did not see at all. This unknown Gervase—and that was another thing! "You call your father Gervase?" he asked, staring down at her wide eyes and calm face.

Miss Ansley nodded. "It is his name."

"But—"

It was that wide-eyed, inquiring look again, and Charles, feeling himself more and more unequal to conversation with this young woman, asked the first thing that came to his mind. "Do you never call him father?"

"Oh." Miss Ansley smiled, the picture of pure mischief. "Only when I am very angry at him. It is something he dislikes above all things, you see."

"He does?" Charles said blankly.

"Oh, yes." Absently Arabella ran her fingers through Sir Rupert's curls as the dog sighed and leaned heavily against her. "He did not really wish to be a parent, you know. It involves responsibility."

No, Charles did not know. He did not know at all. And while he could see why someone might not wish to be a father to this particular young woman, he could not help but think that a father who had wanted to be a father might have raised quite a different daughter, so perhaps Miss Ansley was not as much to blame for her—unusual—behavior as he had at first thought.

Lost in his own thoughts, it took Charles several moments to realize Arabella was watching him in that considering way again, as if she knew something he did not know; as if she had plans of which he was unaware; as if he were a large cheese and she a mouse with great ambitions. . . .

Gulping at the thought, Charles once again bowed, and extended his arm. "Miss Ansley," he said as she regarded the action thoughtfully, "permit me the pleasure of escorting you home."

Charles had never been as happy to see Holmsley, the Hedgwick Hall butler, as he was when the manservant opened the door to them that afternoon and Miss Ansley tripped inside.

On the walk back—and it had been a *long* walk—she had pestered him unceasingly to show her his "cut-them-dead" bow again, adjuring him to teach her how to do it, but as a curtsy.

When he remonstrated with her that it was no such thing—cut-them-dead bows indeed!—she had laughed at him, saying that was *exactly* what it was, and it was too late to gammon her now.

When Charles frowned and said proper young ladies did not say gammon, she clapped her hands and told him Lady Hedgwick had been quite right; he was *just* the person to help her learn how to go on.

When he'd frowned more heavily and made it clear he had no intention of "helping her learn how to go on," as she put it, she'd grinned and said they would see.

They would indeed, he'd replied, and Arabella had laughed. Laughed!

"You know, young lady," he'd told her in tones better suited to his grandfather's years than to his own, "you have a very forward way about you. Many people would find it most unbecoming."

"Oh?" She'd stopped, one hand holding her hat as she'd tilted her head back to stare up at him. Once again it was that wide-eyed look he suspected but could not prove was far from serious.

"And you, Mr. Carlesworth? Do you find my . . . forward way . . . unbecoming?"

She had held her lower lip between her teeth a bit, and had swayed toward him as she spoke. Charles gulped.

He'd been saved from replying by Clorimonde, who'd bounded up to them just then with a stick and an evident invitation to Miss Ansley to throw it. She took it up at once, laughing as the dog raced after the stick and returned it, running around and around them until Charles was half-dizzy watching him. Looking at her animated face, and the way she seemed so wholeheartedly to enjoy the dog and the day, he could not actually say he found her unbecoming; it was just—just—

Not much in the petticoat line, Charles was still trying to puzzle out the "just" when Lady Hedgwick sailed into the hallway demanding to be told where Arabella had been keeping herself. At the sight of Charles she paused and one eyebrow went up as she shot Miss Ansley an inquiring look. Arabella grinned.

"Look, Grandmama!" she cried. "I have met your Mr. Carlesworth, and he has escorted Sir Rupert and me safely home, scolding all the way."

"*Grandmama?*" Charles repeated, stunned.

"*Scolding?*" Lady Hedgwick's other eyebrow rose, and she acted as if she hadn't heard her shocked guest. "Abominable girl! What have you been about that would make Charles scold?"

The words were said in a tone far more fond than forbidding, and Charles stared from Miss Ansley to Lady Hedgwick and back again. He realized now why certain expressions and postures of Miss Ansley's had seemed so familiar to him; although he had never met the young lady before, they were part and parcel of his godmama herself.

"*Grandmama?*" Charles said the word again. "But—but—"

"Yes, Charles?" Lady Hedgwick was watching him expectantly, and Clorimonde added his encouragement to hers with a bark. When no one rebuked him the dog barked again. And again.

"Clorimonde!" Lady Hedgwick said.

The poodle sat down midway between Charles and Lady Hedgwick and grinned at both of them.

"Good dog," Lady Hedgwick approved. Charles ignored him.

"*You* don't have grandchildren!" Charles completed his

thought at last, the words loud in the silence that followed Clorimonde's barking. Arabella giggled, and Lady Hedgwick walked toward the young woman and put an arm around her shoulders, drawing her forward.

"Not grandchildren, Charles," Lady Hedgwick corrected gently. "A grandchild. One."

Arabella, solemn faced except for the laughter dancing in her eyes, made a deep curtsy and rose, extending her hand.

"But—" Charles ignored the hand, his eyes still fixed on Lady Hedgwick, his godmama and one of his oldest friends. "But—you never told me!"

The old lady looked down her nose at him. "I was not aware that I needed your permission to have a grandchild, Charles! Or that I need tell you everything. Or anything!"

Thrown off by her repressive tone, which he had heard many times in his life, but never directed at him, Charles stuttered no, no, of course not; it was just that—just that—

"Yes, Charles?" The tone was even more pronounced, and Charles took a great gulp, his Adam's apple bouncing up and down. From the corner of his eye he could see Miss Ansley was enjoying herself immensely, and once again the wish to throttle the chit rose within him.

"Wish you happy!" The words came out strangled. It was clear from his face that he more pitied that envied anyone related to Miss Ansley, but as he spoke Lady Hedgwick smiled and took his arm.

"Thank you, Charles," she said. "I am most happy to have my granddaughter with me, and to have you make her acquaintance. Now, Arabella dear, run along. I think it is time Charles and I had a little chat. . . ."

"No." Charles was seated in the library, a snifter of the late Lord Hedgwick's best brandy cradled in his hand. His long legs rested on the footstool in front of him, and he was sunk deep into the old leather chair he always occupied when perusing the Hall's excellent collection of books that he'd had ready access to since his earliest years. Everything had been done to assure his comfort, but Charles was not feeling comfortable. Not at all.

Lady Hedgwick sighed as she regarded him. "But Charles—"

"No." He took a larger gulp of the brandy than he'd intended and coughed at the burning sensation. Then he frowned as she started to smile. "Absolutely not."

"Charles, dear," Lady Hedgwick gave him her most endearing smile. She was a handsome woman, and the white of her hair only seemed to make her eyes more blue. "Who is your favorite godmama?"

Charles frowned at her.

"Your *only* godmama."

"That's not fair!"

"The godmama who has allowed you to use her library—*this* library—for years, in pursuit of your dreary Greek studies, and who now asks only one little thing in return. . . ."

"One little thing?" Charles stared at her in horror. "Madam, having spent just over an hour in your granddaughter's presence, I can assure you, this is *not* a little thing you ask!"

"I am persuaded that once you become accustomed to the idea, and more acquainted with dear Arabella, you would enjoy it immensely," she said, again giving him her best smile.

"And I," Charles said, each word distinct, "am persuaded I would not."

"It would be good for you," she offered. "Would get you out a bit more—"

"Good for me?" Charles fairly goggled at her. It occurred to him that he had done a great deal of goggling this day, and he did not like it. Charles did not picture himself as a man who goggled. "I do not believe being *driven to distraction* has ever been *good* for *anyone.*"

"She would not drive you to distraction!"

At Carlesworth's look of incredulous disbelief Lady Hedgwick, known for her honesty, bit her lip and looked away, amending her statement with, "Much. At least—" She straightened, looking hopeful, then sank back into the chair again as she considered. "She would not mean to. . . ."

The skepticism in Charles's eyes made her amend that, too. "Much."

"Perhaps a governess—" Charles offered.

Lady Hedgwick snapped her fingers. "That to governesses!" she said. "It is too late for governesses! She has had governesses! She is a young lady in urgent need of social schooling to make a successful debut in the society she has every right to claim, and it will take all of us—"

"All of us?" Charles set the glass down, aware that it could very well be responsible for the disagreeable buzzing beginning in his head. The words "all of us" made him suspicious.

"Yes." Lady Hedgwick nodded. "Me, you, your grandfather—"

"My grandfather?" Charles rose, and Lady Hedgwick was displeased to see that he was frowning again. "You have enlisted my grandfather?"

She nodded and rose also, disliking the advantage their height difference gave him. "Your grandfather," she said, unable to keep the smile of triumph from her face although she tried, "has said that you will be delighted to help."

"De—" Charles's mouth hung open until her gentle reminder to close it, which he then did with a snap that made his teeth hurt.

"Delighted," Lady Hedgwick repeated. Carlesworth glared at her.

"Well," he said, with the icily civil bow that had elicited Miss Ansley's admiration earlier, and which only made Lady Hedgwick smile, "we shall see about that!"

Stomping from the room, Charles was met in the hall by the impassive Holmsley, who handed him his hat and bade him good day as the butler always did. Wondering how the man could appear so sublimely unaware of the dangerous tilt Carlesworth's world had taken in the last few hours, Charles glared at him, too.

Carlesworth was almost out the door when a muffled bark and the sound of four feet scrabbling on the hall's floors made him turn. Clorimonde was bounding toward him, a large bone, which accounted for the muffled tone, between his jaws. He was followed by Miss Ansley, who was assuring the dog that when he had finished his bone, they would take a nice walk in the garden together, just the two of them. And they would have a wonderful time.

"Clorimonde," Mr. Carlesworth said, stretching out his hand to give the dog's head a solemn pat as the animal came up to him, "run for your life."

Then, not waiting to see if the poodle took his advice, Charles bolted.

❧ 5 ❧

"You might at least have told me, sir."

The Earl of Clangstone left off the close perusal of his leg of mutton to regard his grandson with beetled brow. Charles, the most even-tempered and politest of grandsons, was not given to moroseness, and this peevish tone was most unlike him.

"Couldn't," the earl said, fixing his companion with the keen gaze that, coupled with his prominent nose, years earlier had earned him the nickname Hawk. "She—Clara—made me promise. Didn't want anything said until the chit arrived. Besides . . ." The earl turned his attention to the mutton again. "No need for it to worry you until it was upon you. Nothing you could do, after all."

"No." Carlesworth put down his fork to give his grandfather his complete attention. "I cannot agree to that, Grandfather. There is much I could—can!—do. But I am not talking about Miss Ansley's arrival—although you might have warned me about that, too!"

"About what, then?" The earl, used to taking his supper in peace, was growing exasperated at the way this conversation interrupted his enjoyment of his cook's superb work. More evenings than not he and Charles, both of quiet natures with their minds on different things, spent several perfectly convivial hours in which not more than five or six phrases were uttered at table.

"About Miss Ansley!"

"But you just said—"

"No, no!" Charles frowned impatiently and began again. "Not about Miss Ansley coming. If Lady Hedgwick extracted your promise that you would not tell me about the girl's imminent arrival, of course you could not tell me. No gentleman could. But you might—oh, any time these last—what? sixteen? seventeen?—years have told me about her existence.''

"Oh." The earl spooned a potato from the bowl held for him by a quiet footman, and shrugged. "That." He took a bite, chewing thoughtfully. "It never came up. Besides"—he speared another bite and it rested on the fork he pointed toward his grandson—"before your time."

"She can't be above seventeen," Charles protested.

"What?"

"Miss Ansley. She can't be above seventeen."

"Older," the earl grunted. "Just looks that young."

"Not older than I!"

"What?"

"She can't be older than I!"

"Well, of course not!" The earl grew even testier. Who did the boy think he was, questioning his grandfather? Especially when he made no sense at all. Of course the chit wasn't older than Charles! "Don't be daft, lad!"

"Then how could it be before my time?"

The earl, who up until now had always taken great pride in his grandson's logic and tenacity in getting to the bottom of a problem, began to perceive that the appreciation of logic and tenacity could be carried too far. He frowned as he hunched a still-powerful shoulder.

"Constance, the girl's mother, ran off with Gervase Ansley before you came to live here. It was the scandal of London. Almost broke Clara's and Harold's—the late Lord Hedgwick—hearts. Couldn't hardly be their friend and be nosing that information about, now could I?"

Clangstone was pleased at the righteous note on which he ended his speech, thinking it would properly chastise his grandson so the boy would let the topic go. Alas, Charles had always been remarkably hard to chastise when he felt he was right.

After informing his grandfather that passing vital bits of past history on to his grandson could not, even by the highest sticklers, be condemned as nosing information about, Carlesworth asked where Miss Ansley's mother was now.

The old man sighed, and his eyes grew sad. "Constance died in childbirth," the earl said. "That was before you came, too. She was a lovely girl—always had a smile on her face, and a

laugh not far behind. I always hoped your father would remarry,
and perhaps he and Constance . . .''

Too late the earl saw the flicker of pain that crossed his
grandson's features, and the earl's own softened in response.

"She was a lovely woman, your mother," Clangstone said,
his voice gentle, "but she was gone. And there was Albert, with
two boys, and so lonely, shut up in the country with his children
and his books. And then, of course, before we knew it, Albert
was gone, too. . . .''

For a brief moment the old man rested his chin in one hand,
while with the other he shaded his eyes. After all these years,
Charles was never sure who mourned the loss of his parents
more, he or his grandfather.

After his father was gone he and his brother had come here, to
be raised by the old man who shared with Jack his love of
gaming and with Charles his love of literature, who set their feet
firmly on the path of manhood, and who would have seen them
both depart his house without a word if they wished it because,
he said, they had lives of their own to lead, and he would not lead
his through them.

Jack had gone. It was expected he would. Being the oldest,
Jack would one day come into their grandfather's title. And he
had always been restless, eager for new adventures. At present as
Viscount Chalmsy he was cutting just such a dash in London
as the present earl had when he was young—something Charles
knew the old man found a source of considerable pride.

Charles had stayed. He had no yen for city life; he liked the
country, and he realized his grandfather was slowing down, in
need of a hand to manage the vast estates that would someday be
Jack's. Charles had a head for such things; he was sensible and
bookish like his father, the earl said with a reminiscent smile. A
comfort to a man in his old age.

Just how much a comfort his grandson was seemed forgotten
at the moment, however, and he frowned at Charles as he
continued his tale, knowing he would have no peace until it was
done.

"Lord Hedgwick never spoke Constance's name again. He
ordered the portrait of her that had hung in the long gallery
removed; Clara said once he wanted it destroyed, but that she
would not allow. They wanted to take the child—your Miss
Ansley—to raise, but Gervase wouldn't give the babe up. He

said at the time she was all he had left of Constance, and that while he might not have been responsible to his wife, he would be to his child.''

At Carlesworth's look of inquiry the earl said, ''He wasn't there when Constance was brought to bed with the babe. Off gambling somewhere. They say he arrived home—some rented rooms in Paris—just minutes before his wife died.''

Clangstone took a bite of the now-cold mutton and chewed consideringly, his mind once more returning to his dinner. ''Imagine he regretted it later, though—child to raise, and all. Still, he could have sent her to her grandparents at any time. That was how they left it. For their granddaughter, their door was always open.''

The implied ''but not open for him'' hung between them as Carlesworth thought.

''Miss Ansley said that she did not believe her father had ever really wanted to be a father.'' The words came out slowly as Charles remembered their conversation.

''There.'' The earl nodded head and fork in accordance, pleased to find his perspicacity so quickly confirmed. ''Told you.''

''Ansley.'' Charles frowned at the name, turning it over in his mind as he turned over the piece of meat he'd been playing with for the last twenty minutes. Unlike his grandfather, Charles had little interest in his dinner. ''Ansley. Would that be—''

Clangstone nodded. ''Younger brother to the Marquess of Billswell. Had money in his own right, Gervase did—just as you will.''

Charles listened to the last part of his grandfather's sentence with half an ear, knowing it was important to the old man that he reassure himself every chance he got that while the entail was settled on Jack, Charles would not be left penniless. His grandfather did not believe in leaving everything to the firstborn, and he did believe in rewarding industry, something he was always happy to point out to Jack when Jack most annoyed him.

''His mother left him a snug little property in Kent,'' the earl continued. ''Billswell manages it for him; at least, I imagine he still does. When I went more often into company in London, they used to say the marquess sent all the profit from the Kent property and perhaps a little more besides to his brother for the pleasure of not having Gervase's company.''

"Oh?" Charles frowned. Although he and his brother were very different, sharing few thoughts and even fewer interests, there was a bond between them that such differences did not break. Should he ever know real trouble, he had no doubt that Jack would be there.

Apparently Gervase Ansley had no such dependence on his brother, unless he found himself in such circumstances as might embarrass the family name. In that case the marquess might come to the rescue to save himself rather than his brother. Carlesworth's frown deepened. Miss Ansley, it seemed, could take little comfort in her family. Poor little thing, adrift in the world with her chin up and only her wits and parasol to defend her.

At thought of the parasol Charles's sympathy for Miss Ansley diminished, and he returned his attention to his grandfather.

"No love lost there," the earl snorted. "Although if there's much love lost between Billswell and the world, it's news to me. I don't know the present marquess well, but I knew his father, and he was a man to avoid. Bad *ton*. They say Gervase showed more of his mother than the other boy—had the Ansley temper, but his mother's good heart."

The earl chewed for a moment, ruminating on the late marquess and marchioness. "I danced with the woman once, years ago, at the Ludley's ball. She seemed pleasant enough. Never did know what she saw in Billswell. Suppose it was an arranged marriage, although she might have cared for him. Who knows? I don't think she lived long after that. Hard to remember, now. . . ."

The old man lapsed into reflective silence and Carlesworth, realizing the room had become home to past memories, retained a respectful silence. Hard to remember, his grandfather said.

A vision of a giggling Miss Ansley rose before his eyes, her lips turned up, her brown eyes brimming with laughter, her cheeks flushed from her recent tussle with Sir—*Clorimonde!* The dog's name was *Clorimonde!*

His grandfather now struggled with things hard to remember. A shiver ran down Charles's back at the sudden premonition that his own problem might be things hard to forget.

❧6❧

Charles Carlesworth was not the only young person in the area participating in a heart-to-heart over supper that night.

"You know, Grandmama." Arabella reached for another comfit at the end of her substantial meal and paused, her attention momentarily diverted by the important task before her. Lady Hedgwick watched in amusement as her granddaughter's forehead wrinkled, concentrating on her sweet choice. How she loved to watch the girl eat! And how fortunate that Arabella's small frame did not show the effects of her hearty appetite!

With a sigh and a regretful pat on a portion of her own more ample bulk, Lady Hedgwick reflected for a moment on the inequities of life. Even at Arabella's age she had been given to plumpness, while her husband had been thin as a reed all his life, despite a healthy appetite and a sweet tooth. Gervase Ansley was the same. At least, Lady Hedgwick silently amended, she did not know if Gervase had her beloved Harold's taste for sweets, but when she had seen him last in London it was apparent that time's passing was most seen in his face, not his figure.

Oh, he had the thickening through the chest that comes to many men with age, but she had been forced to admit—only to herself, of course!—that it only made him more attractive. He was a powerfully built man, and even standing still he emitted a feel of tightly leashed energy. There were women, Lady Hedgwick knew, who would find that most attractive, and she heaved a sympathetic sigh for them.

Upon closer inspection she had found he carried perhaps an inch more at his waist, but when she had first entered the sitting room and seen him from the back, staring out the window at the passing London scene, she had caught her breath, for a moment carried back to the day the young reprobate had first come to visit Constance, standing in that very room.

With a quick shake of her head Lady Hedgwick wiped such thoughts away. They did no good, she knew, for she had been through them often enough, in the intervening years.

"Grandmama?" Arabella's questioning voice brought her back to the conversation and with an effort Lady Hedgwick smiled. As she did so the frown now puckering her granddaughter's forehead vanished. One thing Gervase Ansley had done right, Lady Hedgwick thought silently, was raise a caring, sharp-witted daughter. Although whether that was to be laid at Gervase's feet, or at the feet of the young lady herself, the old lady had yet to decide.

Now Arabella was looking at Lady Hedgwick in concern, and it was apparent she had been watching her grandmother's face, noting the sadness that always appeared there when Lady Hedgwick thought of Constance. After all these years . . .

"Yes, my dear?" Lady Hedgwick shook her head again, smiling encouragingly at her granddaughter. Instantly the smile was returned.

"I was just saying, Grandmama, that I do not believe Mr. Carlesworth was as pleased with your plan for bringing me up to snuff as you had suggested he might be."

Lady Hedgwick laughed, and her hazel eyes brightened. "No, he did not seem overly pleased, did he? Dear Charles! It will be good for him, as I told him!"

Her granddaughter's expression was skeptical, and Lady Hedgwick laughed again. "He would be even less pleased, I'm sure, if he could hear you describe his job as bringing you up to snuff, my dear!"

"Oh." Arabella left off eyeing the comfit tray to raise an inquiring eyebrow toward her grandmother. "I take it that is something I must not say?"

"You take it correctly, my dear."

"Ahh." The young lady heaved a sigh, and pulled the tray closer to her. "It is such a confounded nuisance, is it not, to have to watch everything one says?"

"Yes, my dear," her grandmother agreed, her voice firm. "But no matter how—er, confounded—the nuisance is, a lady never says so."

"Oh." Arabella grinned guiltily, and the dimple her grandmother was sure would enchant all of London emerged. "I've done it again, haven't I?"

"You have."

"Well." Arabella took a dainty bite of her latest sweet, and placed it on her plate. "Gervase did tell me not to let anyone turn me into a mealymouthed milk-and-water miss."

Her grandmother assured her there was little danger of that.

"Oh." Arabella sighed, and silence reigned in the dinning room for several moments as the young lady chewed her stuffed date, watched by her grandmother.

"What will we do," Arabella asked when the date was gone, "if Mr. Carlesworth refuses to help us?"

"He won't," Lady Hedgwick replied, with such confidence that Arabella was suspicious.

"Grandmama," she demanded, fixing Lady Hedgwick with her most commanding stare. Her grandmother, who had perfected that stare years earlier, smiled. "You are not going to *force* Mr. Carlesworth to help me if he does not wish to, are you?"

Lady Hedgwick laughed.

"Grandmama."

Such an authoritative tone for such a young lady, Lady Hedgwick thought, and smiled again.

Arabella frowned at her. "I would not wish Mr. Carlesworth to be—coerced—into helping me."

"But my dear," her grandmother corrected, reaching out to pat the small hand that moved restlessly on the linen tablecloth, "of course you would!"

"Grandmama!"

"Besides," Lady Hedgwick amended, realizing the girl was sincere, "it isn't really coercion. In the end Charles will do it because it is the right thing to do, and Charles struggles constantly to do the right thing. He will do it because he wishes to please his grandfather and me, and because he has a good and kind heart. Besides, it really *will* be good for him!"

Arabella looked skeptical again, but contented herself with, "I do not believe Mr. Carlesworth will think so."

"No," her grandmama agreed, chuckling at something Arabella did not see. "I would almost give you odds he will not!"

"But Grandmama—" Arabella protested.

"Enough, child! He doesn't know it yet, but Charles Carles-

worth needs you as much right now as you need him. It will be
an even exchange, never fear!''

Arabella, her curiosity aroused by that tantalizing comment,
pestered—Lady Hedgwick's word, not Arabella's—her grandmother for the next half hour, cajoling the old lady to explain it.
But Lady Hedgwick would say no more than that. Arabella was
such a clever puss she would figure it out before long. Instead,
Lady Hedgwick suggested a game of piquet, knowing that
Arabella, who had learned that game at her father's knee and was
remarkably good at it, was such a keen competitor that the cards
would soon command her full attention. The rest of the evening
was spent in companionable concentration on playing the hands
they were dealt.

A new day brought new perspective for Mr. Carlesworth.

He awoke the next morning to the realization that he had made
too much of Miss Ansley's coming and his godmama's request
the day before.

In the light of a new day it was obvious he had not expressed
himself clearly to the ladies. Once they realized how inadequate
he was to the task they proposed, they would agree he was not
the person for their needs. In fact, they might thank him for his
insight. He might even help them find a substitute—several
substitutes, all better equipped than he. Freddie Blathersham was
an excellent dancer, for instance, and everyone said Thomas
Wooding was a blazing rider to hounds.

Except—Charles, on his way downstairs, paused with his
hand on the banister and frowned. Freddie Blathersham thought
himself a bit too much in the petticoat line for Carlesworth's
taste, and not for the world would he submit Miss Ansley to
attentions she might not quite like. And as for Wooding—well!
The man wore a belcher necktie! Enough said.

Still, Carlesworth told himself, once again starting down the
stairs, there had to be others. His godmama would know. In fact,
she had probably been twitting him a bit when she suggested he
was the very man for the job! More than once Lady Hedgwick
had told him he needed to get out more, to pull his nose out of
his books and stick it straight into life! Probably this was her way
of getting back at him for all the times he had refused her
invitation to accompany her to this ball or that soiree in the
neighborhood—by suggesting that he take on the education of a

young lady about to make her debut. As if he could—or would!

Which, Charles reminded himself more than once as he mounted his horse and cantered over Clangstone land, was the key to the whole thing. He wouldn't. He just wouldn't do it.

That was all he had to remember, and he was secure in the knowledge right up until his encounter with the black stallion and its rider.

At first he did not recognize either the horse or the person it carried, for when he first saw them they were at some distance from him, streaking over the outer edges of Lady Hedgwick's estate, heading right for the hedge that separated Hedgwick from Clangstone property.

"Lady Hedgwick must have a new groom," Charles said aloud, patting his gray's neck as the animal sidled and snorted, its eyes also on the approaching rider. "And a new horse. A magnificent new horse! I wonder what she wants with such a beast? They're out early, too." Charles, who approved of industriousness in grooms, thought that a very good thing. "Usually we don't meet anyone on our morning rides, do we, Thunder? And gad!" There was a pause as Charles watched admiringly. "The boy can ride!"

Cantering forward, he was smiling at the heart that was obviously going to throw the slight youth and the big horse over the Clangstone hedge. It was not a jump for amateurs, and while Charles had made it more than once himself, he would not recommend it to just everyone. Certainly not to a stranger who had never taken it before, and did not know how the land lay.

Charles's smile disappeared, to be replaced by an uneasy frown. He hoped the lad had studied the rolling slopes before attempting the hedge; he hoped it was skill and not foolhardiness heading the black stallion straight down the hill.

Charles leaned forward, his frown deepening. While he was quite sure he had never seen the boy before, there was something familiar about him. If only Charles could see beneath the dark cap that covered hair and forehead. Urging his own horse forward, Carlesworth got his wish sooner than he'd expected. An errant breeze caught the rider's cap and lifted it, and brown hair streamed down the boy's—*girl's! Miss Ansley's!*—back as the large stallion under her rose, its forelegs clearing the hedge, its back following.

The sudden rearing of his gray made Charles aware he had

tightened his grip on his own reins, and he relaxed his hands immediately, giving the horse a pat as he spurred him forward.

The fact that horse and rider had cleared the hedge unharmed and were now rejoicing in it should have filled Charles with relief, but once he ascertained that neither was hurt, his overriding emotion was rage. Pure, unadulterated, deep crimson rage.

"Miss Ansley!" Charles was beside her now, his voice and face as taut as the hand that held his horse rigidly in check while her big black sidled away from them, taking umbrage at the other horse's presence.

"Mr. Carlesworth!" Arabella's cheeks were rose, and her eyes glowed. "Isn't it a beautiful morning?"

"No." Pleasure turned to surprise at Charles's curt tone, and she blinked as he informed her it was not a beautiful morning at all. It had *been* a beautiful morning—quite the loveliest morning of the year, he was sure—right up until he had seen her careening down the hill, putting her life and the life of her horse, to say nothing of Lady Hedgwick's future happiness, in jeopardy.

Arabella's delight at encountering him dimmed and her lips tightened.

"My horse," she said, easily bringing the animal to a stand despite its efforts to put distance between itself and these interlopers, "was never in danger."

"Hmmph!" Charles tried to put into the sound the disbelief his grandfather could inject into a sniff, but it did not come out quite like the old man did it. Even to Charles's ears he sounded no more than peevish, and he tried again.

"And you?" he asked. "Do you care so little about your lovely neck that you would choose to risk it in such a manner?"

Her reaction was not quite what he had expected. Instead of being angry, Miss Ansley's hand went to her throat, sliding around it to lift the hair that had fallen over her shoulder. "Do you really think I have a lovely neck?" she asked.

Charles ignored the question. "And that's another thing," he charged, eyeing her brown tresses with disfavor. "Your hair streaming down your back like a gypsy, and those—those"—he gulped and looked away, out over the horizon—"pantaloons!"

"Breeches," Miss Ansley amended.

"Miss Ansley!"

She nodded knowledgeably. "More than once Gervase has

told me that my poor breeches do not deserve the respect the title pantaloons might give them, worn as they are, and—''

''*MISS ANSLEY!*''

Too late Charles realized he was shouting. Staring down into her surprised face, he clenched his jaw tightly and swallowed a moment before starting again. ''Miss Ansley, I do not believe you are the person to lecture me on the finer points of dress—''

''No,'' Miss Ansley agreed with her best smile, ''that is why you are to lecture me—''

''When you are seen riding about the country in—in—'' He tried but could not bring himself to say the word in her company, settling instead on, ''garb not becoming a lady—''

''But no one has seen me!'' Miss Ansley protested. ''That is why I ride so early.''

Charles frowned. ''What of your groom?''

''I have no groom, so no groom sees me!''

If she thought to win a point with that, she was mistaken. Charles made short shrift of young ladies riding alone, without even grooms to accompany them. ''I cannot imagine why your grandmama would allow—''

The guilty look on Miss Ansley's face made him pause. It was apparent Lady Hedgwick had allowed no such thing. Since he knew Lady Hedgwick was a late riser he deduced it was likely this young minx was back at the Hall, changed into morning dress and looking the picture of innocence, before her grandmother left her room. ''You won't tell her, will you?'' Arabella asked.

''At once!''

''But no!'' She reached a hand out to touch his jacket and Charles, looking down, felt the day grow warmer.

''Well . . .''

Seeing him hesitate, Arabella moved her horse closer, looking up at him with such pleading that Charles had to work to remain firm. ''I do not wish to trouble Grandmama,'' she said. ''Truly I do not. It is just that—sometimes, I think, if I do not get away, I will burst!''

Charles informed her frostily that young ladies did not talk about bursting in public. Arabella regarded him with mournful eyes.

''But that is just it,'' she told him. ''I am not a young lady. Not really. I was born to it, and Grandmama does her best to see I dress the part. . . ." She sighed. "It isn't that I'm not willing to try. In fact, I would like to be, for Grandmama's sake, and for Gervase's, who did his best . . ."

There was skepticism in Carlesworth's eyes, and immediately she fired up in defense of her father. "He did! It is just that Gervase is perhaps . . . more . . ." She was obviously searching for words, and settled at last on one to describe what Gervase was. "—Impatient—with so many of society's ideas that he did not exactly find them worth passing along to me, and now—now—"

"Even your father," Charles said, his voice austere, "must have mentioned somewhere in passing that young ladies do not ride astride in—in—" He eyed her cloth-clad legs, then lamely changed his wording to, "in England."

There was that guilty look again, and Charles pressed his point home. "And if your father did not, I am sure your grand-mama—"

"My grandmama," she informed him, guilt turning to attack as she recalled Gervase's admonition that when one has been backed into a corner, one must always fight one's way out as quickly as possible, "told me you would teach me to ride and act like a lady!"

"It is a task," Charles said, nose in the air, "for which I feel singularly incapable."

"Coward!" Miss Ansley cried.

"Nor," said Charles, descending from the lofty to the deeply goaded in less than fifteen seconds, "do I imagine anyone could do it!"

"Hmmph!" said Miss Ansley, showing him how a sniff *should* be delivered to be effective. She hunched one slim shoulder, and in spite of himself, Charles smiled.

"You do not really mean to tell me," he said in a milder tone than she had previously heard, "that you sneak that horse in and out of your grandmama's stables without anyone seeing you."

"Oh, no!" Miss Ansley smiled, glad to have someone with whom she could share what she believed was an ingenius plan she'd devised for her rides. "I take Tory out in the mornings, before anyone is awake, and I hide my saddle and riding habit—the new one Grandmama had made for me in London—in the copse of trees about a quarter mile from the house, and then, when I have had my ride, I slip into the trees and remove the saddle and don the habit and lead him back to the stable. By that time the grooms are about, but all they ever see is me walking. And I've told them not to worry about me, for Grandmama has given me permission for my morning walks with Tory. So no one knows I have not been perfectly respectable the entire time I was gone!''

"Tory?'' Charles questioned, for the moment ignoring everything else she'd said, including—or especially—the ''perfectly respectable'' part.

Miss Ansley dimpled. ''When we first got him dear Tory would throw terrible fits, and Gervase said he had the temper of a Tory.''

"Oh." Once again, Carlesworth's tone was dry. ''A bit of a Whig, is your father?''

"Oh, no!'' There was that dimple again. ''Gervase isn't anything at all!'' At Charles's look of surprise she amended that to, ''That is, he doesn't care for politics. He has quite bad things to say about Whigs, too!''

"I see.'' Charles was thinking deeply, and as the rest of her speech registered in his mind, his eyes widened. ''Are you telling me,'' he asked, a muscle twitching slightly at the corner of his mouth, ''that you—you—''

Arabella was gazing at him questioningly, and he shook his head. ''Surely you are not—you *cannot* be!—saying that you change every morning in the woods!''

"But of course!'' She laughed. ''I can hardly do so on the main road, can I?!''

"But—'' Charles was goggling again, he knew it. The lady seemed to have that effect on him. ''Really! Miss Ansley! What if someone were to see you?''

"Pooh!'' She waved her hand. ''I hope I am not so green as to allow that!''

Charles hoped so, too. Devoutly. ''You cannot do so again,'' he told her.

Arabella looked at him.

"I forbid it.''

"You *what??*''

Even Charles, with his limited knowledge of dealing with young ladies, realized he had blundered badly. ''If you do so again,'' he extemporized, ''I shall be forced to tell Lady Hedgwick.''

"Oh." A dissatisfied Arabella chewed her lower lip for a moment before brightening. "Does that mean you're not going to tell her now?"

"Well . . ." Charles felt himself wavering.

"Oh, Mr. Carlesworth!" She squeezed his arm before removing her hand and inching her horse away. "I knew you were a right one! Really I did!"

Gratified at being proclaimed a "right one," Charles nonetheless thought it his duty to inform her that was not something a young lady would normally say.

"Oh." Miss Ansley chewed her upper lip again, one hand stroking her horse's neck. "It is all very hard, you know."

Watching her, Charles could believe that it was.

"That is why I have been so happy to have Tory, and my rides. Papa bought him for me two years ago, and he almost didn't think I should bring him, because of course Grandmama has to stable him for me, but in the end . . ." She smiled. "Out here"—one hand swept toward the fields before them—"it is the only place, the only time in England I've felt free since coming."

Charles, who often rode for the same reasons, sighed.

"Miss Ansley," he said, feeling himself slipping into a great abyss, "if you will promise never to don your"—he gulped—"breeches again, I shall do my best to instruct you in riding."

"Really?!"

"You must promise me."

"Of course!"

She looked so innocent that Charles's suspicions were aroused. "And perhaps it would be best if you gave them to me, so that I might burn them."

Arabella assured him that would not be necessary; she would take care of it herself. Something in his face suggested he did not believe her, so once again she went on the attack.

"And does this also mean that you will teach me to dance?" she asked hopefully.

Charles flushed. "Absolutely not. And now—" He turned his horse, heading him toward the nearest gate. "I believe I should see you home."

Arabella, following meekly behind, hid a grin. "We shall see, Mr. Carlesworth," she whispered. "We shall see."

❧ 7 ❧

Charles stood by the road, holding his horse Thunder and Miss Ansley's Tory, and hoping devoutly that none of his acquaintances would pick this particular morning to mend their ways and start about their business well before noon, which would be most unlike them.

His eyes were on the young lady disappearing into the copse of trees near Hedgwick Hall. She turned to wave just before she vanished from sight, and Charles thought glumly that this was the second time in two days he'd returned her to her home. She seemed to have a way of popping up in his life and wreaking havoc there just after he'd decided what to do about her. Now he had contributed to his own discomfort by promising to teach her to ride sidesaddle.

And that was another thing! He ran a distracted hand through his hair. What did *he* know about riding sidesaddle? Heaven preserve them, he would need more help than Miss Ansley!

And that was yet a third thing: Charles's conscience was bothering him. He really *should* tell Lady Hedgwick about her granddaughter's outrageous behavior, because the silly chit did seem to care about the old lady and what she said, and she might listen to her. Charles suspected Miss Ansley would listen only to what she chose to hear him say, but perhaps if her grandmother made it clear to her just how impossible she was being . . .

Still, he'd seen her face when he'd threatened to tell her grandmother about her escapades, and it was clear Miss Ansley *knew* she shouldn't be out riding alone, in *breeches*, so perhaps . . .

His convoluted ruminations were interrupted by an abrupt shove as a big black head reached for the handkerchief in Charles's breast pocket and removed it. "Now, see here," he

said indignantly as he righted himself and glared at the horse.
From behind he heard a stifled giggle, and he turned to find Miss
Ansley surveying him, her eyes bright.

"I should have warned you about Tory," she said, smiling as
she came up to him. "He dearly loves his old tricks."

"Yes, you should have," Charles agreed, reaching for the
handkerchief only to find the horse backing away with it and
snorting. He turned toward Miss Ansley for help, and when he
did it was as if for the first time he really saw her.

She was wearing the new riding habit her grandmama had had
made for her in London. Of a deep forest green, it fit tightly
across her chest—a pleasingly rounded chest, Charles could not
help but notice, before his eyes drifted on—and narrowed to a
tiny waist. The jacket had borrowed its embellishments from the
military, sporting gold epaulets at the shoulders and gold braid
down the arm. More braid encircled the bottom of the severely
cut skirt, and she had looped its short train over her arm. Tory,
for the moment, was forgotten—at least by Charles.

"Mr. Carlesworth," Arabella said after several moments in
which he did no more than survey her. Her look was reproachful.
"You are staring, sir!"

"Oh!" Charles, recalled to his manners by her words, flushed
and looked away, only to look back again. "I beg your pardon,"
said he, who his brother often twitted on his lack of ability to pay
ladies pretty compliments. "It is just that—that—"

"Yes?" Arabella glanced down and behind, to see if she had
forgotten to button something, or if anything else was amiss with
her costume.

"You're beautiful!" Charles gulped, surprising both Arabella
and himself.

"Why, Mr. Carlesworth!" Doubt turned to laughter in her
face, and her rich chuckle bubbled up as she smiled in delight.
"And you, sir, are forgiven! Stare as much as you like!"

"No, no!" Hastily Charles declined that treat. He was sure he
should inform her that was an invitation she must never issue to
a gentleman, but at the moment he felt singularly unequal to the
task. Instead he stuttered on. "I never should have said that—it
was only—"

With difficulty he stopped his stammering, castigating himself
for acting like a callow schoolboy. He might, as Jack said, have
little knack with the ladies, but he knew better than that. "You

surprised me," he said, pulling back his shoulders and looking down his nose in what he hoped was a sufficiently superior way.

"Not as much as you surprised me!" Miss Ansley assured him, her eyes dancing.

"Yes, well . . ." He handed her Tory's reins and she obligingly removed Carlesworth's handkerchief from the horse's teeth, apologizing for the wetness and the slight tear in the corner, Tory not having been totally willing to give up his prize. "Beg you will forget—"

"It is forgotten." Arabella waved one small hand as if to remove the memory.

"I am not in the habit—"

"Certainly not!" They were moving down the lane toward Hedgwick Hall, and Charles had to look around the big black's head for a glimpse of the lady's face. Something in her tone made him suspicious.

"What do you mean by that?" he demanded, stopping in the middle of the road. Miss Ansley stopped, too, her expression surprised as she stroked her horse's nose.

"Why, only that it is apparent you are not in the habit!" she said.

"Not in the habit of what?" His eyes were narrowed, and hers opened further.

"Why, of paying ladies pretty compliments!" She smiled. "It is obvious that is not in your line."

"Well!" Charles stalked forward, and Miss Ansley had to hurry to keep up. "Of all the—"

"But now what is wrong?" Arabella asked, and the breathlessness of her voice made him recall where he was, and slow slightly.

"Just because a fellow is not in the petticoat line—"

"Oh, Mr. Carlesworth," Arabella assured him with a giggle, "no one would ever think that of you!"

Far from being reassured, Charles looked annoyed. "It isn't that I couldn't be, you know!"

"Of course not!" the lady soothed, in far from believing tones, and Charles's jaw tightened.

"I will have you know," he said, "that there is many a lady in London who does not despise Charles Carlesworth as an escort. Not," he added, having just heard his own words and fearing they might make him sound like one of the coxcombs he despised, "that I wish to brag."

"Of course!" Miss Ansley agreed readily. "If Grandmama has told me once, she has told me a dozen times that Charles is a great favorite with all the dowagers, so attentive to their wants, always ready to lend them an arm for the long climb up the stairs."

"Dowagers?" Charles yelped more than repeated the word. "I was not talking about *dowagers*! When I am in London the Almack's patronesses are always after me to attend their dances. Why, Lady Sefton once told me there was no one with whom she would rather waltz, and that, miss, is very high praise indeed!"

Charles had discarded his desire not to appear a coxcomb in favor of the more pressing need to make Miss Ansley realize it was choice that kept him in the country most of the year.

"Dear Lady Sefton," cooed Arabella, who had never met the lady. "Always most polite—"

"She is not!" Charles corrected. "Not polite at all. That is—" He was awfully glad Lady Sefton wasn't there to hear him, feeling she might say something most impolite following his maligning of her character. "Thing is, she likes to dance. Likes to dance with me. So do many women."

"I see." It was the polite but clearly disbelieving tone again, and Charles's color rose.

"I tell you, I am a good dancer!"

"If you say so." They were approaching the stable yard, abuzz with morning activity. Charles ground his teeth at her overly conciliating tone, and several workers nearby stopped at the unaccustomed sound of Mr. Carlesworth's raised voice. They exchanged glances, suspecting the young miss had said something to put the young gentleman off.

Miss Ansley's patent disbelief, in the face of all his assurances, was new to Charles; for years now he had been used to having his statements attended to. Mr. Carlesworth was known in the neighborhood for his honesty, character, and—if he had to say it himself, he would!—wisdom.

"Very well!" Charles said, refraining with difficulty from snatching his hat from his head and stamping on it as he handed Thunder's reins to the head groom. "I'll show you!"

Instantly Miss Ansley's disbelief vanished, to be replaced with honest delight.

"Oh, Mr. Carlesworth!" she cried, in front of the interested groom. "Will you? Will you, really?" She gazed beyond him to a figure clad in black moving slowly through the gardens. Catching his hand, she pulled him, bemused, along behind her as she headed for that figure.

"Yoo-hoo!" she called, further taking Charles aback. "Grandmama! The most wonderful thing! Mr. Carlesworth has just said he will teach me to dance!"

"You don't understand," Charles said a short time later, seated in the library cross from Lady Hedgwick. Miss Ansley had gone to her room to change. "I didn't say I'd teach her to dance."

"And I don't suppose you said you'd teach her to ride, either," Lady Hedgwick said, looking at him with just that expression of disbelief Miss Ansley had shown earlier. How did they do it? he wondered. How did they turn a usually intelligent, careful man into a blithering idiot?

"Yes!" He ran a hand through his hair and tugged at his collar. It was, he decided, an unusually warm June day. "I did say that. This morning when—"

At Lady Hedgwick's look of inquiry he sputtered, remembering his earlier promise not to tell Lady Hedgwick of her granddaughter's morning rides. Lamely he ended, "when I said I would. But I *never* said I'd teach her to dance!"

"And yet she is so looking forward to it." Lady Hedgwick tapped her fingers together. "There must have been a misunderstanding of some sort. You must have said *something*—"

"Said I'd show her I *could* dance, that's what I said. She acted as if I was a regular clodpate who couldn't move one foot in front of the other, and I told her—"

"You told her you are a very good dancer," Lady Hedgwick soothed, and he regarded her with suspicion before giving a slight nod.

"As you should." The old lady nodded approvingly. "You *are* a very good dancer, Charles."

"Yes, well . . ." Her approval brought on his humility. "A gentleman should be able to—"

"Some can't, though," Lady Hedgwick mused. "I know. I have danced with many of them."

"Yes, well . . ." Charles had the suspicion he was being led down another garden path, and brought them firmly back to the point. "The thing is, there is a big difference between telling someone you will show her you *can* dance, and telling her you will *teach* her to dance. And why I *should* teach her, when she has been so disobliging as to doubt my abilities—"

"Yes." Lady Hedgwick heaved a sigh. "You are quite right. There is a great difference between showing and teaching." She leaned forward to pat his hand. "And if you are absolutely set against doing so . . ."

She sighed again, resting her head on one beringed hand. "The dear child is so looking forward to it. And she will be so embarrassed to find she has misunderstood you in this way."

"Hmmph." If Miss Ansley was around long enough, Charles believed he would perfect a disbelieving snort. "No such thing! Hasn't got an embarrassed bone in her body! Misunderstood me, indeed!"

Lady Hedgwick dropped his hand and raised her head, changing her tactics. "It would please me greatly, Charles, if you would do this kindness for my granddaughter."

"The girl," Charles told her, not mincing matters, "is a minx."

Lady Hedgwick looked at him. He tugged his collar. She continued to stare. He tugged the collar again.

"Oh, very well, madam!" he said, exasperation evident. "If only to have done with your plaguing me about it!"

Lady Hedgwick smiled. "You are my favorite godson, Charles," she told him.

"I am your only godson!" he reminded her, rising and standing over her for a moment before taking her hand and kissing it, making her a bow that would not have been despised in the best drawing rooms in London. Her smile broadened.

"But don't think you have cozened me, dear Godmama," he said, stopping at the library door to look back at her, "because what I said is true. The girl is a minx. And so, my dear, are you!"

She waited until he was out the door and she'd heard his footsteps fade in the hall before she started to laugh.

❧ 8 ❧

The Hon. Charles Carlesworth presented himself at Hedgwick Hall the next morning with a feeling of trepidation. He had agreed to teach Miss Ansley to ride sidesaddle, and today they would begin. He had tried to discuss his greatest fear with his grandfather, that fear being that he must appear to *know* how ladies managed with those ridiculous sidesaddles, when he hadn't a clue. He'd tried to figure it out all day yesterday, but the most he could conclude was that it must be much more uncomfortable, and much more difficult to keep one's balance than it was when one rode astride. He wondered why he had never considered that before, but when he tried to ask his grandfather, the old man looked at him as if he'd lost the rest of whatever mind he had left, and after saying, "Don't be daft, lad!" had retreated into a silence broken only by the slurping of his soup.

Charles, wanting to be no such thing, said no more. It was just that he didn't want to be ridiculous, either. There were, Charles was beginning to think, many good reasons for residing in London. Obviously his brother Jack had discovered that years ago.

Charles gazed with longing toward the door, knowing a Carlesworth does not bolt. Still . . .

A slight sound behind him made him turn to find Lady Hedgwick surveying him. "Arabella will be with you directly, Charles," she said, her smile as sunny as the day. "I must tell you again how happy I am that you have agreed to ride with her. It is so good of you, my dear."

Agreed! Charles's glum thoughts must have showed in his face, for Lady Hedgwick smiled more broadly.

"Come now, Charles!" she said. "It is not as if you have been

51

sentenced to the Tower! You *like* to ride! And you are very good at it!''

''Thing is—'' Charles looked toward the stairs to see if Miss Ansley had yet appeared. The surreptitiousness of the movement made Lady Hedgwick look, too. Her eyebrow rose as Charles took a step forward, lowering his voice. ''Don't know, myself.''

''Nonsense!'' If the boy thought to get out of his duty this way, he was much mistaken! ''As if your grandfather didn't toss you up on that nasty gray hunter he had, when you were three! I was there, Charles! Your mother almost fainted away but there you sat, crowing with delight and beating your tiny heels against the animal's neck. And that brute of a horse, standing there as if he liked it! So don't try to tell me you don't know how to ride!''

''No, no!'' Charles glanced nervously toward the stairs again. ''Thing is—sidesaddle!''

''What?'' Lady Hedgwick's brow furrowed; it was not like Charles to talk in puzzles. Sidesaddles, indeed! What had that to do with anything? Why—

Her brow smoothed as enlightenment dawned, and Arabella's step was heard on the stairs. ''Don't worry, Charles,'' Lady Hedgwick said, stepping forward to pat his cheek as the harassed young man looked toward the bend in the stairs where they could soon expect to see Miss Ansley. ''I don't expect you to instruct her in the proper positions for riding sidesaddle. I've already done that! Used to be quite a rider in my day, my boy. You wouldn't remember, but it's true!''

As his face brightened she patted his cheek again. What a serious young man he was! And how men could be so clever and such idiots, all at the same time, would be forever beyond her!

''What you're to do, Charles,'' Lady Hedgwick said in an undervoice as Arabella ran lightly down the steps, ''is accompany the girl on her rides. Be with her as she accustoms herself to the saddle. It doesn't do for her to be out alone.''

At Charles's look of surprise she nodded. ''Yes, I know about that. Very little gets by me, Charles.''

How well he knew, he thought with some bitterness, even as he asked, ''Then why—''

Lady Hedgwick glanced toward her granddaughter, who had stopped on the landing to survey them, her face puzzled as she wondered what low-voiced conversation they could be having.

''I didn't have the heart,'' the old lady said, face and voice soft. "Poor child—she is trying so hard, Charles. A little freedom—"

She gave herself a shake and said more briskly, so Arabella could hear, "But of course it does not do for a young lady to be careening about the countryside by herself, so I am so grateful to you, Charles, for accompanying Arabella on her morning rides."

"Not careening," Charles protested, as Miss Ansley smiled and took another step down the stairs. Both ladies looked at him.

"Young ladies do not careen, even when accompanied by a gentleman," Charles admonished. Miss Ansley giggled as she danced down the last few steps, and Lady Hedgwick favored her with a quick frown that did not fool Arabella one bit.

"You are quite right, Charles," Lady Hedgwick agreed, her face as prim as that of the gentleman beside her. "Young ladies do not careen."

Arabella grinned at both of them.

"You are looking very well today, Mr. Carlesworth," Arabella said. Charles, more than a little pleased he had decided to wear the new riding coat ordered during his last trip to London, said thank you and reached for his hat. The lady waited.

Starting toward the entrance, Charles stopped when he realized that while Holmsley held the door for them, Miss Ansley was not behind him. Half turning, he found her surveying him with disapproval. He looked toward Lady Hedgwick for guidance, but Arabella saw no reason why her grandmother should instruct him when she was there to do so.

"Now," Arabella said, as if to a small child, "you are to tell me I am looking very well, too."

"Arabella!" Lady Hedgwick's exclamation made her granddaughter turn, questioning. "A young lady," Lady Hedgwick said, "does not instruct a gentleman to compliment her!"

"But Grandmama!" Arabella protested. "I am looking particularly well today, and if the last time Mr. Carlesworth saw me in my new habit he could tell me I was—"

"Late!" Charles said, the realization that she was about to blurt out his stuttered comments the last time they'd been together prompting him to action.

In two long steps he had crossed the floor between them and taken Miss Ansley's hand. Tucking it firmly in the crook of his arm, he more dragged than escorted her out the door and down the steps where grooms held Thunder and the handkerchief-stealing Tory.

"Why, Mr. Carlesworth!" Arabella panted, when he at last came to a stop beside her horse. "Had I known how eager you are for our rides—"

"Hush!" said Charles, throwing a harassed glance over his shoulder toward Lady Hedgwick, who had followed them at a more leisurely pace, and who was regarding them with a speculation he could not like.

"Sweet-talker," Arabella replied as she waited for the groom to boost her into the saddle. Mr. Carlesworth, much goaded, surprised her by putting his hands on her waist and swinging her up.

"Well!" said Miss Ansley, settling herself as comfortably as she could.

"Well!" said Lady Hedgwick, her eyes thoughtful as she watched them.

"Well!" said the uncomfortable Charles, swinging onto Thunder. "Let's go, then—"

His horse had taken perhaps two steps when a brown blur streaked by them, turning to rush back at them again, running around both horses, who sidled and kicked more from principle than fright. They had seen this blur before.

"Clorimonde!" Charles roared, reaching for Miss Ansley's horse as he brought his own under control.

Tory, used to the dog but not to having a man roar so close to his ear, reared. Charles watched in horror as Arabella, not yet used to the saddle, left the horse's back and landed with a thud in the dirt.

Instantly he was off his horse, and was starting to kneel beside her when she looked up from where she lay, half sprawled on her backside, her arms supporting her upper body as she stared in stunned surprise at her boots. She blew the feather of her hat, which leaned crazily over one ear, out of her face.

"Really, Charles!" she said.

"Are you hurt?" His face was anxious as Lady Hedgwick hurried forward, crying, "Arabella!"

"And as for you, sir." Miss Ansley turned toward the dog who, finding her in such a position, was trying to lick her uncovered ear off. "Of all the ungentlemanly—"

"Arabella, are you all right?" The fear in her grandmother's

voice made Arabella turn her attention from the poodle to Lady
Hedgwick, and she smiled reassuringly.

"Yes," Miss Ansley said, allowing Charles to help her to her
feet, "yes, Grandmama, I am fine. Even if these three"—she
surveyed Charles, Clorimonde, and Tory with quizzical eyes—
"are doing their best to kill me."

"No!" Charles seemed the only one of the three accused to be
genuinely distressed by the recent incident. "I assure you, Miss
Ansley, I was trying to reach your horse's reins!"

"I see." The tone was her most affable, and only made
Charles, pale a moment earlier, flush. "And you thought you
would accomplish that by frightening him half to death with that
shout they must have heard in York."

"No such thing! I assure you! He was frightened by Clorimonde."

Miss Ansley waved an airy hand, dismissing the poodle.
"Tory and Sir Rupert have an understanding, Mr. Carlesworth.
When they see each other, they act like idiots. I am used to it."

"But—" Charles protested. The lady was brushing off her
habit, but looked up when she heard his voice.

"What I am not used to," she said, adjusting her gloves as she
looked at him, "is *your* acting like an idiot, too. Or at least," she
amended as his color deepened, "I am not completely used to it.
It grows hourly more familiar."

Charles, used to hearing himself described as the most
sensible of young men, stiffened. "I was trying to rescue you!"

"I required no rescuing."

"Your horse—"

"I am quite accustomed to the playfulness of my horse."

"Playfulness!"

"And if it were not for that dratted saddle . . ." Arabella
frowned at the offending article, and walked forward to take
Tory's reins from the groom who now stood, soothing the horse
even as he listened with interest to their conversation. "I would
have had no trouble at all, even with you roaring to wake the
dead and no doubt frightening every horse in Christendom!"

"Roaring to—" Charles felt his mouth hanging open and shut
it with a snap. "The dog—" he started. Miss Ansley looked at
him, and Clorimonde, feeling there was a silence to fill, barked.

"Quite so," said Arabella.

"Well!" Charles bent and retrieved the hat that had fallen

from his head in his haste to dismount and rush to Arabella's aid. "Since my presence is no longer required here—"

Miss Ansley raised an eyebrow. "Are you saying, Mr. Carlesworth, that after all this we are not to have our ride?"

Charles mouth opened and closed again, as he looked from her to Lady Hedgwick, and back again. "I thought," he said, "that is—after your fall—"

He looked to Lady Hedgwick again and she, her eyes anxious, said, "Yes, Arabella. Really, my dear. Perhaps you should rest today, and ride tomorrow. After your fright and fall–"

"Fright and fall?" Miss Ansley was surprised, then touched by the concern in her grandmother's face, and that of Mr. Carlesworth. Her annoyance with the gentleman started to fade. "Pooh!" she laughed. "I have parted company with a horse before, Grandmama, I assure you. Although not"—she eyed Mr. Carlesworth consideringly—"in the recent past."

Charles looked thoroughly miserable, and her annoyance dissipated further. "But as Gervase always told me, 'If you cannot fall, my dear, you cannot rise to ride. And every time you come off a horse, you must immediately get back on—both for yourself and the animal.'"

Miss Ansley was looking at them expectantly as Charles and Lady Hedgwick exchanged glances. They considered this the advice of an unconventional father if the man could see his daughter lying on the ground and risk having a horse put her there a second time.

Mr. Carlesworth, who had thought his heart would stop when Miss Ansley lost her balance on the big black's back, would have been pleased to advise her never to ride again.

"Perhaps . . ." Charles cleared his throat. "Another horse . . ."

He looked pleadingly toward Lady Hedgwick, who seconded him immediately. "Yes!" she agreed. "My sweet Bess is in the stable, and she is used to carrying a sidesaddle."

"Grandmama!" Arabella was looking at them as if she could not have heard right. "Your Bess must be twenty years old!"

"Yes, dear." Lady Hedgwick smiled reminiscently. "Such a sweet mare. I haven't ridden for years, but I couldn't bear to let her go; she always had the most placid disposition."

"But Grandmama." There was a dulcet tone in Arabella's voice that put both Lady Hedgwick and Mr. Carlesworth on guard. "It is too kind of you, I'm sure, to offer Bess, but I cannot accept." At Mr. Carlesworth's frown of inquiry she added, eyes innocent, "I might excite the horse!"

After surveying her granddaughter for a moment with a wistfulness Charles found most touching—as if Lady Hedgwick wished she might wrap the girl in cotton and keep her safe—the old lady gave a reluctant laugh.

"Very well," she said, to her granddaughter's relief and Mr. Carlesworth's consternation, "go on." She looked at Charles expectantly. "I believe," she said, when he made no move, "that you came here today, Charles, to accompany my grand-daughter on a ride!"

❧ 9 ❧

In only a few minutes Mr. Carlesworth and Miss Ansley were on their way down the lane leading from Hedgwick Hall to the main road, their departure being slightly delayed by a spirited argument on the merits of allowing Clorimonde to accompany them on their ride. Charles maintained that the addition of the dog to their party held no merit at all, and Miss Ansley argued that Sir Rupert was a fine companion on any outing, and considered it his doggy duty to accompany her. Nor, she said, would she want him to think even for an instant that he was in her black books.

"If it hadn't been for that blasted dog—" Charles began just as said dog sat back on his haunches and waved his front paws in the air, as if entreating forgiveness.

"It was not Sir Rupert who bellowed in Tory's ear," Miss Ansley said.

Lady Hedgwick, realizing they could brangle on forever without resolution, said, "Oh, go along, do. Clorimonde will be good, won't you, boy?" The last was said in a doting tone that made Charles realize a man's firm hand was required.

"Under no circumstance—" he began, just as Miss Ansley touched her heels to her horse's sides. He watched in confusion as the stallion trotted briskly by him, and Clorimonde, seeing the horse leave, raced ahead. The dog was now leading the way, head and tail up, and Charles looked appealingly toward Lady Hedgwick.

"Really, my lady," he said, "this is beyond permission—"

"Charles," Lady Hedgwick interrupted, "if you are to accompany my granddaughter on her rides . . ."

Stiffly he said he had agreed to do so, and he would; he was a man of his word.

"Well . . ." The old lady was shading her eyes as she

watched the fast-disappearing figure riding away from them. "She seems to be riding without you."

Charles, too, looked toward Miss Ansley's diminutive figure, which was almost to the Hall grounds's gate. With an oath Lady Hedgwick had never heard before on his lips, he touched his heels to Thunder's sides and the gray leaped forward, catching up to the black before the turn to the road.

"Why, Charles," Lady Hedgwick said softly, watching until the two were no longer in sight. "I didn't know you had it in you." When she turned back to the house she was smiling.

In the space between the Hall yard and gate Charles had decided he and Miss Ansley would hold to a sedate pace this morning. He was prepared to be firm when he informed her of his decision, having decided that if he did not hold the line in the beginning, all would be lost.

The young lady considerably surprised him, therefore, by agreeing to his pronouncement, even going so far as to say she thought that would be best. Miss Ansley was finding her bottom a bit sorer than she had first supposed when she rose from her fall, and accustoming herself to this new saddle was not helping the tenderness one bit.

In fact, Arabella told him, perhaps they should not ride very far or very long today; indeed, she did not wish to take him away from the thousand tasks requiring his attention. . . .

Not at all, Charles said politely; he had cleared his whole morning for her riding lesson, and was quite at her disposal. He had expected that to please her, and was surprised by the flicker of dismay that passed over her piquant face before she rallied, saying he was too, too kind.

Charles, who had thought Miss Ansley eager to ride, was puzzled by this about-face, only figuring it out when he happened to glance at her as she shifted position in the saddle, wincing slightly as she did so.

"Of course," Charles said, staring straight ahead as his words brought her face toward his, "if it would not displease you too much, there *are* a few things I would like to do, and perhaps we could ride again in a few days. Not tomorrow, I think, but perhaps the day after, or even the day after that."

A gracious Miss Ansley said no, no, she would not be displeased at all; he must do as he thought best. She realized he was a most busy man, for her grandmama had told her how he so competently handled his grandfather's affairs, and everyone at the Hall spoke most highly of what a responsible and respected young man he was.

Gratified, Charles did not even twit her on her almost eager pronouncement that the day after that would be just fine for them to ride again; she did not wish to claim too much of his time, and she was sure he had many duties to occupy him in the next two days. . . .

Charles agreed gravely that he did, and in mutual consent they turned their horses back toward the Hall, Charles whistling for Clorimonde, who had outdistanced them some time ago.

"Probably off chasing a rabbit," Charles shrugged when Miss Ansley, with a worried glance in the direction the dog had disappeared, asked if perhaps they oughtn't to wait for him. "He'll show up again, never fear."

In that, Charles proved correct. As they approached the small copse of trees by which Charles had waited for his companion only yesterday, Clorimonde streaked by, his mouth firmly clamped on something brown that flapped as he ran.

"What the—" Charles began as the horses snorted and pranced as Clorimonde passed them. He was frowning after the dog, trying to figure out what it was he held, when the poodle made a turn and started back toward them.

"Oh, no!" It was a gasp turned to groan from Miss Ansley, and with concern Charles moved Thunder closer so he could look into her face, which now was covered by one of her hands.

"Are you all right, Miss Ansley?" he asked worriedly, dismounting so he might help her down. "I fear you should not have ridden at all—"

He reached up for her but Arabella dropped her hand and shook her head, refusing to dismount. Her cheeks were crimson, and Charles gazed at her in puzzlement.

"That wretched dog!" she said. "Of all the Sir Ruperts in the world—"

Charles felt something brush his leg and looked down to see the poodle leaning against him, panting heavily.

"—he is the Sir Rupertest!"

At the poodle's feet was the source of Arabella's discomfort, and with raised eyebrow Charles bent to retrieve the remnants of Miss Ansley's breeches.

"Yours, I presume?" Charles said, holding up what remained after Clorimonde had chewed on them, then taken them for a run.

"Yes, well . . ." Arabella reached for them. "Perhaps I can mend—"

"Ah—ah—" Charles held them away from her, and his other eyebrow rose. "I believe, Miss Ansley," he said, "that I am mistaken."

"What?" Arabella frowned as he tucked the breeches firmly under his arm.

"These cannot be yours, after all. I am sorry to have assumed it."

"Well, of course they're mine!" Arabella began.

Charles overrode her, continuing, "Because you assured me you would destroy the breeches I saw you in yesterday."

"Oh." The color in Arabella's cheeks rose further.

"And of course a gentleman knows—just assumes—that when a lady gives her word—"

"But—"

"No more need be said about it."

"But—"

"So obviously Clorimonde has been breeches-snatching from some poor soul who any moment will come storming from the woods demanding his head."

Charles stroked said head suggestively, and a blissful Clorimonde leaned against him, grinning. "There have been many times in our relationship I would have gladly given this beast's head to anyone who wanted it—"

"Mr. Carlesworth!" Arabella began, indignant. Charles continued to stroke the happy dog.

"But I realize Lady Hedgwick is sincerely attached to the animal, heaven knows why, and I would not for the world cause her pain, so—"

"Dear Mr. Carlesworth," Arabella coaxed, reaching out her hand, "do give me my . . ."

The word went unsaid as Charles straightened and, with resolution, said, "Yes, that's it! I will take the evidence of Clorimonde's crime and bury it, so no one can accuse the dog."

"Bury them!" Miss Ansley shrieked.

Charles looked at her. "Yes," he said. "Yes, I am sure you are right. Burying would be wrong."

Her relief was short-lived.

"I shall burn them instead."

"Burn them!!"

"You're right," Charles approved. "Quite right. Thank you, Miss Ansley, for setting me straight. I must see you home at once, and then move immediately to destroy the evidence."

"Mr. Carlesworth—"

Charles, who had already swung himself up onto Thunder's back, looked at her inquiringly. "Unless, of course, you think it would be better to turn them over to your grandmother."

"No!" Arabella did not think that would be a good idea at all.

"No," Charles nodded. "I think you are quite right. Burning is best. Let us go."

Arabella, moving slowly at a walk beside him, slanted a sideways glance toward Mr. Carlesworth. He was looking straight ahead, the slightest of smiles on his lips, as if he had a private joke he was enjoying greatly.

Perhaps, she decided, there was more to the serious young Mr. Carlesworth than she had first thought. Or perhaps this is what Grandmama meant. . . .

Charles, happening to glance her way, frowned slightly. It would appear, he thought, that Miss Ansley had a private joke of her own. Odd, how that made him uneasy!

❧ 10 ❧

For the next two weeks Charles and Arabella rode every other morning, and as Miss Ansley grew more comfortable with the sidesaddle they ranged farther and farther afield, Arabella even attempting a jump one day, to Charles's great consternation.

"Of all the—" he sputtered as he came up with her after she had taken him by surprise and raced away, heading for a low hedge they had passed twice in the past week. "You could have broken your neck!"

"But I didn't!" a triumphant Arabella crowed. Her hand rose to her head, and she patted her hat and hair in satisfaction. "And not a curl out of place!"

No, Charles had to admit, there was not. And with her eyes shining and her skin aglow after the excitement, Miss Ansley presented a most attractive picture; so attractive, in fact, that— that—

Without realizing it Charles leaned forward, only to pull abruptly back as Arabella, sensing his intention, leaned forward herself.

"Don't do it again," he said gruffly, looking away.

"Poor Charles," Arabella teased. "Now you know how uncomfortable a mother hen must be when given a duckling to raise!"

"I am not a mother hen!"

Indignant at her choice of words, Charles turned back just as he felt the hat leaving his head. He reached up to save it but was too late. Miss Ansley had it in her small hands and Tory was prancing away from him while she waved the hat in triumph.

"Here then!" Charles said, spurring Thunder forward. "Give me that, you little minx!"

"Come and get it!" Miss Ansley called and set Tory racing,

heading back up the hill down which they'd just come. Thunder, indignant at being left behind, was not averse to running his hardest when Charles gave him the signal to start, and the two reached the top of the hill together, Miss Ansley reining in then and Charles following suit.

"Oh, wasn't that wonderful!" Arabella said. "I have been longing for such a run these past two weeks!"

Charles, who did not think it wonderful at all for her to be rushing harum-scarum across the green English fields, made his opinion clear as he crammed the hat Miss Ansley had just surrendered to him back onto his head.

"How many times must I tell you, miss," he said severely, sounding for all the world like his grandfather at the earl's sternest, "that a lady does not go careening about the country-side; a lady rides at a sedate pace unless she is fox hunting, and even then society dictates—"

"Pooh!" said Miss Ansley, snapping her fingers at society's dictates, and reaching again for his hat.

Indignantly Charles ducked her teasing hands, then swore under his breath as, with a laugh, she brought Tory up onto his back legs and then applied her small heels to his sides, sending the big black off again. The girl was too hot at hand, that was for certain. Something would have to be done about it, and soon, or—or . . .

He did not have time to puzzle out an "or," for Miss Ansley had disappeared from his view and he set Thunder hurrying after her. He hoped she wouldn't break her foolish neck, for her grandmother would never forgive her, and as to what his grandfather would say—well! He did not want to hear it!

As Charles raced along he ignored the small voice that whispered that he also would never forgive himself if harm came to Miss Ansley. Yet when he crested the next hill and saw Tory standing riderless near a small clump of trees below, the voice could no longer be ignored.

"Arabella!" he called, leaping from Thunder even before the horse had come to a complete stop beside the big black. "Arabella!"

His voice held a hoarseness not usually heard there, and he ran toward the trees, calling as he ran. "Arabella! Arabella! Arabella!"

"Over here, Charles." Her voice held none of the hoarseness

of his; in fact, she sounded quite fine. Unruffled. Serene, even.

Charles felt his fear recede and his temper rise.

"Where are you?" he demanded, striding through the trees.

Her "over here" was unnecessary; he had already spotted the hem of her skirt hanging several feet off the ground. Sitting at the base of the tree which she apparently had ascended, was, of course, Clorimonde!

Of course. He should have expected it.

"What the devil—" Charles began, hurrying to the tree and glaring up. At her surprised glance down he blushed and begged pardon, but continued in the no-nonsense voice he was trying to perfect but which, no matter how he tried, never seemed to work with Miss Ansley. "What are you doing up there? And what do you mean running away like that? And what"—the irritation in his voice was growing with the level of it, for he found himself nearly shouting to be heard—"is that dashed dog barking at?"

He glared from Clorimonde to Miss Ansley and back again, equally annoyed with both.

"Sir Rupert, hush!" Miss Ansley said. "Naughty dog!"

To Carlesworth's surprise the poodle subsided, dropping to his belly at the foot of the tree as if properly chastised. Charles gazed at him in bafflement.

"And you, Charles—really! There is no reason for you to bellow so!"

"Bellow!" Charles was indignant. He did not, he told her, bellow. Ever. He was a quiet young man; everyone said so.

Miss Ansley reminded him of the day he yelled in Tory's ear and Charles glared at her. Yelling, he said, face and back stiff, was not the same as bellowing.

"There!" Arabella, who held something he could not see protectively to her, was reproachful. "You're doing it again!"

"Miss Ansley—"

"Oh!" She smiled. "Are we back to that, now?"

"What?" Confused, he craned his neck another way, trying to see what it was she held.

"You called me Arabella earlier, Charles. Are we back to Miss Ansley now?"

"Miss Ansley—"

The lady shook her head mournfully. "I have waited so long."

"I was worried. I saw Tory standing alone, and I thought—I thought—"

"Ahhhh." It was one of those feminine utterances, long and low and with a depth of meaning behind it he could not fathom. Charles shifted uneasily. "I see," said Arabella, nodding. "You can only call me Arabella when you are concerned about me. But when you are angry I must be Miss Ansley again. Is that it, Charles?"

No, he said testily; no, that was not it. It was just that—that— Confound the chit for not understanding! "It would not be proper," he told her in his best schoolmaster voice, "for me to call you Arabella, when we are not—not—"

Arabella waited several moments for him to tell her what they were not, but when he did not, she sighed.

"Dear Charles," she said, her voice sweet as she gazed down at him. "Do not be such a stick!"

"A stick!" Charles felt his mouth falling open, and shut it firmly. Of all the infuriating women! "Just because I have a care for the proprieties," he began.

"Yes, well." Arabella shifted position and prepared to descend, one foot reaching down for a foothold. "Have a little less care of the proprieties and a little more of this, if you please."

And so saying she reached down her arms and dropped a furry ball into his hands, which reached out automatically to catch it.

"Meow!" said the ball as Arabella followed its descent, dropping gracefully out of the tree.

"It's a kitten!" said Charles.

"Woof!" said Clorimonde, recovering from his guilt sufficiently to resent this furry interloper.

"Pffft!" said the small cat, leaving Charles's hands to claw its way up to his shoulder.

"Ow!" Charles grabbed the kitten by the neck and held it away from him. "He scratched me!"

"Pfft!" said the kitten, indignant at this treatment.

"Woof!" said Clorimonde, making a leap for the cat.

"Sir Rupert!" shrieked Arabella as Charles pulled the terrified kitten to his chest, cradling it there to protect it from the threatening poodle. "Bad, bad dog!" She was holding him around the neck, dragging him back from the cat and its savior. "Shame, sir! Shame!"

The mulish look on Clorimonde's face suggested to Charles that he was in no way ashamed, and Charles grinned.

"Miss Ansley," he said, "how do you do these things?"

"What?" Arabella, concentrating on commanding the poodle to sit, looked up in surprise.

"It was a lovely day," Charles said. "We were out for a ride. A tranquil ride, I thought, to admire the flowers and the sky, to exercise the horses, to allow you to practice your social skills." He looked down at the furry ball he held, and absently scratched the tiny animal's ears, to Arabella's silent approval. "Suddenly we're in the middle of a heated war, with our small David here foolish enough to take on that bumbling Goliath." He nodded toward Clorimonde, who was watching cat and man alertly, waiting for the latter's attention to be diverted.

Arabella grinned. "I heard Sir Rupert barking," she said. "And when I came to investigate, he had your poor little David cornered."

"My—" Carlesworth looked up, startled. "Oh, no!" he said. "No, no!" He held the kitten out toward her, but as he moved so did Clorimonde, and Miss Ansley had her hands full dealing with the dog.

"You are the rescuer here!" Charles said. "If the cat belongs to anyone, he belongs to you!"

"But he likes you so!" Arabella protested.

"No," Charles said firmly. "He does not. I do not like cats, and they do not like me. You can see—" He looked down at the traitorous kitten who, just as he'd uttered his last sentence, began to purr.

"It would appear, dear Charles," Arabella said, "that you have a new pet."

"No!" Charles almost yelped the word. "What would I want with a cat?! I can just hear my grandfather if I were to bring him home, and were my brother Jack to ever hear of it—" The thought made him blanch at the unmerciful teasing he would take. "No. He must belong around here, and we will just let him go."

"But Charles!" Arabella was clearly distressed. "I believe he is lost. And he is so small! Perhaps Clorimonde has chased him away from his mama, and if no one takes care of him . . ." Her eyes clouded over at the thought, and once again Charles held the kitten out toward her.

"Then you take him!" he said. "You like cats. Obviously. He is just what you need to keep you company."

"But Charles." Arabella glanced suggestively down, and as Charles followed her gaze he sighed.

"I already have company," Arabella said. "You know how Grandmama feels about Sir Rupert. And Sir Rupert is making it most clear he does not care for young David, so . . ."

Charles, picturing the old setter used to making its place before his fire, said that he, too, had a dog who would not welcome a feline invader, and—and—

He felt himself losing ground as the kitten purred louder.

"I suppose I could give it to a tenant," he said, looking from the kitten toward Arabella, then back again. One thumb stroked the soft white fur, caressing first one small orange ear, then one small black one. "My old nurse is pensioned off; she'd probably enjoy a companion. Except," he said, frowning as he remembered, "she's visiting her sister in Scotland for several months."

An inspired Arabella suggested he keep the kitten for his old nurse, growing it into a cat, and then, when the old woman returned . . .

Charles regarded her with suspicion. "You think if I keep it around a couple months, I'll keep it forever," he accused.

No, no! She assured him she did not.

"Well, I won't," he told her. "Not forever. You are right; we can't just leave it here, silly little thing. But I am not a man who keeps cats."

"Of course not!" Her words were sober but her eyes danced, and Charles frowned at her.

"Dogs, now. Dogs are a man's animal."

"Woof!" said Clorimonde.

"Some dogs," amended Charles.

Arabella laughed. "Well, then," she said, one arm still firmly wrapped around the poodle's neck, "that's settled, isn't it?"

A reluctant Charles agreed it was, and they walked slowly back to their horses. Miss Ansley held the kitten, to Clorimonde's evident disgust, while Charles put her onto her horse, then mounted his own.

"You won't tell anyone about this?" he demanded as he took the kitten from her and, after a moment, fitted it into the spacious pocket of his riding coat, where it promptly curled up and went to sleep.

"Of course not!" Miss Ansley promised. It turned out she didn't have to.

They were within a mile of Hedgwick Hall when Arabella heard Charles groan and looked up, surprised. Her own attention had been focused on Clorimonde chasing a butterfly in a nearby field, but now she followed his gaze and saw two riders coming toward them. Young men, they were fashionably dressed, and Arabella raised an eyebrow inquiringly.

"Not a word," Charles breathed, raising a hand in greeting, "about the kitten!"

Freddie Blathersham and Thomas Wooding gazed in admiration at the young lady riding with Charles, for a new female in the area, especially such a comely female, was always of interest to them. Their faces brightened when they heard she was staying at Hedgwick Hall, and both promised to call, to Charles's private disgust. Mr. Wooding even went so far as to say that if Miss Ansley would like another riding companion some morning he would be glad to oblige her, for everyone knew what a dull dog old Carlesworth was. The last was said with a good-natured laugh which Charles did not share.

Clorimonde, coming up as the words "dull dog" were spoken, gave an acknowledging woof for his species, causing Mr. Blathersham's and Mr. Wooding's horses to shy. Carlesworth began to feel a bit better about the poodle.

"Thank you, Mr. Wooding," Arabella said, smiling at the gentlemen in a way Charles was sure would have them presenting themselves at the Hall at the earliest opportunity, "but I am quite happy with Mr. Carlesworth's company."

"Oh?" Both Blathersham and Wooding appeared surprised, and regarded their old friend with a respect heretofore reserved for his brother. Charles felt better about Miss Ansley, too, and was smiling as Blathersham asked if he had heard from old Jack recently.

Charles was just saying his grandfather had had a letter from him last week when a meow issued from his pocket. The kitten, awakened from its nap by the cessation of the rocking motion from Thunder's moving, was ready to come out and play.

"Eh?" Blathersham said, looking at Charles in puzzlement.

"I think we'd best be going." Charles gazed beseechingly at

Arabella, who nodded. They were stopped, however, by Wooding's next question.

"Charles," Mr. Wooding said, "I don't mean to pry, but did your pocket just . . . meow?"

Carlesworth laughed. Wooding was a funny one, he said.

"Meow," said the kitten.

"It did!" Blathersham was staring at the pocket in astonishment. "His pocket meowed! I heard it! Didn't you hear it, Miss Ansley?"

All attention turned to Arabella who, watching Charles's anguished face as he anticipated the teasing of his fellows, bit her lip and sighed. "I am afraid, Charles, that they have found you out," she said.

"What?" Blathersham and Wooding chorused. Arabella nudged Tory closer to Thunder, and reached into Charles's pocket, pulling out the kitten.

"It's a cat!" Blathersham said.

"A kitten!" Wooding corrected.

"Oh, bother!" said Charles.

The newcomers started to grin, and Carlesworth reddened.

"A special kitten," Arabella told them, and when she was sure she had their attention, continued. "You asked if Mr. Carlesworth had heard from his brother, Mr. Blathersham. Well, yes, he has. And his brother writes that it is all the crack in London now—all the most fashionable men are doing it—to carry a kitten with them everywhere."

"It is?" Blathersham's and Wooding's eyes grew big. Both yearned to cut a dash in city life, and if Carlesworth's brother thought this a significant enough fashion trend to write Charles about it—well! They had to know more!

Arabella nodded her answer, and was glad their attention was focused so thoroughly on her. One glance at Charles's glassy eyes as he sat as if stuffed, dreading what she would say next, would have made them suspicious.

"But not just any kitten will do," Arabella continued. Charles was appalled she could appear so earnest while telling such a whisker. "It must be a white kitten, like this one. With one orange ear, and one black. That is what makes it fashionable."

"But—but—" Blathersham, who wanted above all else to be a Tulip of the Ton, objected. "Such cats must be remarkably hard to come by!"

"Oh, yes!" Miss Ansley's nod was grave as she agreed. "It is the rarity that makes them so highly prized."

"I see." Blathersham stroked his chin, considering. "I don't suppose you'd care to part with yours, Charles."

Before Carlesworth could agree, Miss Ansley had assured the young gentlemen he would not. "Nothing," she said, with a warning glance toward Charles, "could part Mr. Carlesworth from this cat. Nothing."

Blathersham's face fell.

"You might have told us, Charles," he complained. "Trying to steal a march on your friends—"

"Tell me, Miss Ansley," said Wooding, who had been thinking deeply. "Does the kitten have to be just like this one? That is, if it were white but the left ear were black and the right orange, instead of vice versa—"

Arabella gave it as her opinion that that would be allowed, then looked toward Charles for confirmation. "Isn't that your understanding, too, Charles?"

Charles looked at their anxious companions and gave a wooden nod.

"Of course," Carlesworth cautioned, as the two began listing aloud all the places they might look for such a kitten, "you know how these fashions are. Here one day, gone the next."

He was trying to warn them without giving himself or Miss Ansley away, but his words had the opposite effect.

Wooding and Blathersham exchanged startled glances, and nodded. "Then we'd better be looking!" Blathersham said. "Before the fashion is gone!"

Lifting their hats in polite farewell, the two cantered off, leaving Charles staring in disbelief after them.

"Gudgeons!" he said, when they were out of sight.

Miss Ansley giggled. "It is as Gervase always says," she informed him. "You need only say it is fashion for people to follow it." She held the kitten to her cheek for a moment before returning it to Charles with a smile.

"Next time you need only tell them you no longer have the cat with you because it is no longer fashionable to carry one."

"Perhaps," said Charles, stroking his chin, "I'll tell them that instead, all fashionable men now own monkeys."

"Own or are?" Miss Ansley asked, her eyes twinkling.

Really, Charles told her, some days he just didn't know. . . .

❧ 11 ❧

"Yes, my old friend," Charles said that night as he gazed into the mournful eyes of his longtime library companion, "I fear you are right."

The old setter, whose head rested on his master's knee, emitted a heavy sigh, and after staring for several more moments at the interloper asleep in Carlesworth's lap, rose and ambled over to its place by the fire where it settled with its head pointedly averted from that painful sight.

"I know," Charles said, continuing to speak softly to the dog as with one finger he stroked the kitten's soft white fur and scritched it under its chin. This so pleased the small ball of fluff that it stretched and purred in its sleep, shifting slightly to make its chin more accessible to this agreeable activity. "It is all her doing, you know. Everything has been at sixes and sevens outside the house since she arrived, and now—now—" Charles had stopped his finger's movement, which had awakened the kitten, and that small animal put one paw suggestively on her new master's finger, to see if he might start the scritching again. "Now she has invaded my home, too."

The dog made no answer, and Davida—for such, upon closer inspection, she had been shown to be—ignored Carlesworth's ruminations in favor of continuing her nap.

When he had first arrived home Charles had taken the kitten to the kitchen, having decided, after he left Miss Ansley, that his cook would be delighted with such a pet. His cook had had other ideas, however, and perhaps that was why, after consuming what the butler Roberts described as a monstrous meal for one so small, Davida had had little trouble slipping out of the kitchen in search of her savior.

Repeated efforts to restore her to the more restricted area

failed; Roberts informed him that every time the kitchen door opened the little cat came scooting out in search of Mr. Carlesworth. And, continued Roberts, who liked cats, it was clear she was a sly one, for she seemed to have an instinct for heading straight toward whatever room Mr. Carlesworth was occupying. She had managed that at suppertime, slipping into the dining room when one of the footmen entered, and considerably surprising Charles's grandfather by appearing on his table along with the soup.

"Eh?" the old man had said, some of his consommé slopping over onto the tablecloth as the kitten made its way from floor to table leg to table top.

"Oh, for goodness' sake!" Charles exploded, which drew the kitten's attention. Without a single glance at any of the interesting objects occupying the table, she scampered toward Charles, purring loudly. Unfortunately, the most direct line to Charles was through his soup, and in seconds a surprised Davida had leaped from her watery footbath onto his clean linen.

"That's a cat!" his grandfather said as the exasperated Charles grabbed the animal by the scruff of the neck and held it away from him, using his napkin to dab first at his waistcoat and then at the kitten's feet.

"You've had a cat in your soup!" the old man continued. "There's a cat in my dining room, and he has been in your soup!"

"Mr. Carlesworth, I am so sorry," began Roberts, hurrying forward to relieve him of the furry bundle. "I don't know how she got in here, sir, but as attached to you as she is—"

"What the *devil*," exploded Charles's grandfather, "is a cat doing in my dining room, and in your soup?"

Charles, who had resumed his seat when Roberts took his new pet, looked up and said, "That is Davida, Grandfather. She is a present from Miss Ansley."

"Meow," said Davida.

"Oh." His grandfather looked from Charles to the cat and back again. "Giving you presents, is she?"

"Ha!" Charles waved away the footman who had removed his soup bowl and was preparing to deposit another before him. "Foisting them on me, more like!"

"Meow, meow," said Davida, her small claws gripping Roberts's arm as he prepared to take her from the room.

"Ow!" said Roberts, so far forgetting himself as to show pain and emotion in front of his employers.

"Meow, meow, MEOW!" returned Davida, sounding for all the world as if she were being tortured.

"Oh, very well!" A goaded Charles stopped the butler with a word. "Give me the confounded cat and let us enjoy our supper in peace!"

A relieved Roberts was only too happy to do so, and quiet was restored to the High Point dining room. It was broken only at the end of the meal when Charles's grandfather, who had sat in thoughtful silence through several courses, said, his brow furrowed, "Didn't know you wanted a cat, Charles."

His grandson stared at him in disbelief.

"Could have had one anytime these last ten years, you know. Didn't mean to deprive you."

"But I didn't!" Charles said.

His grandfather looked pointedly at the kitten, who had made its way to Charles's shoulder and chose to reside there, purring loudly.

"I don't want this cat!" Charles said, one hand absently patting it as he rose. "I have never wanted a cat. But Miss Ansley—"

"Yes?" his grandfather prompted, when he didn't continue.

"Miss Ansley rescued this cat," Charles said. "From Clorimonde. But then she couldn't take it home, because of Clorimonde's dislike of the cat. I suppose he dislikes all cats. Principle, you know. So she said I must take it. I didn't want to take it. Wanted her to take it. Wanted to leave it where we found it. But no, she said, I must take it. So take it I did. Then we ran into Blathersham and Wooding on the road. They heard the cat. It was in my pocket. She told them it is all the crack in London to be carrying around a small white cat with one orange ear and one black ear—told them Jack told me so; well, it is just the sort of thing Jack would nose about, for a lark, but—and then she said the ears can be interchangeable—"

His grandfather's eyebrows, which had begun an ascent with his first words, were alarmingly high at the end of his confused speech, and Charles sighed.

"The long and the short of it, Grandfather," he said, "is that now, I have a cat."

"And the thing is," Charles now mused to the old dog and

sleeping kitten in the privacy of his library, "it wouldn't surprise me at all if within a week Blathersham and Wooding are calling at Hedgwick Hall to see if Miss Ansley thinks they've found a cat stylish enough to bring them into fashion, too."

In that prediction, Mr. Carlesworth underestimated his friends. Mr. Blathersham was at Hedgwick Hall the next morning, a small wicker basket perched precariously on his knees as Arabella and her grandmama entered the room.

"Lady Hedgwick!" Blathersham said, rising in a hurry and almost dropping the basket. "Miss Ansley!" He reached for the ladies' hands in turn, bowing deep over each.

"Miss Ansley, I—" he began, then paled slightly as Clorimonde entered the room and made straight for Mr. Blathersham and his basket. The dog took one good sniff, and growled.

"Clorimonde!" said Lady Hedgwick.

"Sir Rupert!" said Miss Ansley.

"Pfffft!" said the contents of Mr. Blathersham's basket.

"Oh, no!" said Mr. Blathersham, paling further.

"Woof!" said Clorimonde, who by now was on his hind feet with his front feet propped on Mr. Blathersham's shoulders. That gentleman brushed him off and, basket held high, sought refuge on one of Lady Hedgwick's prized Queen Anne chairs.

"Mr. Blathersham!" said Lady Hedgwick.

"Sir Rupert!" repeated Miss Ansley, trying her best to collar the dog.

"Beg pardon!" said Mr. Blathersham, still holding his basket high. "But if perhaps Clorimonde could be persuaded to leave the room—"

By now Holmsley, drawn to the morning room by the sounds of unseemly excitement emanating from there, had sailed onto the scene. After one quick gasp of shock he set himself to the task of restoring order by the simple expedient of attaching both hands to the collar Clorimonde wore and, with the help of a quickly called footman, dragging the dog from the room.

"Woof, woof!" said Clorimonde, still hurling defiant accusations at Mr. Blathersham and his basket as the door was shut upon him.

"Well!" said Lady Hedgwick, when the poodle had been ousted and a modicum of decorum returned to her usually quiet morning room. She glanced at her laughing granddaughter, then moved her gaze to their guest, and her eyes narrowed.

"Mr. Blathersham!" she said.

The young man, busy mopping his forehead, paused in midmop with a polite, "Yes, my lady?"

"Mr. Blathersham, you are standing on my Queen Anne chair. My *prized* Queen Anne chair!"

"Oh!" Mr. Blathersham leaped down as if his feet were scorched. "Beg pardon," he said. "Exigency of the moment— not meaning to offend, but—" He patted his basket. "Couldn't hardly let Clorimonde get these beauties, now could I?"

He looked so proud of himself as he hugged the basket to his chest that Lady Hedgwick forbore to point out that there might have been better ways to fend off the dog than standing on her furniture. Instead, curiosity aroused, she asked just what it was he had in that basket, anyway.

Mr. Blathersham turned toward Miss Ansley. "Yesterday, Miss Ansley," he said, "when we met on the road, you said one must have a white one, with one orange ear, and one black, but I have been through every barn and kitchen within miles of my home, and no such one is to be had, I assure you!"

The expression on her grandmother's face was almost more than Arabella could bear, for the old lady was looking at their guest as if he had lost his mind. Schooling her features to a look of polite interest, and averting her eyes from Lady Hedgwick's, Miss Ansley managed a polite, "Oh?"

"So I was wondering." Mr. Blathersham began to open his basket, and beckoned her closer, so she could peer inside. "Do you suppose one of each would do?"

"Oh, Mr. Blathersham!" Arabella reached for the orange kitten peering up at her with big blue eyes. Beside it sat a white kitten, and one tip-to-toe black. "They're darling!"

"Well, I rather thought so," Mr. Blathersham confided. "Always liked cats, you know. Thing is, wasn't all the crack. Not supposed to like cats. Supposed to like dogs. A manly thing, you know. And since I couldn't find a white one with one black ear and one orange, I thought perhaps if a fellow carried one of each color . . ."

He was looking at her with such a hopeful expression that Arabella had to turn away, biting her lip hard to maintain her composure. She cuddled the orange kitten to her cheek for a moment more before turning back to him, shaking her head regretfully.

"I don't know, Mr. Blathersham," she said, "it is a unique idea, to be sure, but . . . When the fashion is for one thing, it seems so few substitutes will do. . . ."

His face fell, and he took the orange kitten from her and placed it back in the basket, stroking its fur softly as he did so. "Was afraid of that," he mourned. "But you never know. I thought—I hoped—"

His thoughts and hopes were never put into words; just then the morning room door opened and Holmsley intoned, "Mr. Wooding, my lady!"

Mr. Blathersham closed the lid of his basket and whipped it behind his back as Mr. Wooding tripped into the room, carrying a large orange cat in his arms.

"Lady Hedgwick!" Mr. Wooding began. "Miss Ansley—" Too late he spied the other gentleman, and the smile on his lips faded slightly. "Blathersham," he said.

"Wooding."

Mr. Wooding regarded Mr. Blathersham with suspicion. "What's that you've got behind your back, Blathersham?" he questioned, moving a bit to the right and craning his neck to see.

Mr. Blathersham turned to the left, and countered with, "What's that you've got in your arms, Wooding?"

"Oh!" Mr. Wooding looked down at the cat, who only looked disgusted, and flushed. "Thing is, thought I'd ask Miss Ansley—"

"It ain't a white cat, Wooding."

"No, but—"

"And it ain't a small cat."

Stung by his friend's cavalier comments, so true and therefore so unwelcome, Mr. Wooding turned appealing eyes to Miss Ansley. "Belongs to my aunt Agatha," he said, stroking the animal in his arms. "I know it's not white, or small, but it's orange with sort of whitish ears, and I thought—I thought—"

He watched Miss Ansley shake her head sadly, and sighed.

"Didn't think at all," Blathersham snorted, drawing his friend's fire.

"Oho!" said Mr. Wooding. "And what's that you've got in your basket there, Blathersham?" Mr. Blathersham looked guiltily down at the basket he had absently swung from behind his back to his side.

"Nothing," said Mr. Blathersham.

"Meow!" said the basket.

"Oho!" said Mr. Wooding. Mr. Blathersham began to realize he had never liked the way Wooding said oho, and was about to take exception to it when Lady Hedgwick entered the conversation.

"Gentlemen!" said Lady Hedgwick. "What on earth—"

Behind the two young men Arabella was signaling madly and Lady Hedgwick, after frowning at her granddaughter for several seconds, changed that to, "Would you care for tea, gentlemen? And some cream, perhaps, for your cats?"

When they failed to recognize the sarcasm in her last sentence and actually seemed in danger of accepting her invitation, Lady Hedgwick continued, her voice thoughtful, "Not, of course, that I am used to entertaining cats—nor to having people bring them here to shed hair all over my furniture without a by-your-leave— nor to having people standing on my furniture, when it comes to that. . . ."

Mr. Blathersham, gulping, thought of an engagement elsewhere that required his urgent attention. Not willing to leave Mr. Wooding behind—for that young gentleman showed a real inclination to moon after Miss Ansley, which Mr. Blathersham had every intention of doing himself, and so did not want to leave his friend to steal a march on him—he suggested that Mr. Wooding's aunt Agatha might be missing her cat, and might want it back soon.

Mr. Wooding started, and gulped himself. Yes, he stammered, with a bow to Miss Ansley and another for Lady Hedgwick, that might be true; he had not exactly gained her permission before taking Old Lolly off for this visit. . . .

Smiling, Arabella assured him he would be wise to return the cat at once, perhaps even before his aunt missed it.

Mr. Wooding, thinking too late of Aunt Agatha's often caustic tongue, said yes, that would be a fine idea, to be sure. He followed Mr. Blathersham from the room in good order.

"And now, miss," Lady Hedgwick said, as soon as the door closed behind the two young men and their feline friends, "you will tell me what this was all about. Immediately!"

Arabella did, providing such a highly colored version that by the end of her recitation both ladies were in stitches, tears rolling down their cheeks.

"And the thing is," Arabella said, burying her head in a pillow on the low sofa on which she sat, "only Charles has the truly fashionable cat in the district, and he is not one bit thrilled about it! While these gentlemen—"

"—are running all over Christendom," her grandmother continued for her, wiping at her eyes. "Oh, Arabella! It is too, too naughty of you!"

"I know," Miss Ansley agreed, sitting up and hugging the pillow to her chest, "but poor Charles! If you could have seen his face! He didn't want to take the kitten, and did so only out of the goodness of his heart—and because I hounded him so! I really could not let his friends roast him about it forever! So when the opportunity presented itself—" She giggled and wiped her eyes. "Seize the opportunity, Gervase always says."

"Hmmm." Lady Hedgwick was watching Arabella's merriment with interest. "So Charles took the kitten. . . ."

At her granddaughter's look of inquiry, Lady Hedgwick's eyes opened wide. "It occurs to me, my dear," she said, "that there may be times that Gervase is quite right."

Arabella, with no reason to doubt it, merely smiled and nodded.

❧ 12 ❧

"And you should have seen Mr. Wooding's cat!" Arabella's face was merry as she told Charles about her visitors that afternoon. They'd ridden out from Hedgwick Hall perhaps two hours earlier, Arabella having been invited to join Charles on a visit to several of his grandfather's tenants. That done, they had stopped for refreshment in a shady spot beside one of the small streams Charles had fished as a boy, his grandfather's cook having thoughtfully provided them with a half dozen of his famous cherry tarts.

"The poor cat looked so disgusted. It was obviously much more used to curling up on a pillow somewhere than to being carried about the country! It had gotten hair all over Mr. Wooding's bottle green coat. And it was so *big*."

"His aunt Agatha's cat." Mr. Carlesworth nodded. He knew the animal. "Nasty old thing. Hope it bit him."

"Charles!"

"Likes to bite," Charles explained. "Might as well bite Wooding. Bit him before. I saw it. Went to pay a duty call with Wooding one time. Old lady gave the cat a sweet, Wooding tried to filch it, cat bit him. Didn't blame it. Hope it bit him again."

"Charles!"

"Well, *I'd* bite him if he were carrying me about the country."

"Charles!" Arabella burst into laughter at the picture and Mr. Carlesworth, after a puzzled moment, joined her.

"Wouldn't carry me about the country, of course."

"I should hope not!"

"But if I were a cat—"

Arabella grinned. "I am glad you are not a cat, Charles," she told him, biting into the last of the cherry tarts. "I would miss

83

you. Not," she continued, when he would have replied, her head tilted to one side as she considered, "that I wouldn't have liked you as a cat, for I am sure you would be a very good one. And I suppose if you were a cat I could still talk to you. But you couldn't talk back. Not," she said, considering him thoughtfully, "that there wouldn't be days when that would be a blessing. . . ."

"Now see here!" Charles began, indignant.

"And I couldn't tease you if you were a cat," Miss Ansley said, "for that would be cruelty to animals, for a cat can't tease back. And I am never unkind to animals."

"No," Charles snorted. "Only to me!"

Miss Ansley dimpled. "Poor Charles." She reached out a hand to cover his. "Has it been so terrible for you, these past few weeks?"

She looked so anxious for a moment that Carlesworth, thrown off balance, stuttered no, no, of course not—he had rather enjoyed—

Then he saw the twinkle growing in her eye, and frowned heavily. "You're doing it again, aren't you?" he said.

"Doing what?" She was the picture of innocence, her eyes open very wide, which only increased his suspicions.

"You're teasing me again. You always do that."

"Yes." She grinned. "I cannot help myself, Charles. You are so easy to tease. And it is such fun."

She should, he told her, have more respect for her elders.

Arabella's grin broadened.

"I am at least six years older than you!" Charles said, reading her expression correctly.

Her grin vanished, to be replaced by a look of pure surprise. "So *old?!* Why, Charles! I had no idea! I hope our rides haven't been too much for one of your advanced age."

"Now, stop that!" He glared at her as threateningly as he could, to no avail.

Miss Ansley giggled. "I cannot help it, Charles," she told him, pressing her lips to try to control the growing laughter. "When you are being so ridiculous—"

A frosty Charles asked just what was so ridiculous, and Arabella grinned again.

"I am eighteen, Charles," she told him. "Nineteen soon. If you are six years older, that would make you twenty-four, which hardly qualifies you as an elder—unless you are talking about your stuffy old attitudes.''

"It makes me older than you!" Charles began, responding to the first part of her argument before he grasped the last, and stiffened. "And my attitudes," he said, his eyes narrowing, "are not stuffy."

Now it was Miss Ansley's turn to choke and she did so, the last bit of her cherry tart catching in her throat and sticking there. She did not recover until an exasperated Charles patted her several times on the back in an effort to dislodge the stuck crumb.

"Oh, really, Charles!" she said. "Don't be ridiculous! Even Grandmama and your grandfather are not as strict in their notions of how I should go on as you are!"

"That is because they never see just how abominably you behave!" Charles said.

"Well . . ." The dimple appeared at the corner of Miss Ansley's mouth, and a roguish glance agreed that might be true. "Still . . ."

The dimple grew more pronounced.

"Do you remember last night, Charles, when you and your grandfather came to dinner and your grandfather was telling us how Grandmama used to set them all the pace at the fox hunts, riding neck or nothing across the fields?"

Charles nodded. He did.

"Can you tell me, Charles," Miss Ansley was looking up at the sky, as if the words were only idle musings, "the difference between riding neck or nothing and careening?"

"A lady," Charles said, his tone repressive, "does not careen."

"Does she ride neck or nothing, Charles?"

He frowned. "Apparently," he said, "if she is your grand-mother." Intuiting her next question, his tone grew more repressive still. "Not," he said, "if she is you."

"Well, why not?"

Words and voice were both indignant and—if he had it correctly—a trifle hurt, and Charles looked at her in surprise.

"Well—" he started.

"I am a very good rider, Charles!"

He agreed she was.

"Even with that stupid sidesaddle!"

He agreed again. She had grown, he said, most proficient.

"Well then, why is it every time I give Tory his head in the run I long for, you ring such a peal over me that anyone listening would believe that at the very least I'd tied my garter in public?"

"Miss Ansley!" Charles flushed. "I do not ring a peal over you! I just—"

"And that's another thing!" Arabella said. "Why is it that you are always calling me Miss Ansley? That day you thought I was hurt you called me Arabella, which I very much like, but no, now it's back to Miss Ansley, even though I call you Charles."

"Yes, well—" He coughed. "I believe I have told you more than once that you should not—"

"But that is foolish!" Arabella cried. "You are my friend—" She stopped suddenly and her forehead puckered slightly. "You *are* my friend, are you not, Charles?"

She looked so anxious that Charles was thrown off balance— something, he was sorry to say, that seemed to occur much too often in Miss Ansley's presence.

Of course he was her friend, he said. But that did not mean—

"Then why should we not address each other as friends should and do?" The interruption was more a demand to be told than a question, and as Arabella's tone sharpened, Charles's words came slower, and low.

People might not understand, he told her.

Arabella snapped her fingers. "Pooh to people!"

No. Charles shook his head. She could not say pooh to people, especially not when she wished to take her place in society. Especially not when—

He stopped, appalled at what he had been about to blurt out. It was something he knew, something his grandfather and her grandmother knew, but never spoke of. There was no need. And not for the world would he say it to Arabella, whom he was trying to protect.

"Especially not—" she prompted.

Charles shook his head. "It was nothing," he said.

"Especially not," her words were quiet, "when you are the daughter of Gervase and Constance Ansley, and their reputations precede you."

"No!" He tried to deny it, but she read it in his eyes.

"My father loved my mother very much," she said, looking away from him and off toward where the horses grazed. "Once,

on the anniversary of her death, my father was in his cups—
something I saw very seldom, in all the years I was with
him—and he told me my mother was the closest thing he ever
met to heaven's inhabitants.'' She grinned. ''He told me also that
I am only a little like her—in looks, but more with the devil of
the Ansleys to my temperament.'' Her grin grew. ''That is why
I sympathize with the task my grandmama has set you, Charles.
Even though I try very hard to be good, I know your job is not
easy.''

A skeptical Charles said he had not noticed her trying all that
hard to be good, and Arabella's rich bubble of laughter rose,
causing Tory to prick his ears and gaze inquiringly toward them.
When neither made a move toward him, he resumed his grazing.

''Well, perhaps not very hard, Charles. But occasionally I do
realize how disruptive my presence is to your peace of mind.
Still,'' she said, tilting her head to the side, considering, ''I
daresay it is good for you!''

An indignant Charles wanted to know just what it was about
him that made people feel having his peace continually disrupted
was good for him, but Miss Ansley ignored the question,
choosing instead to continue her story.

''My father was very sorry, later, that he persuaded my mother
to run away with him to Gretna Green. He was sorry for the
scandal. He wanted to give her all the best, he said, but he felt,
in the end, he had given her all the worst.''

''Then why—'' Charles started. She ignored him.

''But he was young, and hot-blooded and hotheaded. He still
is hot-blooded and hotheaded, although with time he has learned
to hide it better. And perhaps he gained better control of his
temper.'' She thought a moment, her forehead wrinkled. ''He
tells me, whenever I lose my temper, that age helps, and the
realization that you cannot control the world no matter how
much you try, so little is worth getting angry over, so long as you
get even.''

She sighed. ''My father sees it as justice, but I think there is
a revenge in getting even that I cannot quite like, don't you,
Charles?''

Unsure just who they were getting even with, Charles cautiously said that he rather believed it depended on the circumstances. Miss Ansley beamed at him.

''That is just what I like about you, Charles,'' she approved.

"You have a great deal of sense. Of course it does. I am sure Gervase would agree with you if he were here right now."

From all he had heard of Miss Ansley's father, Carlesworth rather doubted that, and was glad they did not at this moment have to put it to the test. Instead, he waited for Arabella to continue her story.

"My mother was courted by many men, Charles. Both my father and Grandmama have told me so. She was very beautiful, you know—Grandmama has an old portrait she has hung in my room. I am not really very much like her, although I have her eyes."

She looked expectantly toward him, and Charles said at once that they were very fine eyes. He ventured to add it was apparent Blathersham and Wooding thought she was quite taking, too, and Miss Ansley giggled.

"Oh, I am well enough," she said with the shrug he had come to recognize as part of her. "Grandmama says I will be the toast of London—if I listen to her and you and your grandfather—but Grandmama is prejudiced, and I only hope I do not disappoint her.

"My mother, on the other hand . . ." She looked dreamy, and proud. "My mother had many suitors, many with excellent titles and connections and much bigger fortunes than Gervase's. Her father—my Grandpapa—wanted her to marry elsewhere. Gervase had a reputation even then, it seems, and Grandpapa had given another man leave to address my mother."

Miss Ansley looked at Carlesworth then, and her eyes were very bright. "You would never ask, let alone encourage, a woman to flee with you to Gretna Green, would you, Charles?"

Carlesworth, who could not imagine fleeing with a woman anywhere, wrinkled his forehead as he tried to picture it. At last he shook his head no.

"Of course you would not." Arabella laughed, but behind the lightness of the sound was a deeper note—of what? he asked himself. Bitterness? Disappointment?

It occurred to him—he didn't know why the thought came now, but it made him uneasy—that his brother Jack would have said yes in an instant. It was just the sort of ill-considered, highly romantic thing Jack would do when in a passion, without a thought for all those hurt by the action. And then later Jack would come to his grandfather and Charles, looking for forgiveness and help back, help in atoning for his mistake. And he would get it. Oh, yes. He would get it. No matter how disappointed they might be in him, he would always be their Jack, and when he needed help, they would give it.

Gervase Ansley had not been so lucky.

Struck by the unfairness of it, Charles shook his head again, then looked up to find Miss Ansley watching him closely. It was clear she had misunderstood the action, but before he could speak she continued.

"My mother loved him, Charles, so she went with him. I have a diary she kept. My father gave it to me on my sixteenth birthday. That and this locket"—she touched her neck, and Charles saw there the gold medallion she always wore—"is all I have of her. It is only through reading her words that I have come to know my mother at all. Yet Charles," she said, looking straight at him now, her gaze clear, "through it I feel I came to know her quite well. She was happy with my father, Charles. Happy I was to be born. Happy in their rented rooms in Paris. And she never, ever regretted her decision." Miss Ansley's voice wavered slightly before steadiness returned. "Only society's reaction to it."

Her hand went to the locket again and she sat back, looking toward the stream, her eyes full of thoughts of far away. "Pray God, Charles," she said into the lazy afternoon, as he sat very still, listening, "that in your lifetime someone loves you as my parents loved. I do."

They sat for perhaps half an hour, neither speaking, Miss Ansley staring at the gurgling stream and seeing memories there, Mr. Carlesworth staring at Miss Ansley. The sun was casting long shadows when at last she rose and said, "I believe we should be getting back, Mr. Carlesworth. Grandmama will worry."

"Yes," said Mr. Carlesworth, rising, too. "I believe you are right, Arabella."

❧ 13 ❧

"What is it, lad?"

Charles, lost in thought that night as he sat in the library with Davida on one leg and an open but unread book on the other, started and glanced up.

"Grandfather!" he said, laying down the book and picking up the cat as he half rose. The earl waved him back into his chair and took the one opposite him, peering at his grandson in concern. "I didn't hear you come in."

"Obviously." The old man's tone was dry, and Charles's look questioning. "Nor did you hear the three questions I addressed to you at dinner."

"Oh." Charles settled Davida more comfortably on his lap, happy to reposition the tiny claws that extended and retracted as she purred her contentment at his presence. He gave the earl his full attention. "Was there something you needed, Grandfather? Something you would like me to do for you?" He glanced around the room, and his eyes fell on the tray Roberts had so thoughtfully provided moments earlier. "A glass of brandy, perhaps?"

The earl, after a moment's more close inspection of the younger man, allowed that a glass of brandy might be quite nice. "And one for yourself, Charles."

Carlesworth rose to pour the required drinks, and the disgusted Davida, deprived of her favorite perch, gazed about for several seconds, blinked twice at the earl, and hopped from the floor to his footstool, and from the footstool to his knee.

"Here now!" said the earl.

"Meow!" said Davida.

Charles, stopped in mid-pour by his grandfather's voice, turned to see his pet walking daintily up the earl's leg, where she turned and placed her front paws on the arm the old man had resting on the chair.

"Davida!" Charles said. "Get down."

"Meow!" said Davida, ignoring him. She rubbed her small head against the earl's empty hand, and when he did not seem to take the hint, encouraged him again. Clangstone smiled.

"Persistent little thing, isn't she?" he asked, raising his other hand to pet her. Satisfied, Davida settled herself comfortably on his leg and closed her eyes.

"Please, sir." Charles had the brandy poured now, and was returning to his grandfather. "You can put her on the floor."

"No, no." The earl waved the hand not stroking the small cat and shook his head. "She's all right. Never thought I cared much for cats, but this one . . ." He ran one finger from the kitten's nose to the middle of her back, to Davida's obvious enjoyment. "This one has spirit."

He looked up, and his eyes were remarkably keen as he said the small cat and Miss Ansley had a great deal in common.

"What?" Charles, about to be seated, stopped in surprise.

"Spirit," the earl said. "They both have courage—determination."

"Yes." Charles's frowning gaze was directed at the small cat, but the earl had the certain feeling the expression was for someone else. He watched as his grandson settled himself in the worn old leather chair that had been Charles's father's, and sighed. Sometimes Charles reminded the earl so much of the boy's father that he could hardly bear it. Take the way he dealt with his problems, for instance. Turned them all inside and tried to puzzle them out, instead of going to those who loved him and wanted to help.

The earl sipped his brandy and frowned himself. He loved the boy too much to be shut out. "So," he said, when Carlesworth seemed no closer to speaking. Charles looked up politely.

"Yes." Charles leaned forward, setting the brandy on the small cherry table beside his chair. "There was something you wanted me to do, Grandfather."

The earl nodded. "I want you to tell me what's bothering you, lad."

Charles looked surprised. "Bothering me?"

The earl heaved an inward sigh. For such a clever young man, there were times Charles was really remarkably obtuse. "You sat through supper without hearing me, boy. Now I walk into the library and find you sitting here, a frown on your forehead and your book open, but your mind obviously somewhere else." He sat forward, moving the small white cat, who issued a disgusted meow in annoyance and jumped down, stalking over to the fireplace, where she settled herself between the paws of the old dog lying there. The setter rolled its eyes toward Charles, as if to say "Now see what you've done," but otherwise did not move, and Carlesworth smiled to see how quickly his new pet had made yet another conquest.

The earl smiled, too. "Quite a way about her, isn't there?" he said.

Charles nodded.

"That's like Miss Ansley, too."

Carlesworth's smile diminished, and the earl thought he understood.

"Driving you daft, is she?" he asked.

"What?"

The puzzlement in his grandson's face made it clear that that was not it, and it was several seconds before Carlesworth even understood his grandfather's meaning.

"Oh. No!" He shrugged. "Actually, we are getting along quite well—when she is not being totally impossible!"

The earl chuckled. "Growing into quite a lady, isn't she?"

Charles grinned. "Why do you say that?" he asked. "Are all ladies impossible?"

"Without a doubt." The earl sipped his drink. "At least, the best of them!"

"Then Arabella," Charles said, tapping his glass thoughtfully, a slight smile on his face, "is certainly one of the best of them!" He sat for several moments more, and as the earl watched the smile faded to a slight frown. Carlesworth's eyes took on that moody look again.

"Actually," Charles said, picking up his brandy and sipping it carefully, "I think she always has been. A lady, I mean. And one of the best. It's just that not all her actions would be considered quite"—he searched for a word for several moments—"orthodox—by society."

There was silence in the room again and the earl, his eyes on his grandson, settled back into his own chair and sipped his brandy slowly, trying to decipher Charles's last utterance. If

Miss Ansley was not the cause of his grandson's distraction, then what?

"Charles."

Carlesworth's head came up, and he focused on the face in front of him. "Sir?"

"I want you to tell me, Charles, what you were thinking about when I came into the room just a few minutes ago. And during dinner."

"Jack."

"What?"

Clangstone was surprised. What did his other grandson have to do with all this? Puzzling it out, he thought he knew, and sipped his brandy reflectively. "Oh." The earl sighed. "Have you had a letter from Jack, then? What kind of trouble has he gotten himself into this time, that you must be thinking about him so?"

Charles ran a hand through his hair, and sipped his brandy again. No, he said, it wasn't that. As far as Charles knew, Jack was just fine. But Charles had been thinking about Jack, and Gervase Ansley, about his grandfather and father and even Charles himself.

"What?" Now the earl really *was* confused.

"Today, Grandfather, Arabella told me about her mother and father. She told me she is proud to be their child. I've been thinking all night about the things that make us who we are. For instance." He held up the book at his side, looking first at it and then at the earl. "Would I love reading so if father hadn't started me so early, and if it hadn't been the chief pleasure I enjoyed with him, one of the few ways he let me into his life after mother died? Would I ever have taken up Greek if he hadn't—hadn't—" Charles put the book down and looked away.

"Hadn't loved it so," his grandfather supplied. Charles nodded.

"And Jack," Charles continued. "Would Jack be living the life he lives now if it wasn't so expected of him as the future earl? Would he take so many risks, do so many of the things he does, if the pattern hadn't been set early on, when taking risks was how *he* garnered father's attention? And what would have happened to us when father died if it hadn't been for you?"

What would have happened to me, the old man thought silently, as he looked into the troubled young eyes across from him. What would I have done if you hadn't come to put life back into this old house, and into this old man who was left without either wife or son to comfort him in his old age?

"You saved us, Grandfather," Charles said. "Who knows who we would be, if not for you?"

"Charles." The earl shook his head, leaning forward to lay one hand heavily on his grandson's knee. "You give me too much credit, lad. You would be who you would be."

"No." Carlesworth shook his head. "You saved us. I turned inward after father's death, and Jack raged out, and you pulled us both through. You gave us our heads as much as we were able to use them, but you always—always—held the reins."

"Until you were old enough to drive," his grandfather said, the words soft.

Charles nodded. "The thing is, Grandfather," he said, the words slow, as if he considered each one carefully, for the first time. "We were lucky, Jack and I. Father was lucky, because he grew up a child whose father loved him." Charles picked up his brandy and this time finished off the glass, putting it down with a slight clink that sounded loud in the quiet library.

"The thing is, Grandfather," Charles repeated, leaning forward, his arms on his knees, his face showing intent in the light of the candle beside him, "who held Gervase Ansley's reins?"

It was not easy for either the earl or Charles to talk of such things, for both were private men, neither of whom had much experience or comfort in talking about their feelings. Yet they sat late into the night probing Charles's question of what it is that makes people who they are, and the candles were sputtering in their holders when the men at last rose to retire. Davida, roused by the sound of their movement, also awakened and demanded to be taken up with them, sitting at the bottom of the steps and meowing loudly until Charles, who had at first refused her and climbed the stairway sans one small cat, returned in exasperation to pick her up and carry her upstairs with him. His grandfather, waiting for him at the top of the stairs, grinned.

"Looks like she's got you wrapped around her little paw, Charles," he said.

Charles shook his head. "Females!" he said.

"Meow!" said Davida, licking his hand approvingly. "Meow! Meow! Meow!"

* * *

Now the earl thought of last night's conversation as he sat at Lady Hedgwick's table, exchanging a conspiratorial wink with her as Charles and Miss Ansley brangled over Tory's ability to beat Thunder in a fair race, Arabella holding that the run they'd had that morning, in which her mount reached the top of the hill a half-nose ahead of Mr. Carlesworth's, was certain proof that the big black was superior. Charles indignantly disputed her claim with the spirited rejoinder that she'd had a two-length head start, hurling her challenge at him when his horse was heading in the other direction, and after she'd already begun her run.

"Ha!" said Arabella.

"Yes! Ha!" retorted Charles. "You know it's true, Arabella."

"Grandmama!" the young lady entreated, turning appealing eyes toward Lady Hedgwick, who laughed and begged them not to bring her into their argument, for she was sure both horses were equally wonderful, although in her opinion neither held a candle to her dear Bess.

After looks that showed they were clearly astonished she could even *mention* Bess in a conversation extolling the superiority of their mounts, the two turned in unison to the earl.

"Grandfather—" Charles began.

"My lord—" said Arabella.

Clangstone smiled. "I had a black stallion once," he said. "Do you remember him, Clara? Big, rawboned brute—could carry me for hours and never flag. He would have left both your horses in the dust. I remember one time—" And he was off, Lady Hedgwick adding to his story whenever she could, while Arabella and Charles rolled their eyes and waited.

When Clangstone's story seemed at last at an end Arabella, her eyes alight, proposed a race. With witnesses. Along the main road. The earl looked at her in surprise.

"No, no, my dear," he said, shaking his head and smiling at her enthusiasm. "You must not have been fully listening. The horse has been dead twenty years. He couldn't possibly race!"

Charles, his voice dry, said he rather thought Miss Ansley was proposing a race between her Tory and his Thunder. He added that he would be happy to oblige the lady, at her convenience.

"Oh." The earl chewed thoughtfully on his chicken, and shrugged. "I suppose—if you wish."

Unexpectedly it was Lady Hedgwick who interrupted to say,

in the firmest voice Charles had yet to hear her use with her granddaughter, that no, there would be no race. All three of her companions looked at her in surprise.

"But Grandmama—" Arabella began.

"No." Lady Hedgwick remained firm. A race would, she said, be dangerously close to careening, which she and Charles were both agreed was unacceptable for a young lady. Besides, it would invite all sorts of vulgar persons they might encounter along the road to view her granddaughter in a less than favorable light, and that she would not allow.

"Oh." Charles, appealed to in that way, could not argue, although he did later tax her in private about her opposition to a contest along their usually quiet lanes. So did her granddaughter.

To both she returned the same answer, saying to Charles, "You know how proud Arabella is of that horse," and to Arabella, "You know how proud Charles is of that horse." After each had nodded, and she was sure of their attention, she paused dramatically, then asked, "Would you really want one of you to lose a race for no better reason than that the other might win?"

Each, in turn, when the question was put to them that way, also grew thoughtful, and while in future days heated discussions continued over who had the superior mount, with Mr. Carlesworth coming out ahead in their runs one day, and Miss Ansley another, the idea of a definitive race with witnesses, to settle the question for all time, was never mentioned again.

❧ 14 ❧

Two days later Charles arrived in the afternoon to take Arabella driving. He was not in the best of moods, for he was there under duress.

Miss Ansley had told him that she thought it would be a splendid notion if he were to teach her to drive, and, when he told her that under no condition would he do so, considering it unsafe and unseemly for a lady to take a team in hand, she had smiled sunnily and said, well then, never mind, she would ask Mr. Wooding instead.

It was just that Mr. Blathersham had said Charles had the best hands in the country, and the best team, and she had a desire to ride behind what Mr. Blathersham said were the most splendid grays born, but never mind, if Charles did not care to teach her, Mr. Wooding had already said he was most eager to be of service.

"Don't be ridiculous!" Charles snapped.

Charles saw Arabella's hands tighten slightly on Tory's reins as Miss Ansley's eyebrows rose. They were out riding at the time, and too late did Charles remember that it was not politic to call the lady ridiculous.

"That is—" He frowned. "Wooding can't teach you to drive. Cow-handed. Hate to say it, but there it is."

Miss Ansley sighed. "That is what Mr. Blathersham said," she confided. "But I thought perhaps he was just the tiniest bit jealous, and so might not—"

Charles did not wait to hear what Mr. Blathersham "might not," demanding instead to be told just what Blathersham had to be jealous of Wooding about. Arabella opened her eyes very wide and stared at him.

"Why nothing, Charles. But you know how young men are."

His frown grew. Of course he knew.

Just when, he demanded, had Wooding been making these offers to take Miss Ansley driving? And when had Blathersham been so much about that he had time to be growing jealous?

Arabella informed him serenely that the gentlemen came regularly to tea at Hedgwick Hall; or rather, they came to visit and stayed to tea.

"Oh, they do, do they?" Charles snorted.

"Yes." Miss Ansley giggled. "Grandmama says if they came any more frequently, and stayed any longer, she would have to build a wing on the house for them!"

"What?"

Arabella glanced at him sideways and smiled. "She is just joking, Charles," she said.

"Well, I don't think it's very funny!" He was staring straight ahead, glaring at the road. "If they are importuning you in any way—"

Oh, no! They were not importuning, Miss Ansley said, far from it. The truth was, she found them endlessly amusing.

"Amusing!"

Arabella looked at him in surprise.

"Why, Charles," she said. "Do you not?"

No, he informed her, he did not. He did not find them amusing at all. In fact, he wasn't at all sure he liked them above half.

Now it was Arabella's turn to have her mouth hang open. "But Charles," she protested, "I thought they were your friends!"

A grumpy Mr. Carlesworth did not know why she'd think that.

"You've known them forever!"

Knowing someone forever did not make them a friend, he informed her.

"You introduced us!"

Hunching a shoulder, he wondered aloud what else he could do, when they'd come smack up to them in the road. Manners were, after all, manners, no matter who one was dealing with.

"They speak very highly of you."

Charles shrugged.

"And they admire your brother Jack immensely."

Well, that just went to show, Charles said. Two rattles admiring a third. He was surprised her grandmother did not have a greater care as to who she let call upon her granddaughter.

"Why, Charles!" There was a teasing grin on Miss Ansley's face. "If I did not know you better, I would almost believe you are jealous!"

An austere Mr. Carlesworth had informed her that it was no such thing. Jealous! Of two such fribbles! Nonsense!

"Then you won't mind if Mr. Wooding teaches me to drive."

"Mind?" Charles's brows snapped together. "Of course I'd mind! I just told you—the man is cow-handed. He couldn't teach you anything. Shouldn't even take you up beside him. Might overturn you. You wouldn't like that. Wouldn't like it at all. I wouldn't like it, either. Nor would your grandmama."

No, Miss Ansley agreed, she would not. She was watching him thoughtfully. Perhaps, then, Mr. Blathersham might teach her.

"Blathersham!" Charles snorted again. He had been right when he first met her, he thought; Miss Ansley's continued presence in the neighborhood had improved his snort immensely. "Blathersham can barely walk, let alone drive!"

"Really?" Miss Ansley said politely that she understood Mr. Blathersham to be one of the most graceful young men in the neighborhood, particularly on the dance floor.

"I said *I'd* teach you to dance," Charles reminded her.

"When?"

"What?"

"When will we start, Charles? It has been several weeks since you agreed to teach me, and while I have not wanted to plague you—"

"Ha!" said Charles.

"—if you are not going to do so, I must find someone else."

"I am going to do so," the harassed Charles replied. "Told you I would, and I will. Just wanted to get you comfortable riding first."

Now it was Miss Ansley's turn to say, "Ha!", and she did. "You were hoping I would forget, Charles," she said. "Admit it."

Charles, who had been hoping just that, would admit no such thing. She was unduly suspicious, he told her, and that was not becoming in a young lady.

"Ha!" said Miss Ansley again. Charles frowned.

"When?" she demanded.

"When what?"

"When will we begin our dancing lessons?"

Charles's frown grew. "My grandfather and I are invited to supper at Hedgwick Hall Monday next," he told her. "We will begin then."

"And when will we begin our driving lessons?"

"There will be no driving lessons."

Arabella sighed. All right, she said, if he would not teach her, she would have to choose between Mr. Blathersham and Mr. Wooding. Who would he recommend?

"Neither," said Charles.

She appeared to think deeply. She did not want to learn to be cow-handed like Mr. Wooding, but Mr. Blathersham had told her just yesterday that his team had come up lame.

"I don't doubt it," Charles muttered, and at her look of inquiry, added, "I've seen him drive."

"Oh." Arabella pondered. "Well, then, I suppose it will have to be Mr. Wooding. . . ."

"No!" The word was forceful, and she looked at him inquiringly.

"Are you saying I should prefer Mr. Blathersham, Charles?"

"I'm saying you should prefer neither."

"But Charles." It was Arabella at her most reasonable.

If there was one thing he disliked more than Arabella at her most unreasonable, it was Arabella at her most reasonable, thought Charles, and ground his teeth.

"If you will not teach me and I must learn—"

She turned a deaf ear to his pungent comment that she need not learn at all, and only regained her hearing when he said at last, in far from graceful tones, that all right, if she must drive, he would teach her, for he wasn't about to have her breaking her neck before he had a chance to wring it.

Miss Ansley smiled. "Why, Charles," she said. "You say the sweetest things."

A muscle in Mr. Carlesworth's jaw twitched, and he kneed his horse slightly, hearing a low ripple of laughter behind him as he rode ahead.

It was that feeling that he'd been outmaneuvered that put Charles in not the best of moods when he arrived at Hedgwick Hall to pick up Arabella. Nor was his mood improved when, upon entering the house, he was escorted to the morning room, only to find Wooding and Blathersham there before him.

"Ah, Charles," Lady Hedgwick said, smiling at the sight of him. She held out her hand and he moved forward to take it, bowing with a grace that Blathersham and Wooding watched enviously. When he straightened he cast them a glance that said he dared them to match it, then turned toward Miss Ansley and offered her his arm.

"I believe, Arabella," he said, making marked use of her name, "that we have an engagement."

"Yes." She rose gracefully, placing her hand on his arm as she smiled at her crestfallen visitors. "You must excuse me, gentlemen, but I must go. We would not wish to keep Mr. Carlesworth's team waiting."

"Oh?" Blathersham cocked his head knowingly. "Got your grays with you, Charles?"

No, Mr. Carlesworth said, he did not. He was driving his grandfather's chestnuts today.

"Oh." Blathersham nodded. Good horses, he allowed, but not nearly as spirited as Mr. Carlesworth's grays.

"Oh?" said Miss Ansley, a challenge in her violet eyes.

No, said Mr. Wooding, no they were not. Not up to his bays, either.

Charles grinned. "Thomas," he said, "I've driven job cattle up to your bays."

"Oho!" said Mr. Blathersham, as Mr. Wooding flushed.

"Now see here—" Wooding started.

"Mr. Carlesworth," Arabella interrupted, "is going to teach me to drive."

"Oh." Mr. Wooding cast reproachful eyes her way. "I hoped I was to have that honor, Miss Ansley."

Arabella smiled. "I know you offered, Mr. Wooding, and I thank you. But Charles here"—she patted his arm as she moved with him to the door—"was so eager and so insistent that he be allowed to teach me, that I did not have the heart to refuse him. Isn't that right, Charles?"

She gave him her brightest smile, and only Charles and Lady Hedgwick saw the laughter in her eyes as he agreed. Stiffly, but he agreed.

"Yes, but—" Mr. Blathersham was not known for his keen mind, but every once in awhile it retained some bit of information he would dredge from it later, usually just when someone most wished he would not. He looked at Charles questioningly. ''I thought you always said you'd never let a woman drive your horses. Said you didn't think women should drive. Said—''

Charles, watching the laughter fade from Arabella's eyes, and seeing a militant spark grow there, interrupted hastily. ''Yes, yes—well.'' He grinned. ''After all—not my horses!''

Blathersham seemed to understand that completely, which worried Charles, and Lady Hedgwick laughed, but Miss Ansley only pursed her lips and gazed speculatively at Charles in a way that made him gulp and look elsewhere. Wooding's assurances that she could drive any of the cattle in his stable, anytime—that he would consider it a rare honor—made her smile almost as much as they rankled Charles, and as the two walked down the steps toward Carlesworth's phaeton, Arabella said she was glad there was one man there, at least, forward thinking enough to realize she was likely to become the most competent whip around.

Charles laughed.

''I beg your pardon?'' Her voice distinctly frosty, Miss Ansley glared down at him as he helped her up into the phaeton his grandfather had had built for him last year, and which was his pride and joy.

''My dear,'' he told her, his lips turning up in amusement, ''it is a foolish teacher who does not keep at least one or two tricks to himself.''

Arabella considered that, found it fair, and was willing to compromise. ''One of the most competent,'' she offered.

Charles, who had by now taken his seat and sent the team smartly down the drive, said his grandfather also had the reputation of a remarkable whip. In a burst of confidence Arabella confided that she would be quite happy simply to become a notable whip—almost as notable as her father.

''Oh?'' Charles turned his head in surprise. He had not thought of that before. ''Your father is a notable whip?''

Arabella nodded.

''Then why did he not teach you?''

Her lips twitched slightly, and she stared straight ahead. ''Because, dear Charles, my father has the stuffy, antiquated notion that women should not drive!''

❧ 15 ❧

For a moment Charles dropped his hands and the team broke into a canter. Miss Ansley's kind advice to mind his horses did not draw a response, but the team was checked, then hauled to a halt as Charles turned disbelievingly toward her.

"Your father would not teach you!" he said.

She shook her head.

"But you have plagued me—"

"Not *plagued,* Charles!"

"Blackmailed!" The way he said the word made it clear he considered that worse, and he was further incensed when Miss Ansley smiled.

"*Persuaded,* Charles," she amended.

"Of all the unprincipled pieces!" He frowned at her. "Your father obviously is better able to resist your persuasion than I am!"

Arabella touched his hand sympathetically and her head nodded up and down, her eyes kind. "Well, yes. But he has known me all my life, you know. And I am so very much like him that he knows exactly what I am doing, sometimes even before I do."

Well, said Charles, he wished *he* had that ability to know exactly what she was doing. Seconds later he contradicted himself with no, no, he did not, for on further thought he realized such knowledge would be frightening. Arabella smiled coaxingly.

"Dear Charles," she said, and when he had his full attention, smiled again. "Dear Charles, as interesting as all this is, it is not teaching me how to drive!"

Despite his qualms on the subject, after only two lessons Charles was forced to admit that there were perhaps some women who could be trusted with prime cattle, and with not overturning themselves or their passengers in the ditch. That Miss Ansley was one of those women was apparent, for she handled a team as if she were born to it. By the end of two weeks she was driving his grandfather's chestnuts well up to their bits, and pestering Charles unmercifully to entrust her with his precious grays—something, he assured her, he did not ever intend to do.

They were heatedly discussing that as they bowled down a familiar lane one morning, Charles maintaining that Miss Ansley was not going to drive his grays now, or ever, and she holding just as stoutly to her belief that he was only being stubborn, pigheaded, and selfish in not letting her do so.

"Selfish?" Charles, stung, wanted to know who it was who had taught her to drive, anyway.

"Only because you felt you must, to keep me from driving out with Mr. Wooding," Arabella rejoined, her color as high as his own.

"You know, Arabella, there ought to be some things a man can keep to himself just because he wants to, without being called selfish, and if his horses aren't one of those things—"

"I'm not asking you to *give* them to me, Charles!" Arabella said in exasperation. "Just let me drive them!"

"Why is it so important to you?" he demanded. "Why isn't this team enough?"

"Why is it so important to you that I should not?" she countered.

This time Charles did not allow himself to be distracted, as he had been so many times before. "I asked you first."

Miss Ansley regarded him deeply for several moments, then grinned reluctantly. "I want to drive your horses, Charles," she informed him, her eyes twinkling, "because you have said I cannot."

"Well!" He made it clear that was just as he'd thought, and he considered it a pretty childish reason, too. Arabella's grin grew.

"And why do you not want me to drive your horses, Charles?"

"You might injure their mouths," Charles said, with perfect disregard for the truth. After seeing her in action for several weeks, he knew Miss Ansley had the lightest hands in the neighborhood.

"Pooh!" said Arabella.

"And that's another thing!" This time Charles *did* allow himself to be distracted, hoping to distract her, too. "This habit you have of saying pooh every time I say something you don't quite like—"

Arabella interrupted to say she did not say pooh every time he said something she didn't like, because there would be days she would be saying it all the time, which she did not. No, she only said pooh whenever he said something particularly stupid.

"Well!" said Charles. Not until Miss Ansley's arrival had anyone in the neighborhood taken it upon themselves to tell him not only that he was being stupid, but when. He considered it one of her least attractive features.

Another of her least attractive features surfaced as Arabella returned to their original topic. Not for the first time did Charles deplore this bulldog tenacity she exhibited in focusing on something and not letting it go until she was satisfied with the response.

"Come now, Charles!" she said, her nose in the air and her tone that of a governess speaking authoritatively to a naughty child. "What is the reason, really? You know your horses will take no hurt from me, especially if you are right here beside me! So what is it really that makes you so stubborn?"

He was not, he told her, stubborn. But they were *his* horses—

"Ahhhh." Miss Ansley was smiling that superior little smile that almost always raised his temper, and Charles's glare was forbidding as he asked just what that was supposed to mean. "You are telling me, Charles," she said, her eyes on a distant phaeton that had just emerged from a small stand of trees down the road, "that you will not let me play with your toys."

"No such thing!"

"And that—that—"

Charles's indignation turned to surprise and then concern as Arabella so far forgot herself as to drop her hands. She was sitting, her eyes wide, her mouth open in a perfect O, and he thoughtfully took the reins, pulling up the team even as he looked about for the cause of her distress.

"What—" he began, as Arabella breathed, "Sir Rupert!"

"What?" Charles glanced about in annoyance. He had handsomely bribed one of the stable boys to keep the dog occupied and locked up while they were out on their drives, his grandfather's team not being as tolerant of barking brown streaks as Thunder or Tory, and having a tendency to kick out whenever the dog came close to them. If the poodle had escaped his captor Charles would have something to say to said captor, thank you. "Where?"

"There!" Arabella was pointing, but a frowning Charles could not see the dog, try as he might.

"I don't see the dratted beast," he said, looking past the approaching vehicle toward the trees. "Did he go into the trees, because if he did, we can turn here, and—"

"Not *that* Sir Rupert!" Arabella said, looking at him as if he were daft. "No, no! *That* Sir Rupert!"

Charles thought it only fair to tell her she was making no sense at all as, once again, he followed her pointing finger. It was aimed directly at an oncoming phaeton in which sat Blathersham and a stranger. Even as Charles looked the stranger beamed and raised his hat, half standing as Blathersham dragged his team to a halt beside them.

"Miss Ansley," Blathersham said. "Charles."

It occurred to Carlesworth that his old friend did not appear very happy, and his gaze shifted from Blathersham's usually placid, smiling face to the man beside him, and back again. Blathersham was not smiling now. In fact, he looked like a hound who had just returned from an unsuccessful fox hunt. Charles raised an eyebrow, and Blathersham responded to it.

"Charles," Blathersham said, "let me make you known to Sir Rupert Omsley. Cousin, you know. Distant cousin. Very distant. Mr. Carlesworth."

"Mr. Carlesworth!" Sir Rupert said, reaching out a hand even as his eyes remained fastened on Miss Ansley, who was frowning at him in a way that would have told anyone with even a particle of sense how little she appreciated his regard. Sir Rupert did not seem to notice.

"Omsley," Charles said, touching the fingers briefly before returning his questioning gaze to Blathersham.

"Ran into him in town," the unhappy Mr. Blathersham said. "Been up to London, you know—business." It was apparent from the new coat he wore that Mr. Blathersham's business had been a visit to his tailor, something he considered quite pressing two or three times a year, as Charles remembered. Carlesworth smiled. "Came back with me. Don't know why."

"But Freddie, you do!" Sir Rupert said, slapping his cousin on the back in a way that made the already morose Blathersham frown deeper. "Once you told me about the new beauty in your neighborhood, I knew I could not be elsewhere!"

Blathersham, speaking as if his cousin were not there, said to Charles, "Says he knows Miss Ansley. Says they were almost engaged in Belgium. Says he knows if he just presses his suit now, she'll be his. Sounds like a hum to me, but there it is!"

"Freddie!" said Sir Rupert, for the first time alert to the growing light in Charles Carlesworth's eye. It was a martial light, and Sir Rupert did not like martial lights. He had not liked the one that appeared in Miss Ansley's father's eye each time Gervase Ansley looked at him, either, but close questioning of his cousin had elicited the information that no, there was no Gervase Ansley visiting at Hedgwick Hall. It was just the young lady and her grandmama. Freddie had neglected to mention any Mr. Carlesworth, and Sir Rupert frowned at this rather large gap in his cousin's story, wondering for the first time if there might be others.

"Freddie!" Sir Rupert laughed. It was not a lighthearted sound, and trailed off badly. He slapped his cousin on the back again. "How you do run on! Miss Ansley will think—"

"No," said Arabella, cutting him short. She had retrieved the reins from Carlesworth and now held them in her determined and competent hands. "Miss Ansley will think no such thing, because Miss Ansley does not think of you, sir, at all. Good day, Mr. Blathersham!" She gave a curt nod and headed the earl's team down the road at a smart pace, moving them along in the opposite direction from that in which Mr. Blathersham's vehicle was pointed.

"Isn't she something? So spirited! So beautiful," Sir Rupert marveled, holding his hat to his chest as he gazed admiringly after the disappearing vehicle. "And so happy to see me, too!"

"Ho!" said his companion. "Didn't seem happy to me!"

Sir Rupert put his hat back on his head, and gave his cousin a superior smile, which his cousin resented heartily. "That, Freddie, is because you do not understand the intricacies of the female mind. My presence here has shocked her. She did not expect me, and has not had time to realize her happiness. I doubt even Miss Ansley yet knows how delighted she is to see me."

Freddie, fuming, wanted to say that he might not understand

the intricacies of the female mind, but he did at least understand when a person behaved as if he had no mind at all. He was afraid, however, that the words would not come out quite as withering as he would like, so he said nothing, bending his brain instead to the task of deciding what could be done at his home to make his cousin uncomfortable enough to keep his visit short. The unhappy knowledge this his mother would not cooperate in making any relative unwelcome weighed heavily on Mr. Blathersham, and he sighed.

Sir Rupert, thinking he had silenced his cousin with his great wisdom, smiled his most superior smile and condescended to say nothing.

❧ 16 ❧

Had Charles been there to hear Sir Rupert's last statement he could have corrected him, and would have been happy to do so. As they bowled along the lane at a rate that could only be called less than prudent, it was apparent Miss Ansley did indeed know just how delighted she was to see her old suitor, and she was not delighted at all.

At all.

"I wish," she said, her jaw clenched, her eyes alight as he urged the horses to lengthen their stride, "that my father were here. He would run the man through!"

She turned hopeful eyes toward Charles, who told her sharply to mind her team. Reluctantly she slowed the pace, then looked at him again.

"That," said Charles, his tone still sharp, "is exactly why I will never let you drive my grays!"

"What?" Miss Ansley's mind had wandered far from that point, and she was surprised to have him return to it.

"No matter the provocation, a good whip does not take the irritation out on his—or, in your case, her—team!"

"Oh!" A guilty Miss Ansley slowed the horses even further. "You are right, Charles, I know. I am so sorry." She looked worriedly at the horses. "You don't think they've taken any hurt, do you?"

He relented enough to say no, he was sure they had not, and so sorry did she look that he did not even add that he would not have allowed that to happen. Charles had been quite prepared to take the reins if Arabella's temper had outrun her team any further.

"It is just that—" She handed him the reins and leaned back against the seat, her arms folded tightly in front of her, her face

111

drawn in a forbidding frown. "To see him here, when I have been so enjoying myself! And to hear him saying those ridiculous things! Oh! He is so dense, Charles! So thickheaded! And now he will moon around me forever, and without my father to shoo him away . . ."

Charles, who had great faith in Lady Hedgwick's ability to shoo anyone she did not care to have crossing her doorstep, said optimistically that Arabella was making too much of it. She turned hopeful eyes toward him.

"Charles," she said, one gloved hand coming out to rest on his own, "do you ever fence?"

Carlesworth, who thought he had come to expect anything from her, had not expected this, and found himself coughing as her face went from hopeful to frowning.

"I suppose," she said, when he stopped, "that means no."

Well, Charles said, not exactly. He did fence, a little. When Jack was home, because his brother enjoyed it above all things. But—as her eyes grew hopeful again he raised one hand in warning—that did not mean he was going to call Sir Rupert out for having the temerity to live, and bring his life into their neighborhood.

It seemed, the dissatisfied Miss Ansley said, a good enough reason to her.

Charles laughed. "I am surprised you did not have your father teach you to fence, if you think it so helpful," he said lightly, and was considerably taken aback when she said he had.

"*What?*"

"I fence." Miss Ansley read the doubt in his eyes, and her chin came out. "I do!"

"Of all the whiskers!"

"It is not! And I have my own little walking stick with the neatest blade—I'll show you!" Her face fell. "Except that my father took it with him when he left London. He said my using it here simply would not *do*."

"I should think not!"

"But it would be so handy!"

"You're serious, aren't you?" Charles was watching her in amazement, and Arabella met his surprise with her own.

"But of course! You do not know how annoying Sir Rupert can be!"

Charles, who thought she was making too much ado over

nothing, tickled himself and further enraged his companion by his one-word reply.

"Pooh!"

Carlesworth was not laughing a week later, however, as he stood by the wall watching Sir Rupert squire Arabella down a country dance gotten up for the guest's entertainment after the dratted fellow suggested it to Blathersham's mother, a vastly good-natured women of kind heart and little sense who, not wishing their young relative to die of boredom, as he had informed her he was likely to do in the country, had arranged the small party for perhaps thirty guests.

When her plans were made known to her son he had very much shocked her by saying the fellow could just die then, if he was that bored, and when she had chastised him for it, Mr. Blathersham had finished with an uncharacteristically pettish, "Well, let him go back to London, then, if he likes it so much there!"

But that Mrs. Blathersham could not allow; it would not be polite. And so a party had been arranged.

Since it was Arabella's first dance after her lessons with Charles she was more than a little excited, saying philosophically that the new dress promised by her grandmother would, perhaps, make up for Sir Rupert's presence.

That it had not was small comfort to Charles as he stood watching them, his back against the wall, his arms crossed across his chest, and on his face so forbidding an expression that Mr. Blathersham, approaching him from the left for a commiserating chat, had thought better of it, and gone off to drown his sorrows in his mother's punch.

Between watching Arabella's steps to make sure she did not disgrace him, and watching the way Sir Rupert alternately ogled and cajoled her, paying florid compliments Charles could not like, Mr. Carlesworth was not having a good time. That Miss Ansley's whole demeanor made it obvious she did not care for the compliments, either, helped very little.

Besides, at her first dance Miss Ansley should have been dancing with him. It was he who had let her step all over his feet while her grandmama pounded on the piano and his grandfather barked orders like a general, telling them to bow this way and that, to step and step until Arabella was quite confused and even

Charles, who knew the steps and was always said to perform them most gracefully, wasn't sure he could follow them anymore.

During a break for tea that night at Hedgwick Hall Charles had taken her aside and told her to ignore the directions his grandfather gave and follow his lead; she had a natural grace that would see her through. Miss Ansley had smiled gratefully for the compliment and the advice, and when her grandmama had returned to the piano, Arabella had locked her eyes onto Charles's and allowed nothing to distract her as she followed the pressure of his hand and one or two directions hissed in her ear to combat the earl's trumpet tones as she moved through the country dances.

They did so well then that Charles's grandfather, pleased, congratulated himself on his own abilities as an instructor, and offered to partner her through a set which, when completed, was pronounced perfect by a beaming Lady Hedgwick, and quite good, really, for no more experience than she'd had, by Charles.

Miss Ansley's face fell at the latter, and Carlesworth was immediately called to order by his grandfather, who said he was just jealous that the earl and Miss Ansley did a better job of it than he himself had done. And, Clangstone added awfully, if that was how Charles talked to the young ladies, it was no wonder all of London did not consider him a lady's man.

"But grandfather," Charles protested, his cheeks growing red as he heard Lady Hedgwick snort and Miss Ansley giggle, "I was just trying to be fair. Arabella doesn't want me to pay her pretty compliments, she wants me to teach her to dance."

He had turned to Miss Ansley for confirmation, only to have her purse her lips and look toward the ceiling, wondering aloud if it would be so impossible to do both.

"Not for a man with address!" said the earl with a bow toward the lady and the offer of his arm as he prepared to lead her through a country dance again.

"I have address!" Charles protested, but they were already walking away, and it was left to Lady Hedgwick to give his arm a sympathetic pat before she took her place again at the piano.

Yes, it should have been him partnering Arabella now, instead of the odious Sir Rupert. After all, it was Charles who had taught her to waltz, when she begged and plagued so heartily for him to do so, taking her in his arms and whirling her about the room again and again, until the motion—yes, he was sure it was the motion—had made him unusually flushed and light-headed. There was something about his hand at her waist and the soft smell of her hair that seemed to add to the reeling feeling, and when the music ended Charles had looked down to find Miss Ansley looking quite as flushed as he felt.

"Arabella," he had said softly, bending toward her, one hand still on her waist, the other holding tight to her small fingers.

"Yes, Charles?" she had prompted, seeming to sway forward herself as he hesitated. Her eyes were bright and questioning, and he didn't know what he would have done if his grandfather hadn't coughed, reminding him they were not alone in the room, and had not been.

Releasing Miss Ansley as if she burned him, Charles had taken a step back and adopted his most formal tone. "You must not waltz until you have been approved by the patronesses of Almack's," he told her. "Do not forget."

"Oh, Charles!" Arabella rolled her eyes, and shook her head as if disgusted. Before he could determine what she had to be disgusted about, she had driven that question from his mind by her next comment. "Sometimes you are such a stick!"

"A stick?!"

Charles heard his grandfather cough again, and he knew the earl and Lady Hedgwick were regarding them with ill-concealed amusement. Liking to be laughed at as little as anyone, Charles said that was a fine way to talk when he was only trying to help, which was what she'd asked him to do, she and her grandmother, if she would remember, and—and—

"Yes, Charles," Lady Hedgwick agreed, coming forward, her voice soothing. "We remember."

"So why I must be called a stick—"

"Because you are." Miss Ansley disregarded her grandmama's warning head shake, and was only too happy to tell him. "All stiff and straight and not able to bend these silly societal conventions to let yourself speak."

"It is these silly societal conventions you asked me to teach you, Miss Ansley, and if I am not to your liking as a teacher, well—let me just remind you that this was not my idea. And I would be happy to withdraw my services at any time!"

"No," said Arabella, her color high as she ignored the last part of his speech to focus on the first. "Because you couldn't have an unconventional idea if it was given to you on Grand-mama's silver salver! And why you are forever prosing on as if I am the only one to benefit from our time together, when—''

''Arabella!'' Lady Hedgwick had interrupted then, wanting to crack the combatants' heads together almost as much as she wanted to gather them into her arms. They looked like two ruffled roosters, standing there, leaning forward, hands on hips, while Clorimonde, who had wandered in sometime during the dancing, now placed himself between them and snuffled wor-riedly, looking from one to the other and back again.

''Yes, Grandmama?'' Miss Ansley's color was still high, her eyes bright, and it was apparent she was not going to take in good part any censure of her conduct, any more than Charles would. Instead, Lady Hedgwick rolled her eyes at the earl and took another tack.

''You are upsetting Clorimonde.''

''*What?*''

Both Arabella and Charles looked at her in surprise. Then they looked down at the poodle whimpering between them.

''Oh!'' Arabella dropped to her knees beside the dog and put her arms around him. ''There, there, Sir Rupert,'' she said. ''Charles didn't really mean it.''

''Nor did Arabella,'' Charles said, dropping his hand onto the poodle's head. The two exchanged glances and then sheepish grins, and Lady Hedgwick drifted toward the earl under the guise of offering him tea.

When they were out of hearing of their grandchildren the earl looked back and said with a soft smile, ''I wouldn't be young again for anything, would you?''

Lady Hedgwick looked back, too, and sighed. ''Perhaps,'' she said.

The earl patted her hand. ''Then perhaps,'' he said, changing his mind, ''I would, too.''

Things had gone pretty well after that, with Charles and Arabella alternately riding one day and driving the next, and regular dancing lessons that were really more enjoyable evenings than necessary practice. In fact, they had had just such an evening last night, at the end of which Arabella, fanning herself on the terrace to which she and Charles had adjourned while her grandmother and his grandfather nourished themselves inside with a glass of Lady Hedgwick's best wine, had looked up at the sky and asked, "Charles, would you say I have eyes that outshine the brightest stars in the sky?"

"Good heavens, no!"

The reply, while truthful and quick, was not all Miss Ansley had hoped it would be. Or perhaps it was the shocked tone in which it was uttered to which she took exception.

"Why not?" she demanded.

Charles looked at her in surprise. "Not the sort of thing I *would* say," he told her. "Not at all in that line. You know that."

Arabella turned her gaze heavenward again. "Sir Rupert says it."

"Sort of thing *he* would say." Charles settled himself on the low stone wall on which she already sat and, always ready to instruct, asked if she was familiar with the constellations.

As a matter of fact she was, but at this moment Miss Ansley was more interested in conversation than instruction. Which was just as well, because when she did not reply, it gave Charles time to think, which led to his next question.

"When does he say it?"

"What?"

"That nonsense about your eyes—when does Sir Rupert say it?"

"Oh." Miss Ansley smiled. "He was here this afternoon for tea."

Charles frowned. "He was here yesterday afternoon for tea."

Miss Ansley nodded. "He is here every afternoon for tea," she said, her tone so placid that Charles's frown deepened.

"Thought you didn't like the fellow."

"I don't!"

"Then what are you doing having him to tea every day?"

There was a dissatisfied note in his voice that pleased Miss Ansley, even if she found his question most unfair. She made it clear that Sir Rupert's frequent visits were not her idea. In fact, she reminded him, she was the one who had asked him to run Sir Rupert through when he first arrived in the neighborhood, but no, Charles would not do that one little thing for her. . . .

Charles, who did not think running a man through was a little thing, quibbled for a moment on that point before saying, perhaps more authoritatively than he otherwise would have, that she ought to send the man to the right-about.

"Oh?" Disliking his tone, Arabella's own voice sharpened. "And how am I to do that, pray? When he comes with Mr. Blathersham, who is your friend! And Mr. Wooding, too!"

Mr. Carlesworth was willing to see Mr. Blathersham and Mr. Wooding sent to the right-about, too.

"And when it is my grandmama's house, and they behave perfectly civilly, which is something I cannot say for you."

Charles asked indignantly just when he had behaved uncivilly, then was sorry he had as Miss Ansley reeled off a catalogue that ended with their present conversation, saying for good measure, "And grandmama is there all the time. When the other young gentlemen visit, I mean."

"*She* ought to send them to the right-about," Charles conceded, willing to stretch a point.

Arabella frowned again. "She will not. She says I must learn to deal with such things. And she is right!"

"Deal with such things as idiots saying your eyes are brighter than the brightest stars?" scoffed Charles.

"And what is so idiotic about that?" Arabella demanded, rising to stand over him, her hands pressed together in front of her as if that was the only way she could keep from sending him tumbling backward into the bushes. Charles eyed her uneasily and rose, too.

"Well," he said, trying to retrieve a situation he sensed was fast getting out of hand, "you know—said it in the daytime! No stars out then! Besides." He was sure this was the clincher. "Not true. No one's eyes can shine brighter than the stars. You stand over there," he said, pointing, "away from me, and I can't even see your eyes in the dark, but that star's light is coming to us from who knows how far away, and we see it as clearly as—as—"

Something—what he was inwardly coming to call his Arabella sense—told Charles it was just as well he could not see the lady's eyes in the dark, and he ground to a halt, gulping and saying as an afterthought, "That is—very pretty eyes, you know; I've always thought so, but, brighter than stars . . . no." He shook his head decisively. "No."

Miss Ansley, complaining of a headache, had taken her leave of him there, and had retired to her room, leaving their grandparents to eye him speculatively as they sat sipping their wine and he prowled the music room aimlessly, picking up first one thing and then another for a distracted inspection in which he saw nothing of what he actually held.

"Charles," Lady Hedgwick had finally said, "is something wrong?"

No, he had told them, no. It was just something about stars in Arabella's eyes. That idiot Sir Rupert had told her that her eyes were brighter than stars, but Charles had assured her it could not be. And by the way, did Lady Hedgwick think she should be letting such a fribble attend her granddaughter in that way, and—and—

Lady Hedgwick had shaken her head. "Charles," she said. "Charles, Charles, Charles."

His grandfather had seconded her. "Charles, Charles, Charles."

The earl, too, had shaken his head, risen, and said, not looking at his grandson again, "Come, lad. Let's go home."

Now Charles stood, watching Arabella trip down one country dance and then another with Wooding and Blathersham and that confounded Sir Rupert, and every other young buck in the neighborhood who Mrs. Blathersham had invited to her party, but when Charles, who had every right to Arabella's hand, approached her, she had already promised this dance or that one away. In fact, she had told him, nose in the air, that she wished he had solicited her hand earlier, as the other gentlemen had done, for then perhaps she could have worked him in. . . .

Worked him in! After all he'd done for her!

So here he stood, taking what comfort he could in the fact that Arabella did not seem to be enjoying this dance with Sir Rupert any more than Charles was enjoying watching the two of them dance it together. For some reason his mind flitted to the feel of her in his arms as they'd waltzed—thank goodness there would be no waltzing for her here!—and the warmth of her hand in his as they'd stepped their way through the country dances, and Charles found her ill-concealed displeasure with Sir Rupert was actually no comfort at all.

As the dance ended Charles muscled his way to her side and held out his hand. Making his finest bow he completely ignored Sir Rupert, who still held her hand in preparation for the dance beginning again. Charles said, "I believe, Miss Ansley, that this is my dance!"

"Now see here—" Sir Rupert began, but Arabella cut him off.

"Why yes, Mr. Carlesworth," she said, her face very prim, "I do believe it is."

She curtsied to Sir Rupert, who was trying to explain that he wished to dance with her again, and took Charles's hand as the music started.

"Thank you!" she whispered as they took their first steps. As his face relaxed a little her lips turned up mischievously. "It is about time, you know," she told him, as they started to part in the dance. "I thought, Mr. Carlesworth, that you would never ask!"

So surprised was Charles, who had been refused not once, but three times, that he did something he had never done before. Mr. Carlesworth missed a step in the dance.

❧ 17 ❧

"You really are a little minx, you know," Charles said the next morning as they rode companionably over Hedgwick land. He did his best to sound disapproving, but Arabella was not deceived. She lowered her eyelids before peeping up at at him, and he grinned.

"Why Charles," she said, "what an unkind thing to say. I have no idea what you mean."

Yes, he assured her, she did. She knew exactly. After all, it was she who had refused him every time he'd asked her to dance last night, only to beg him, in the end, to rescue her from Omsley.

"I did not beg you!"

Mischief had been replaced by indignation in Miss Ansley's eyes, but Charles held firm. "Your eyes did."

"Yes, well." Arabella bit her lip and sighed. "I thought I could do it, Charles, just to teach you a lesson, but I could not." She shuddered. "Sir Rupert! Ugh!"

The dog running at her side looked up questioningly, but when she addressed him no more, veered off in search of a rabbit.

"And to think I danced with him twice! And he wished to partner me again! Well, that was when I decided that if you hadn't learned your lesson, Charles, I had learned mine!"

Her social mentor informed her she should not dance with any man more than twice in one evening before adding, his grin starting to fade, that he did not know what lesson she thought it was she needed to teach him. Arabella looked at him again, and shook her head.

"I do not know where you get your reputation for wisdom, Charles," she said. "And if you cannot figure out what lesson I am talking about, I certainly shall not tell you!"

Before he could question her further she was off, touching her heels to Tory's sides and leaning forward, letting the horse run straight out on the level fields ahead of them.

"Well!" said Charles, spurring Thunder after her. The big horse needed no encouragement, and in short time he had caught the big black and was passing him, to Arabella's evident disgust.

"No fair, Charles," she said, when she reined in beside him minutes later as he stood waiting for her beneath a shade tree. He was patting Thunder approvingly, and his welcoming smile turned to puzzlement at her words.

"No fair?"

"Your winning like that." She gave her own horse a pat, and invited Mr. Carlesworth to help her down so they could walk a ways on this fine day. Charles willingly did so, but raised a quizzical eyebrow as he asked if she would have wanted him to let her win even if she hadn't deserved to.

"Of course!" Arabella said promptly. "Didn't you know a gentleman always lets a lady win?"

"Who told you that?"

"Mr. Wooding." She batted her eyes at him. "And Mr. Blathersham. And Sir Rupert. I trounced them soundly at piquet several nights past, one right after the other, and they all very gallantly volunteered that they had let me win!"

She smiled at the memory of the way the young gentlemen had chided each other on being beaten by a woman, only to be beaten each in turn themselves. And how they then had redeemed their pride by announcing it was not poor playing skill, but chivalry, that took the day for Miss Ansley!

Watching her face Charles asked, frowning, just when this had been, and Arabella looked at him sideways, a small smile on her face.

"You are not my only guest, Charles," she informed him.

"No, no! Of course not! It is just that I know you have been so busy—"

"You have been very busy, too, Charles. Grandmama tells me she has invited you and your grandfather to dine with us twice now, but each time you have had some excuse."

Yes, well, Charles said, there was so much work to do. He had his grandfather's estates to run, and with their morning rides one day, and their afternoon drives the next, and now dancing—

Arabella stopped, and for a moment all trace of laughter was gone from her face. "Tell me, Charles," she said, "are you angry with me—seriously angry?"

A startled Carlesworth stuttered of course not, whatever had given her that idea?

Arabella, after regarding him searchingly for several more moments, sighed and started forward again. "I have had the feeling, Charles, that perhaps—perhaps you are trying to avoid me."

No, he assured her, it wasn't that; it was just that he was . . . busy.

Watching her bent head, and the way the light played on the curve of her cheek and reflected off her thick lashes, it was all he could do not to tell her the real reason. The more Mr. Carlesworth enjoyed her company, the more he realized how much he would miss her when she was gone, off for the little season that would launch her into the society she was preparing for and so richly deserved to enter. Her grandmother felt the little season would give her some acquaintances to make her comfortable for the full season when the cream of society returned to town in the spring.

At one time Charles could hardly wait for her to go so that he could return to his well-ordered life, but now—now he had decided he would start to pull back a little so he would not miss her so much, later. After all, she had others to call on her. She had made the acquaintance of several families in the neighborhood, and of course all the young bucks . . .

Charles frowned. Funny how knowing she was not left alone when he was not there did not make him as happy as it should. He would think about that later. For now, he turned the subject with a light, "So they let you win at piquet, did they?"

Arabella's rich laughter bubbled up. "Charles," she told him, "my father taught me how to play cards before I had reached my tenth birthday!"

"Oh." He digested that bit of information, and started to grin. "Something of a sharp, are you?"

A modest Miss Ansley studied one gloved hand and said she liked to believe she could hold her own.

"Oh?" Charles studied his own gloved hand with the same care, remarking to the world at large that he considered himself something of a piquet player, too, and if someone should ever care to try her skill—

Arabella looked up eagerly. "Really, Charles?"

He nodded, grinning. His grandfather, he said, had taught him to play early on, to while away the long winter nights.

"I bet I can beat you!"

Well, Charles said, if she did, it would be because of superior skill.

"Why, Charles," she teased, "no chivalry?"

No, Carlesworth said, none. And, he added shrewdly, he rather suspected that was just as she wanted it, because they both knew very well that the only thing that would make Miss Ansley more frustrated than not winning was being patronized by someone allowing her to win.

Arabella laughed. "You know, Charles," she said, "I begin to think that you, like my father, are coming to know me too well."

"Oh, no!" Carlesworth put a hand to his forehead, pretending to shudder, and Miss Ansley giggled.

"Who would have thought, Charles," she asked, after they'd walked for several minutes in companionable silence, enjoying the tranquil day, "when you came barreling into me perhaps— what?—ten weeks ago now, that someday we would be walking along, enjoying each other's company so, getting along as well as we do?"

The words were innocent enough, but there was something about the way they were said; almost too innocent, really, and Charles felt his Arabella sense start to vibrate. Well, he said cautiously, it was better than getting bashed with a parasol.

Miss Ansley laughed. "Come now, Charles! You must admit I had reason to believe you were not quite sane, staggering through the hedge like that, and knocking me down without a by-your-leave!"

Charles said he would admit no such thing, because it wasn't true. Had he known, however, that a by-your-leave would have made it acceptable to her to be knocked down, he certainly would have said it, and saved himself a bashing.

Arabella giggled. "And then there was the time you shouted in Tory's ear, and he dumped me off his back, Charles. That was not very good of you, either."

Charles made his thousandth apology, and waited.

"Of course, I have never held either of those incidents over your head—"

"Ha!"

She gazed reproachfully up at him. "Now, Charles."

He shook his head at her, and told her to cut line.

An innocent "I beg your pardon?" was her return.

Charles grinned. "You want something, Arabella. What is it?" Miss Ansley bit her lip, pondering. Either he really was coming to know her well, or she had botched this badly.

"You remember, Charles, when Sir Rupert came, and I asked you to run him through?"

Carlesworth said firmly that was something he still would not do. Nor—if this was what she wanted, he would not do it!—would he fence with her. No matter what she said.

Arabella shook her head. She had removed her bonnet and was swinging it by its ribbons as they walked along. The sun, picking up red highlights in her soft curls, was playing tag with the shadows they walked through, and Charles, enjoying the sight, did not hurry her, but waited.

"No, no," she assured him. "It's nothing like that. Although I wish you would fence with me, I enjoy it so!" She glanced up, but at his firm head shake she shrugged and said, "Oh, very well. It's just that . . ." She sighed. "Charles, Sir Rupert is plaguing me to marry him again."

"He *what?*" Charles exploded with an anger that made Miss Ansley blink, then quickly curb the soft smile that followed her initial surprise. "The impertinent nodcock! I hope your grandmother sent him off with a flea in his ear the minute he applied to her!"

Arabella looked guilty and Charles paused, his eyes questioning. The question grew when she said nothing.

"Arabella?"

She looked up at him.

"Arabella, he did apply to your grandmother?"

"Well . . ." She looked down at her hat and swallowed, pulling the ribbons through her fingers several times before looking up again. "Not exactly . . ."

"No?"

He watched as she pulled the ribbons still harder, and a sense of foreboding set in. "Arabella?"

"Now, Charles." She laid a hand on his arm. "You can understand that I would not want him plaguing Grandmama. After all, she is so busy with planning our wardrobes for the fall, and making all the arrangements for our travel, and then, of course, she wants to give a small party before we go, and—well—" She gulped. "Then he said that ridiculous thing about not wanting to apply to a female, which almost *did* make me send him off to Grandmama, so she could give him the setdown only she can, but—"

She shook her head resolutely. "I knew it would not do. So I told him, Charles, that he must speak with you." The words came out low and fast, as if she were rushing at a fence and determined to throw her heart over it. "I said that you are standing as sort of a guardian to me here, and—and—"

"You told him what?"

Arabella looked up into his eyes and then down, gulping again. "It seemed like such a good idea at the time, Charles," she assured him. "For there you were last night, frowning at us like the strictest guardian imaginable. You frowned even more than my father, Charles, and Sir Rupert was terrified of him! So I thought—I thought—"

A withering comment that she had not thought at all brought the color into her cheeks, but Arabella pushed bravely on. "I thought he would lose courage and take himself off to London, for I've already told him I would never marry anyone of whom my dog disapproved."

"What?"

Arabella looked at him questioningly.

"Of whom your—*dog*—disapproved?"

"Oh, yes!" She smiled sunnily. "Sir Rupert quite abhors him, you know!"

"He doesn't like the dog?"

"No, no! Sir Rupert doesn't like him!"

"What?" A thoroughly confused Charles asked her to begin again, and Arabella explained that Sir Rupert the dog did not like Sir Rupert the man at all, which could mean that Sir Rupert the man did not like Sir Rupert the dog, either, but that was neither here nor there.

No, Charles said, it wasn't. But what Sir Rupert the dog's preferences had to do with anything he did not know.

Arabella looked at him in surprise. "But Charles!" she protested. "You do!"

No, he assured her, he did not. If he did know, he would be the first to be aware of it.

"But you do!" Arabella assured him. "If we have discussed it once, I'm sure we have discussed it a hundred times—how

animals seem to have a sense about people, and to know who is
to be trusted, and who is not!''

"Oh." Yes, Charles agreed, they had discussed that. But what
it had to do—oh. She was looking at him in that where-has-your-
mind-gone-begging way again, and Charles stopped. Of course.
"Clorimonde doesn't like the fellow."

Arabella giggled. "He despises him! We have to lock up poor
Sir Rupert whenever the other Sir Rupert comes to call!"

Charles's suggestion that they were locking up the wrong Sir
Rupert was met with hearty agreement from Miss Ansley, and a
loud woof from Clorimonde, who had come to see if they offered
any more agreeable sport than the promising rabbit scent he'd been
following. At the sound both Tory and Thunder shied, which
seemed to give the dog considerable pleasure. He barked again.

"Clorimonde!" roared Mr. Carlesworth.

Miss Ansley nodded. "That is just what he says when Sir
Rupert comes. Except he punctuates it with several growls, and
an occasional showing of teeth."

"Oh?" Charles patted the dog's head approvingly. "I didn't
know he was that discerning!"

"Oh, yes!" Arabella's nod was eager. "Once, he even took
Sir Rupert's hat and carried it out to the stable and buried it!"

Astonished, Charles asked how she could know that, if the hat
was buried. Miss Ansley beamed seraphically up at him.

"There is an excellent view of the stable yard from the
music-room window!"

"And you never said anything while this was going on?" The
tone was dry, and she opened her eyes very wide at him.

"But Charles!" she protested. "Had I told Sir Rupert his hat
was being buried, I would have had to interrupt him, and
Grandmama *assures* me that gentlemen hate to be interrupted
when they are going on. And on. And on!"

"Ahhh." Charles understood, and chucked her under the chin
in commiseration. "Given to long-winded periods, is he?"

Arabella nodded vigorously. "The longest!"

Charles grimaced. "Thank you! And now you have sent him
to me. As your guardian!"

"Dear Charles," said Miss Ansley, catching his hand and
holding it for a moment against her cheek. Mr. Carlesworth was
not deceived.

"Pooh!" said dear Charles.

❧ 18 ❧

After Charles's conversation with Arabella he expected a visit
from that dratted Omsley fellow, as Sir Rupert was coming to be
known in his mind, at some not-too-distant date. He had not
expected the visitor to be waiting for him when he rode home
just after noon that same day, however, and he was not pleased
to see him. It's just like the fellow, Charles thought, perhaps a
tad unfairly. Doesn't give a man a chance to prepare for him, just
comes bumbling in. Carlesworth's eyebrows drew together and
his lips compressed as he made his guest a curt bow.

Omsley, who had been nervous enough before Carlesworth's
arrival, took one quick glance at Charles's forbidding face and
felt his stomach churn. Sir Rupert dropped his cane three times
before Charles had even crossed the hall to shake his hand, and
he dropped it again when Carlesworth expressed regret that a
two o'clock meeting with his grandfather's solicitor, down that
day from London, would not allow them long to converse.
Perhaps if Sir Rupert would care to return another time?

Charles said the latter hopefully, wishing for more time to
fortify himself for this latest situation Miss Ansley had gotten
him into, or for time to make a bolt for the city, he wasn't sure
which.

A moment later his lips turned up a bit in self-derision, and he
gave an inward laugh. Yes, he did. Charles Carlesworth was not
a man to bolt when a friend was in distress, and he realized with
a start that the infuriating Miss Ansley, besides being the bane of
his existence more days than not, was also a friend. And a valued
one. Being plagued by this clodpate—

Carlesworth's brow grew darker as he waited for Sir Rupert's
reply. That gentleman, watching the emotions playing across the
face in front of him, gulped and almost took himself off, except

for the fact that he wasn't sure he could bring himself to the sticking point again if he left, and so . . .

A quick glance in the mirror just across from him—for Sir Rupert purposely had chosen the one chair in the hall that faced a mirror—assured him that he was looking his best, and reminded him that he was a very fine fellow, really, and that once Carlesworth knew his mission he would no doubt be so happy Sir Rupert had come that he would postpone the meeting with the solicitor and offer his guest a glass of wine to celebrate. Of course, Miss Ansley's father had not been happy, and Mr. Carlesworth was looking quite as forbidding as that frightening gentleman at the moment, and—and—

Sir Rupert gulped. "Beg a moment now!" he said.

Charles nodded. Of course he would, plague take the fellow. "Very well." Charles turned and walked away, pausing only when he realized no one was following him. He glanced back over his shoulder to see Sir Rupert fiddling with his cravat, watching his reflection in the mirror as he brought the folds more to his liking. He patted his hair back from his forehead as Charles rolled his eyes.

"This way," Carlesworth said when the other man, after his careful ministrations, had straightened and, seeing Charles watching him, favored him with a tentative smile. The smile was replaced by a nervous twitch at Charles's curt tone, and Sir Rupert dropped his cane again.

"Of course!" Omsley said, bending to retrieve it. When he straightened Charles was already striding down the hall, and Sir Rupert had to hurry to catch up. When his host stopped and threw open a door off to the left, stepping back so that Omsley could precede him into what Sir Rupert saw was a well-appointed library, Sir Rupert was feeling out of breath and—he hoped not, and looked around for a mirror to check, but could find none—mussed.

Gervase Ansley had also made him feel mussed.

"Please." Charles stopped by the desk for a moment, but motioned Sir Rupert toward the fireplace. "Have a chair."

A grateful Sir Rupert, glad for the chance to sit down, was halfway seated when a "Meeeeeeooooooowww!" from below, and a sharp sting in his posterior region made him straighten abruptly, his protuberant eyes starting from his head even more than usual.

"For heaven's sake, man, have a care!" Carlesworth snapped, striding across the room to lift something from the chair Sir Rupert had chosen. The indignant Omsley watched as his host cradled the object gently, saying, with a frown toward his guest, "Are you all right, Davida?"

"Meeoooooowww," spat the kitten, one small paw coming out, claws extended, in an effort to reach Sir Rupert.

"There, there," said Carlesworth, rubbing her small head with his thumb.

"That's a cat!" Sir Rupert said, in full comprehension of the situation.

"Well, of course it's a cat!" Carlesworth continued to stroke the kitten, which by now had curled itself into the crook of Charles's arm, from where it could hurl *pfft! pfft!* insults at the intruder opposite them.

"She scratched me!" One hand went gingerly behind him as Sir Rupert said the words, and Charles, looking up, had to bite back a grin.

"You're lucky that's all she did," he said. "You almost sat on her, you dolt!"

"Now, see here!" Sir Rupert, who liked being called a dolt as little as any man, and who liked being scratched by small white kittens with one orange and one black ear even less, was about to embark on a biting speech on the way guests should be treated in country homes when it occurred to him that such behavior, satisfying as it might be, probably would not be the best way of winning Carlesworth to his side in his suit for Miss Ansley's hand.

Swallowing his words with difficulty, Omsley managed a weak smile for the kitten and took a step forward to pat her head, calling her a pretty little thing. The ungrateful Davida took a swipe at his hand and Sir Rupert leaped back, yelping.

"Ow!" he said, sticking his thumb into his mouth, then pulling it out again so he could talk. "She scratched me again!"

"Yes." Carlesworth agreed. "She did."

"Of all the—"

Carlesworth carried the kitten to the window seat and settled her on a cushion there, listening to her purr a moment before he strolled back to the fireplace and, indicating the chair opposite him for his guest, took a seat. "It would appear, Sir Rupert," Mr. Carlesworth said gravely, "that animals do not like you."

"What?" Sir Rupert, still sucking his finger, was distracted, and it took him a moment to focus on the words. Then he sighed, and his face fell. "Oh," he said, and sighed again. "She told you about the dog, did she?"

Charles nodded.

"Then I suppose she told you why I am here?"

Charles considered disclaiming, just to see how his guest would proceed. After a short struggle he decided not to prolong the poor man's misery—or, more to the point, his own—and nodded again.

"Well?"

Sir Rupert was sitting forward, his sore thumb forgotten as he waited for Charles's answer. The expression on his face put Carlesworth forcibly in mind of a hound he'd had once; not the brightest of creatures, it was always getting in trouble, but always hopeful someone would like it, anyway. Yes, Charles thought, surveying Omsley's face further; he understood what Miss Ansley meant. As Sir Rupert tilted his head slightly, Charles caught a definite likeness to Clorimonde.

"Sir Rupert," Charles said.

"Yes?"

"Sir Rupert—"

"Yes?"

"Oh, for goodness' sake, man, give me a chance to speak!" Feeling harassed, Charles spoke more sharply than he normally would have, and watched as the other man's face fell. He felt as if he'd kicked Lady Hedgwick's canine companion.

Miss Ansley, Charles thought grimly, owed him a great deal for putting him through this.

An abashed Sir Rupert begged pardon, and waited. And waited.

Charles, it seemed, was having difficulty finding the right words to blight a man's hopes forever.

When Sir Rupert thought he had waited long enough, he smiled crookedly and said, "She named her dog after me, you know."

Charles blinked. "I . . . beg your pardon?" he said.

Sir Rupert smiled. "She named her dog after me," he repeated. "After she left Belgium, and told me—oh, I don't know, perhaps five times—that she never wished to see me again, I thought—it did occur to me that, perhaps—she really did not like me very much. But then, when I heard from Cousin Blathersham in London that she was here, and I came, and she'd named her dog after me—'' He looked at Charles hopefully. ''It says something, doesn't it?''

Drat the chit! Charles thought. And drat Omsley, too! What kind of fellow would take having a dog the likes of Clorimonde named after him as a sign of affection? Charles cleared his throat.

''Well,'' Carlesworth said, ''it does say something. . . .''

Sir Rupert's nod was triumphant. ''I thought so!''

''But not what you hoped.''

''What?'' Sir Rupert looked puzzled, and Charles cleared his throat again.

''Miss Ansley,'' Carlesworth began carefully, ''is sometimes given to a certain . . . um . . . whimsical streak, a love of the ridiculous that shows up in small jokes and—and—''

Charles saw Omsley's puzzlement grow, and felt more harassed than ever. Clearing his throat, he began again. ''It is possible,'' Carlesworth said, ''that I am not the person you should be discussing this with.''

Smiling, Omsley assured him he was; Miss Ansley had said so. Carlesworth spared an unkind thought for Miss Ansley before going on.

''Yes, but—'' Charles waved a hand helplessly. ''Perhaps her father . . . ?''

Omsley's eyes widened in alarm. ''Is he here?'' It was apparent from Sir Rupert's expression that he would not welcome that intrusion. ''In the country??'' Omsley darted furtive glances over his shoulder as if Gervase Ansley might materialize in the room at any moment.

No, Charles said, he was not. It was just that—that—

''You ever meet Gervase Ansley?'' Sir Rupert asked. His hands and chin were resting on his cane as he held it before him, and his eyes were fixed on Carlesworth's face.

''I have not had the pleasure,'' Charles said.

Sir Rupert shook his head vigorously. ''No pleasure,'' he told Charles. ''I can assure you! Damned nasty fellow, Ansley! Has this way of looking at you as if he were just judging what sort of thrust it would take to do you in. Like he can just feel the sword in his hand, and is waiting, waiting. . . .'' Omsley shuddered, then confided, ''Devil of a fellow with a sword, is Ansley.''

Sir Rupert, staring at the man in front of him, thought a moment, then eyed Charles anxiously. "You fence?" Sir Rupert asked.

Charles said he did.

Sir Rupert gulped. "Ever been out?" he asked, the words so carefully casual that Charles had to bite the inside of his mouth not to smile.

"I do not," Mr. Carlesworth said, inclining his head gravely, "believe in dueling."

"Oh!" A relieved Sir Rupert smiled. "Neither do I!"

They sat for several moments, Sir Rupert nodding as Charles looked at him, and Charles nodding back—he had no idea why. At last Charles said, "Sir Rupert, it will not do."

"Eh?" Sir Rupert's mind had been on what could have been a potential hazard to his health, had Mr. Carlesworth proved as bloodthirsty as the frightening Mr. Ansley, and was not easily recalled.

"You and Miss Ansley," Charles said. "It will not do."

"But—" Sir Rupert moved indignantly, and dropped his cane again.

"Pfft!" said Davida, disapproving from her place on the windowsill.

"Why not?" said Sir Rupert, his tone belligerent as he picked up his walking stick.

Charles shook his head. "It simply will not. Miss Ansley—"

There was that hopeful look again, and Charles sighed.

"Miss Ansley," he said, "does not wish to wed. You."

"Perhaps not now—" Sir Rupert began.

"Never."

"Never?"

"Never."

Sir Rupert sighed. "That's a very long time." He stared off into space for several moments, then sighed again. "It's the dog, isn't it?" he asked, face glum.

Why not, thought Charles, and nodded.

"Dog won't live forever," Sir Rupert said hopefully.

"She will get another one." Charles's voice was firm, dashing his visitor's hopes.

"Other dog might like me," Sir Rupert suggested.

Charles considered, found that fair, and asked if other dogs normally *did* like Omsley. The gentleman shook his head from side to side, and the glum expression returned.

"Well, then . . ." Charles said, shrugging and holding his hands wide.

"Don't think a dog ought to make the decision," Sir Rupert said, sitting up very straight and showing more resolution than Charles had believed him capable of.

Carlesworth nodded. "No," said Charles slowly, "nor do I. But the thing is, the dog has not."

"Oh." Sir Rupert thought. "Her father, then . . ."

Carlesworth was tempted to leave it at that, for it was clear Gervase Ansley had put a more than healthy fear into his daughter's suitor. If Sir Rupert thought Ansley stood behind the refusal, that might be the end of it.

Still, Charles thought, as disgusted as he was with Omsley, it was clear the man meant well, and cared for Arabella as much as any man who placed his tailor first in his life could. He deserved to know the truth.

"Sir Rupert," Charles said. "Both her father and I do Miss Ansley the honor of believing she knows her own heart. And that heart is not yours. Believe me, sir, over the past few weeks I have come to know Miss Ansley well, and I tell you truthfully the two of you would not suit."

Sir Rupert was watching him closely, and frowned at the last words. "Because you say so?" he asked, the pugnaciousness of his expression putting Charles so forcefully in mind of Clorimonde when he had a stick in his mouth and would not let go that Charles had to cough to cover a laugh. Why was it Arabella could be outrageous without retribution, but it was Charles who now stood in danger of paying for her outrageousness, he wondered.

When Carlesworth had mastered his voice he nodded, face grave. "Because I say so, if that is what you need to hear to realize the hopelessness of your suit. But most of all, because Miss Ansley says so."

"Oh." The fight went out of Omsley's face, to be replaced by a depth of disappointment Charles would not have credited to him.

"Well . . ." Omsley heaved himself to his feet, no longer looking at his host as he said, "I have already taken too much of your time, I fear, Mr. Carlesworth, and will no longer trouble you. I had thought—I hoped—'' He smiled crookedly. ''I thought how well we would look in a carriage together—an open carriage, with green cushions, and me wearing my claret coat, and her in pink. . . .''

Charles, who thought marrying because it would present a pleasing picture in a carriage was perhaps the oddest reason he had yet heard for entering holy matrimony, could only blink at his guest's vision.

Sighing, Omsley made his way toward the door as Charles rose to escort him, and said, shocking Charles considerably, ''But then, I've seen the way she looks at you, seen the way she laughs when you're about. I'd hoped I was wrong, but it's plain to me now. It's you she fancies, isn't it? And you fancy her. Well, then!''

Sir Rupert reached out a hand as Charles held the door for him. He gave Carlesworth's fingers a brief shake, trying to recover what dignity he could, under the circumstances, and take his leave as a gentleman. ''I wish you very happy, I'm sure.''

''*What?*'' said Charles.

Thinking he understood, Omsley replied, ''Oh! I see! Don't want it nosed about yet, do you? Well, you can depend on me. Mum's the word.''

So saying, he left the room a shaken man. Had he but known it, he left an even more shaken man behind him.

❧ 19 ❧

Arabella was surprised to find Charles less than forthcoming on his conversation with Sir Rupert. He astonished her considerably by saying there might have been more to the gentleman than they gave him credit for, and he hoped that someday Omsley would settle on a lady quite unlike Arabella but who Sir Rupert also felt looked good in a carriage.

Miss Ansley had not seen Charles for three days, having received no more than a terse note from him the evening of their last ride, saying the matter she had referred to him had been taken care of, and she need worry about it no longer.

She had half expected him to arrive to tell her about it that evening, and when he did not, she was sure he would come the next day. He did not appear then either, and when his grandfather paid a visit the day after, calling to take Lady Hedgwick to tea at the Southebys, he had no information for her other than that Charles had locked himself up in the library with the account books, saying he had a tangle to unravel—a tangle, the earl later told Lady Hedgwick with a chuckle, that he did not at all believe had anything to do with the account books—and did not wish to be disturbed until he had done so.

"Has the household in a rare taking," Clangstone told Arabella with a satisfaction she did not understand. "Even raised his voice to his valet, and all because the poor fellow asked him if he was sure he wished to wear the scarlet waistcoat that day!"

Arabella's brow furrowed. "That doesn't sound like Charles!" she said.

Carlesworth's grandfather chuckled. "Isn't," he agreed, with a great good humor she could not understand. "Isn't like him at all!"

The old gentleman was beaming, as was her grandmother,

who had joined them by this time, and Arabella's frown deepened. "But—" she began.

Her grandmother leaned forward and kissed her cheek. "Good-bye, my dear! We must go, we'll be late! You're sure you don't wish to join us?" Arabella shook her head in answer to the question. Mrs. Southeby's fear of sunlight's injurious effects on the complexion caused her to keep her receiving room in virtual darkness, the windows so heavily draped that guests had to half grope their way to their seats.

The only time Arabella had accompanied her grandmother there she had tripped over an unseen footstool and tumbled into a cherrywood table, knocking a knickknack to the floor. Mrs. Southeby had said, in one of those fainting voices that Arabella always found suffocating, that dear Miss Ansley was not to worry herself about it, it had only been her favorite. . . .

Her grandmother had assured Arabella that she would, in time, come to learn the placement of all pieces of furniture in the darkened room, thus avoiding such accidents. Arabella found that hard to believe, and did not care to take the chance again, remembering the disapproving glances of Mrs. Southeby's sister, maid, and housekeeper as they picked up the pieces of "one of madam's prized possessions."

Fixing her large eyes upon the earl Arabella said, in a voice that brooked no excuses, "I am sorry Charles is having so much trouble with his accounts. I do hope, however, that he will find the problem soon, and will not fail to join me tomorrow morning for our usual ride. If he cannot, please tell him I will ride over in the afternoon to see if I might help him unravel his knot."

Aha! thought the earl. He delivered the message with alacrity that evening when his grandson joined him at the supper table to sit frowning at his soup.

"What?" Charles said, snapping to attention as the earl politely delivered what to his delighted old ears sounded a great deal like a threat.

"That's what she said, dear boy," Clangstone repeated, spreading butter on his bread with pleasure. He was coming by degrees to delight in the difference Miss Ansley's presence in the neighborhood was making in his dining room. Gave it an excitement that hadn't been felt there in years.

"Well, I don't see—" Charles began, met his grandfather's limpid gaze, and frowned further. "I have work to do, you know!

I can't be forever junketing about the neighborhood with Miss Ansley just to keep her amused!''

''Promised Lady Hedgwick,'' the earl pointed out with a fairness his grandson did not appreciate. ''Promised Miss Ansley, too.''

''Hmmph!'' said Charles. ''We shall see!''

And, the following morning, they had. The earl had chuckled, watching his grandson ride out. He would never know if it was Charles's sense of fairness, or the young lady's threat, that had torn Carlesworth from his books, pronouncing—somewhat grumpily—the mathematical problem there resolved, but Charles had gone.

Now the two were riding down the country lane not more than two miles from Hedgwick Hall, and Arabella could only stare at Charles as he made his pronouncement regarding Omsley. Her small pink mouth formed a soundless O before she closed it and gazed reflectively at his stern face. Charles was not looking at her, but staring straight ahead, a slight frown on his forehead.

''You are funning me,'' she said, expecting his lips to turn up as they always did when he tried to tease her and was found out.

Charles shook his head.

''But Charles—''

''Arabella, I do not wish to say another word about it!'' His face turned toward hers in annoyance, increasing her surprise. ''It is no little thing to quite cut up another fellow's hopes, you know, and I do not thank you for placing me in that position! Sir Rupert Omsley will not bother you again! I suggest you be thankful for that, and turn your thoughts to other things!''

They rode in silence for several minutes after that, Miss Ansley taking Carlesworth's advice and turning her mind to what on earth had occurred between the two men to make Charles so testy. It was a topic Mr. Carlesworth would not have appreciated her considering, had he known, for Mr. Carlesworth did not wish to discuss Sir Rupert's conversation with Miss Ansley at all.

He was afraid that if he told her part of it, she would weasel the rest from him as she almost always did, drat the chit, and Charles was strangely loath to have Arabella learn the last words uttered by Sir Rupert. That she would think them a very good joke he had no doubt, and that may have been what hurt most of all. At any rate, Charles did not wish to find out.

For Charles Carlesworth—cautious, correct, clever, conscientious Charles—had realized, in a blinding light, that Sir Rupert Omsley was right. Not in what he said about Arabella's face lighting up when Charles entered a room—Carlesworth had seen nothing of that! But the man was right when he realized Charles felt a great deal for his charge. It was more than he would like, Charles knew, just as he believed it was much more than circumstances should allow.

What, wondered Charles, would his godmama, to say nothing of his esteemed grandfather, think were they to find that Arabella Ansley, the young lady they had placed in his hands for careful coaching before she burst upon the London scene to make a brilliant match (and Charles was sure it would be brilliant; she was such an engaging little puss, all wide-eyed naivete one minute, and full of her own quaint, worldly wisdom the next) was fast becoming—had already become—the object of his affection?

The peals they would ring over him! The accusations he would find in their eyes! He paled at the thought. Charles, to whom duty was everything, to have so far forgotten himself—no!

Carlesworth shook his head to clear it of that vision. It would not do. They had entrusted him with a mission and Lady Hedgwick's precious granddaughter, and he could not—would not—betray that trust.

Arabella, watching him, saw the headshake and her brow furrowed further. Charles looked for all the world like a man struggling deeply with himself. Like a man in danger of losing his best friend, and already mourning the loss.

She put one small hand out to touch his arm, an action that so surprised him that he communicated his surprise to Thunder, who snorted and bridled.

"I say!" said Charles.

Arabella apologized. She had not meant to startle him, only to ask if he was feeling quite the thing.

Charles looked at her.

"I saw you shake your head just now," she began, then broke off as he colored and set his lips in a firm line. "Charles." She touched his arm again. "Are you all right?"

"Quite," he said.

"If something is bothering you—"

"The only thing that is bothering me," Charles said, with more truth than tact, "is you! I'll race you to the tall tree!"

He had already given Thunder the signal to start and Arabella, not about to refuse a challenge, was soon after him, her mind storing away that curious statement for later examination. Although she believed Charles had wanted her to think it referred to her cross-examination at the moment, she had an inkling—a precious inkling!—that there might be more to it than that.

They arrived at the tall tree with Arabella and Tory no more than a half-length behind Carlesworth, and they were just catching their breath, their cheeks flushed and Arabella laughing, when Mr. Blathersham and Mr. Wooding cantered around the bend in the road and came straight toward them.

"Oh!" said Arabella as the two slowed their mounts. "Mr. Blathersham! Mr. Wooding! Good day, gentlemen!"

Both made quite credible bows, really, for being on horseback. Carlesworth was puzzled by the way they looked Miss Ansley and him over, then exchanged knowing glances before Mr. Wooding inquired whether they had been riding long.

"Perhaps an hour," Carlesworth said.

Mr. Wooding looked at him. "Ahhh," he said.

"Ahhh," seconded Blathersham. The two men looked at each other again, and nodded. Mr. Blathersham turned toward Arabella.

"Miss Ansley," he said, "my cousin has been recalled to town. He asked that I make you his apologies since he did not wish—I mean, was not able—to call on you personally to take his leave. But he asked me to remember him to you, and to ask you to believe him always your most faithful servant. He also asked that I give you his best wishes for your future happiness."

Arabella, surprised by quite the longest and certainly the most formal speech she had ever heard Mr. Blathersham utter, thanked him graciously and invited the gentlemen to turn their horses and ride back to Hedgwick Hall to join them for a light luncheon she was sure would be waiting when they arrived.

To her surprise, both young gentlemen colored alarmingly.

"No wish to intrude," blurted Blathersham, while Wooding followed with, "No doubt you wish to be alone."

Carlesworth sat his horse stiff and glassy-eyed.

Omsley! he thought. Omsley! His friends' actions made it

clear Sir Rupert had imparted his suspicions to his cousin before leaving for London. And Charles had relied so heavily on the man's assurance of discretion. He'd actually believed the man would keep his suspicions to himself!

Alas, Sir Rupert, like so many people, considered himself the soul of discretion. He had not meant to mention his interview with Carlesworth at all. But when Blathersham had made some rather slighting comments about Omsley finally coming to his senses and realizing Miss Ansley had no interest in him while so many other engaging young bucks—and here Blathersham had polished his quizzing glass in a most self-congratulatory way— were at hand to claim her attention, Sir Rupert had abandoned his initial plan in favor of putting his cousin in his place with a few well-chosen words that turned the smug look of satisfaction on the young man's face to one of incredulity, followed shortly by crushing disappointment.

Belatedly aware of what he had done, Sir Rupert left the Blathersham home with a caution to his cousin not to be bandying the news about until the lady and the gentleman she'd chosen—who knew why?—were themselves ready to announce it. After all, he'd promised discretion. . . .

Blathersham agreed, of course, saying indignantly that he did not bandy. In his mind, he didn't; he only told Mr. Wooding, who only told young Lord Eversett, who only told Mr. Critch-field, who'd just happened to see . . .

Well, that was how such things circulated in the country.

Charles's fears were confirmed when Wooding moved his horse close enough to Carlesworth's as the four went their separate ways to hiss, "Never knew you to be a man to steal a march on his friends like that, Charles. Might have told us!" before he rode on.

Miss Ansley, who had heard part of the message, stared after the two with puzzled eyes. "Whatever," she said, turning her gaze expectantly toward Charles, "was that all about?"

Carlesworth, his color high, shrugged and said perhaps the two weren't hungry.

"But they are always hungry!" Arabella argued. "Grand-mama says her cook has had to buy twice the amount of food she used to, before I came! Besides—" She realized too late she had allowed herself to be diverted, and frowned suspiciously at her companion. "That is not what I meant!"

"Oh?" Charles inclined his head politely, as if for all the world he did not know what she was talking about, and Arabella's frown grew.

"Just now, Charles," she demanded, "what was it Mr. Wooding was talking about just now?"

"Haven't the foggiest," Charles averred, shaking his head as if he, too, were puzzled by Wooding's cryptic pronouncements. "You know the fellow—all about in his head! Doesn't know himself what he's saying half the time!"

Arabella's frown deepened. "I believe," she told him, her stare awful as she turned it full upon him, "that Mr. Wooding knew *exactly* what he was saying. What's more," she continued, as Charles tried to disclaim, "I believe that *you* know exactly what he was saying, too!"

Charles, desperate to avoid further questioning, threw down the challenge of a race back to Hedgwick Hall and was off, leading Miss Ansley on a merry chase that could only be said to come desperately close to careening.

❧20❧

As they rode neck or nothing into the Hedgwick Hall stable yard Charles knew he had only postponed, not ended, Arabella's questioning. He had hoped that a plausible story would present itself to him during the race back, but so uncooperative was his brain that he had not gotten past *This cannot be happening! It cannot! It cannot! It cannot! Where did I go wrong?* when he was forced to rein in Thunder in preference to running himself and the horse into the stable.

"Charles!"

He had just dismounted and handed his horse's reins to a Hedgwick Hall groom when Arabella's voice was heard. Turning, he saw her sliding off her horse as another groom hurried to help her down. She was coming toward him, a militant look in her eyes, as he gulped, waiting in resignation for what would come next.

What came next surprised him, however. Miss Ansley's gaze, so intent on his face, flickered and slid past his shoulder. Her eyes opened in surprise and "What on earth?" escaped her lips as she stopped a few feet from him, her gaze drifting beyond.

Startled, Charles turned to see what had so captured her attention, and his own jaw dropped. The splendid curricle with its matched bays that had so excited Miss Ansley's attention might be unknown to that young lady, who even now was moving toward it, intent on examining the team and the bang-up equipage they drew, but it was well known to Charles.

"Jack!" Carlesworth said, shocked, as perhaps the handsomest gentleman Miss Ansley had ever seen this side of her father came around the team and stood regarding her and Mr. Carlesworth. The gentleman's face held open admiration for the lady before him, and his gaze, when transferred to his brother, took on a quizzing look that Carlesworth could only regard with fore-boding.

"Jack?" Miss Ansley said, turning back to Carlesworth in surprise. Charles nodded.

"My brother," he said, in far from happy tones. Jack's quizzical gaze sharpened. "Viscount Chalmsy."

"Ahh!" Arabella's face lit up, and she took a step forward, holding out her hand. "My lord! I have heard so much about you!"

"And I you, Miss Ansley!" Jack said, taking the small hand and raising it to his lips in a manner Arabella very much approved, but which Mr. Carlesworth surveyed with much less favor. "That is," Jack said, straightening from his bow and favoring her with his most dazzling smile, "I assume you are Miss Ansley."

She assured him his assumption was correct. Charles, recalled to his duties by his brother's amused air, made formal, if stiff, introductions.

"What are you doing here, Jack?" Carlesworth asked, the question so blunt that Arabella was quite taken aback by his unsmiling countenance and sharp tone. Viscount Chalmsy's smile widened.

"Always so good to see you, too, dear boy," the viscount murmured, causing Mr. Carlesworth to color.

"Of course it's good to see you," Charles started. "Always is. Thing is—didn't expect to see you. So seldom do."

Jack grinned. "True," he said. "Too true. It occurred to me, sitting up there in London, that it had been too long since I paid you and grandfather a visit, to say nothing of our ancestral home. But alack—" One hand went to his chest, as if to cover his heart, and Carlesworth's brow furrowed; the gesture made it clear that something was as smoky here as he'd first expected. "When I arrived home, neither you nor grandfather was there. Our esteemed Roberts having informed me that both of you were invited to Hedgwick Hall for luncheon, I of course drove here immediately, believing that Lady Hedgwick would not mind my addition to her party if it kept us from being separated a moment longer."

Arabella, who shrewdly sensed there was more here than met the eye, watched Charles speculatively. That he was not pleased to see his brother was apparent, and surprised her. Charles always spoke so highly of the viscount, so why . . . ?

Then, too, there had been something calculating in the way Viscount Chalmsy surveyed her when first they met, something hard and speculative in that look that wasn't quite hidden behind the urbane air he wore as naturally as the well-fitting driving coat and hat that completed his man-about-town image to perfection.

When Charles seemed as if he would say nothing forever, Arabella stepped into the breach with a declaration that the viscount had been quite right. There could be no doubt Lady Hedgwick would be delighted to see him, and they would be pleased to add him to their luncheon table.

"In fact," she said, smiling from one of the gentlemen to the other as her brain worked feverishly to try to make the puzzle pieces fit, "I imagine luncheon is even now ready. Shall we go in, gentlemen?"

With a great flourish Jack offered her his arm. Charles stood frowning at them both in a way that made Arabella's brain work even more furiously. Now what? she wondered. Jack, also watching his brother's face closely, had no such trouble reading that expression. He grinned.

"Coming, Charles?" he asked over his shoulder as he led Miss Ansley away. Arabella, too, was looking back and Carlesworth, his mouth tight, said no, he rather thought he wouldn't. Perhaps he'd ride on home. . . .

"But Charles!" Arabella protested, stopping to turn toward him, forcing Jack to stop, too. "Grandmama is expecting you."

"Oh, that's all right," Jack said, with an airy wave of his hand that dismissed his brother directly. "If Charles has to leave, I am sure we can manage to amuse ourselves without him." He had recaptured her hand and replaced it on his arm, and was even now turning her back toward the house. Carlesworth, glowering at the viscount, changed his mind.

"You're right!" Charles said, coming forward to offer his arm to Arabella, too, in spite of his brother's already established claim. "It would be most impolite of me to cry off at this late date."

"It would be quite all right, Charles," Viscount Chalmsy assured him, amused.

"No," Carlesworth said, glaring at him, "it would not!"

Again Charles offered his arm to Arabella who, feeling a bit like her parasol tugged between her grandmama's poodle and her, compromised by placing one hand on Charles's arm and one on Jack's.

As Charles stood frowning at his brother, and Jack stood smiling back, she looked up at both of them, noting that while she had always considered Mr. Carlesworth quite tall, his brother was even taller, and with shoulders that must be the envy of many of the viscount's acquaintances.

"Gentlemen," Arabella said, wondering mightily what was going on, "shall we go in?"

Lady Hedgwick tried later that afternoon to recall when she had ever hosted a luncheon that amused her more. Both she and Lord Clangstone had cried out in delight when Jack entered the morning room with Arabella and Mr. Carlesworth, accepting without a blink the viscount's tale that he had grown tired of the city and longed for the sight of his ancestral home. No one even mentioned the fact that when Jack had last visited, he had craved the city's excitement so that in less than two days he had set off for the metropolis again, claiming a most important, albeit heretofore forgotten, engagement.

"Came seeking peace and verdure, did you, Jack?" Charles had asked, at his most dry, as his brother waxed poetic on the beauties of the country as opposed to the dreary walls of town.

"But of course, brother mine," Viscount Chalmsy replied, with a smile Arabella found tantalizing, but which made Mr. Carlesworth strongly wish to box his brother's ears. That he would have no luck in doing so, Viscount Chalmsy being well known for his punishing right at Gentleman Jackson's Boxing Saloon, did not in any way deter Charles's wish to try.

What did deter him, however, was the fact that they were in Lady Hedgwick's morning room, and her estimable butler had just announced luncheon, and everyone, including himself, would think he had lost his mind if he so far forgot himself as to take a swing at his smiling brother.

During the meal Viscount Chalmsy kept up a steady stream of conversation, flirting with Arabella and providing Lady Hedgwick with just those tantalizing tidbits of London gossip she most liked to hear. He told his grandfather of those of that gentleman's acquaintances he had last seen at White's, all of whom asked after the earl and hoped he would be making a sojourn in the city soon.

''Well, well!'' Gratified, Clangstone said that perhaps he should consider such a trip during the coming season.

''You should,'' Lady Hedgwick assured him at once. ''Come and bear Arabella and me company! You, too, Charles!''

Charles remarked to the room at large that he had no real taste for town life, finding London—and here he looked directly at his brother—too full of fribbles and wastrels for his taste.

Viscount Chalmsy laughed. ''Such a dull dog, Charles!'' Jack said. ''Sometimes I wonder that we can be brothers!''

''No more,'' said Carlesworth, at his most polite, ''than do I!''

The earl, who heard the savage undertone in the younger voice, frowned, his eyebrows coming together as he glared a warning at first one young man, then another. Carlesworth, his eyes fixed on his brother's face, did not see his grandfather's warning, but Viscount Chalmsy did, and gave an imperceptible shrug. A moment later he turned the conversation to London's latest scandal, and soon had everyone but his brother in stitches as he moved from one topic to another, his exaggerated explanations and droll expressions adding zest to the meal for everyone except Mr. Carlesworth, whose appetite, should anyone have cared to notice, seemed to have quite deserted him.

Jack had driven himself back to High Point, leaving Hedgwick Hall after his grandfather and Charles, to Mr. Carlesworth's great annoyance. Charles had tried to outwait Jack, only to find it couldn't be done. Charles really did have work to do while Jack. . . .

When the viscount did at last return home late that afternoon he was halfway to the house when he encountered his brother, who stopped his progress by the simple expedient of stepping from the shadow of the tall hedge that surrounded High Point's extensive gardens. Jack's eyebrows rose.

''But Charles!'' he said. ''How nice of you to wait for me! And in such a theatrical manner—lurking in the shadows!''

Mr. Carlesworth frowned at him, refusing to rise to the clear bait offered by the word ''lurking.'' ''What are you about, Jack?''

Viscount Chalmsy grinned. ''I don't know what you mean!''

"Why did you have to stay at Hedgwick Hall after we left? What are you about?"

Viscount Chalmsy opened his eyes wide in a way that once again made Mr. Carlesworth wish to hit him. Charles, surprised at these violent emotions heretofore largely unknown to him, balled his hands at his sides and waited.

"Well, if you must know," Jack said, stepping around his brother to continue his leisurely pace toward the house, "I stayed long enough to walk in the garden with Miss Ansley, and to invite her to drive with me tomorrow."

"To drive—" Charles fell into step beside Jack, only to stop him again, this time by taking his arm. "Why?"

Jack's look was all innocence. "Many young ladies like to drive."

Again Carlesworth refused to be diverted. "Why are you here, Jack?"

The smile disappeared from Viscount Chalmsy's eyes, to be replaced by a reckless light Charles had seen there many times before, and never liked.

"I was in London yesterday, Charles," Chalmsy said, his voice soft. "In White's. Minding my own business. Reading the newspaper. Waiting for a card table to open, so that old Mannering—you know Mannering—and I could play. And who comes up to me but a fellow I hardly know—and do not care to—who, with a great deal of familiarity I do not like tells me he has been in the country lately. Has, in fact, visited my home. Spoken at length with my brother. Spoken intimately, he said."

"Omsley," Charles said, closing his eyes. When he opened them again Jack was watching him closely.

"You know him, then." The words were even softer, and did nothing to decrease Carlesworth's uneasiness. Charles nodded.

"Imagine my surprise," Jack continued, "when our so dear friend"—he ignored Charles's interruption stating Omsley was not and never would be his friend—"told me, in the strictest confidence, of course, that there were soon to be nuptials in my family!"

Charles rolled his eyes and heard his brother's voice grow softer still. "I find, Charles," Jack said, "that I do not enjoy hearing such information from strangers."

Viscount Chalmsy's hand was on his brother's arm now, and Charles gave it an impatient shake. His tone was belligerent as he said that in the first place, Omsley was an idiot; in the second place, it was all a hum; and in the third place, Charles owed his brother no explanation; Jack did not run his life.

Jack had no trouble agreeing with the first part of his brother's statement, reserved judgment on the second, and was clearly skeptical of the third.

"Oh, for goodness' sake!" Charles said, exasperated. "Not that I see what interest it is of yours—"

Viscount Chalmsy, who up until this moment had never struck Carlesworth as the most careful of brothers, looked enigmatic but said nothing, allowing Charles to continue.

"—but I have been helping Arabella—Miss Ansley—learn how to go on a bit in society, at Lady Hedgwick's request—and grandfather's—"

"You?"

The disbelief in his brother's voice caused Charles's frown to descend again, and he nodded.

"You??" Jack laughed. "And who is going to teach *you?*"

A stiff Charles said that he did well enough, thank you.

"Well enough!" Jack was amused. "If you mean by that you can waltz without stepping on your partner's feet—"

"Listen, Jack," Charles interrupted, "just because I do not waste my time in every gaming hell or at every sporting event within easy driving distance of London—"

Jack grinned. "Some of them are not in easy driving distance," he corrected. "One adjusts. But go on."

Although Charles glared at the viscount he did not return to his original topic, saying that Omsley had come there in pursuit of Miss Ansley and had misunderstood when Arabella directed him to Charles as the person to talk to, to—to—

Jack's eyebrows were raised. "Let me guess," he purred. "To solicit her hand?"

Charles said defensively it was not really that, it was just— just—

Viscount Chalmsy stood waiting.

"All right," Charles said at last. "But it isn't what you're thinking. That is, yes, I told him she wouldn't marry him. Well, what woman in her right mind would? But it wasn't because— even though he thought—"

Jack's eyebrows had risen almost to his hairline, and Charles bit back his stutterings with difficulty, taking a deep breath before he began again.

"In several weeks," Carlesworth told his brother, his voice cold, "Arabella will be going with her grandmother to London where, I hope, for her sake as well as Lady Hedgwick's, she will be a tremendous success. And I"—he was smiling, but it was with an effort that made Jack's eyes, open so wide seconds before, narrow suddenly—"very likely will never see her again."

"Ahhhh." Jack was watching him much more closely than Charles would like, and Carlesworth was happy when his brother turned his attention to his fingernails, which suddenly seemed to require his full concentration.

"And I suppose," Jack said, slanting a quick glance up before studying his nails again, "that you will be relieved by that. Happy, even, to see her go."

"Of course," Charles said, falling into step beside his brother as they started toward the house again. "I must be."

Jack nodded, and his voice was reflective, as if he thought of something else. "Of course," he said. "Of course."

❧21❧

Viscount Chalmsy sat watching the sun dapple the leaves above his head as he leaned against the old oak tree that had been the refuge of his youth. He had found it the month after he and Charles arrived at High Point to live with their grandfather following their father's death. He had never mentioned to anyone that this tree, among the stand of perhaps thirty, was his, for it was not in keeping with the care-for-little image he cultivated, and had been well on his way to perfecting even as a child.

Charles had found him here more than once when they were growing up and Jack was in disgrace with their grandfather for something or other, but Charles had always assumed it was the stand of trees that drew his brother. They offered a safe and easy place to hide, for once inside their circle a person could hear others pass not more than twelve feet away, yet never be seen.

Not even Charles, with his eyes that saw much and his mind that discerned more, had tumbled to the fact that it was always *this* tree to which Jack was drawn. There was something about it; its strength, perhaps; the obvious fact that it had survived longer than any of those around it, and would, bar a disaster, still be standing after the others were gone. At least, that was how Jack liked to think of it, when he needed a continuity and stability other than that provided by his brother and grandfather.

He was not thinking about the tree now, however, and his frown was not for the sunlight on leaves. As Jack sat, breaking small twigs into pieces and throwing the pieces away, his frown was for the rare mess it seemed Charles had gotten himself into.

The viscount had come to High Point two weeks ago for the very reason he had told his brother when he arrived. He had not taken it in good part to hear from a near stranger that one of his kin—and one of the only two relatives he cared about—was contemplating matrimony. Plus, knowing his brother, he had assumed from the way Sir Rupert rhapsodized about Charles's so-called intended that his brother, not as up to snuff when it came to women as the viscount believed himself to be, very likely had been taken in by a fortune hunter in search of a comfortable meal ticket.

True, Charles's fortune would not be as great as, say, the viscount's, but Carlesworth's wife would never starve, and there was more than one woman in the world, Jack thought cynically, who was looking for a good-hearted, courteous, kind husband she could depend on and, perhaps, easily dupe and easily lead. That the assumption that Miss Ansley was such a woman did not flatter his brother any more than it flattered Miss Ansley had not even entered the viscount's mind.

So Jack had set off from London with the impetuousness well known to his brother and grandfather, intent on separating Charles from what he had decided, by the time he was forty miles out of the city, must be one of the worst self-serving hussies ever put upon the earth.

The viscount had suffered a jolt, therefore, when he first met Miss Ansley. He knew within minutes that there was no doubt she was a minx, but try as he might he could detect no hardness in her character that would suggest she was out to feather her nest at his brother's expense.

Besides, when that dolt Omsley had told the viscount of Miss Ansley's presence in the neighborhood, he had failed to mention that she was Lady Hedgwick's granddaughter, and that the old lady doted on the puss. Since Jack had known for years that Lady Hedgwick also doted on his brother, the viscount realized that Lady Hedgwick would wish Carlesworth harm even less than the young lady who alternately listened to and brangled with his brother.

And if that was not enough, it was clear that Lord Clangstone found Miss Ansley charming. In fact, his grandfather had been as blunt as Charles in warning Jack that Miss Ansley was a friend of the family and not a young miss with whom the viscount might be wishful of setting up one of his shocking flirtations.

Jack, far from taking offense, had grinned and said he had heard more than one story of his grandfather's own shocking flirtations since going up to London, causing the old man to grin, too, before warning the viscount again that Miss Ansley was off limits to dangerous Jack. Clangstone had further surprised him by asking, his brows beetled, just what Jack was doing there anyway, saying in the rough tone he often used when he was worried, that if his grandson had outrun the constable, he had only to tell him.

Touched, Jack had disclaimed at once. In fact, he told his grandfather, he had had quite an amazing run of luck lately. But when he broached the subject of Charles and Miss Ansley, saying rumors about the two had brought him to High Point, the earl had surprised him by becoming uncharacteristically terse, saying only that Jack should keep his nose out of what he didn't understand.

That miffed the viscount, who was only trying to understand, and made him more determined than ever to get to the bottom of what was going on in his ancestral home. For that reason he had ignored his grandfather's subtle suggestions—and his brother's far-from-subtle ones—that he might be happier back in London, since he had made it known more than once that he found the country such a bore.

Jack, used to having his arrival greeted with excitement and a demand to know just how long he could stay, grinned at both of them and remarked seraphically that since those nearest and dearest to him found such delight in the country, he intended to remain with them until he had unlocked the secrets of their joy.

The three of them had been standing on the flagstones of High Point at the moment, and he had been gazing rather abstractly at Miss Ansley as she stepped down from the carriage that had brought her grandmama and her to visit. His statement had caused his brother to take a hasty step forward, fists clenched, and if the earl had not taken hold of Charles's arm and half dragged him down the steps, the viscount really believed his brother would have tried a turnup with him. In Jack's opinion that only showed how disturbed Charles was, since they both knew, and even Charles would admit, that when it came to physical contests the viscount outweighed his brother both in size and experience.

In addition, Charles normally had little taste for fisticuffs, his gentle nature giving him a much greater tolerance for the foibles of his fellow men than the viscount exhibited. Usually the most patient of fellows, Charles had shown an uncharacteristic incli-nation to have his cork drawn since Jack's arrival. Chalmsy had found that his brother, who usually declined to be baited, knowing from long experience that it was just the devilry in Jack that made him try to rouse the slow-to-anger Charles to fighting pitch, could be brought to the boiling point by a chance remark not even meant to raise Charlesworth's ire.

And what had brought about this change in his brother's even temper? There could be only one thing, Jack believed, and that was Miss Ansley.

Chalmsy believed Charles's declaration that the young lady was going to London for the little season and that Carlesworth believed he might never see her again, but what he did not understand was why, if that thought pained his brother as much as it seemed to, Charles did not make a push to fix his interest with the young lady.

His suggestion to his brother that Miss Ansley might hold a larger spot in his affections than Charles cared to admit had been met with such revulsion, heightened color, and that unusual willingness on Carlesworth's part to take umbrage and demand satisfaction that Jack, far from being convinced, had only been determined to investigate further.

To do that, he turned his attention to Miss Ansley.

He had taken her driving several times, looking always for signs of a gazetted fortune hunter. All he had encountered, however, was a charming young woman who viewed him with a friendliness reserved for the brother of Mr. Carlesworth, and a knowing eye that made it clear she knew a great deal more about the viscount than that gentleman might have liked, and was having none of his practiced compliments.

At least, that was the message she delivered when she and Jack were alone, or in the drawing room with others, sans Charles. When Mr. Carlesworth was present, however, her demeanor changed, and Jack might flirt with her as much as he liked. Indeed, the lady could be said to encourage it, calling his brother's attention to this or that droll thing the viscount had said.

Such machinations were not lost on Chalmsy; in fact, he rather appreciated them, having practiced just such tactics successfully more than once himself. He had taxed her about it, though, on their last drive, after they had come across Charles riding down the lane. Carlesworth had frowned at sight of them, and Miss Ansley, who had struck the viscount as more than a little distracted since she had entered Jack's curricle, had perked up dramatically at first sight of the viscount's brother. She'd rattled on to Jack at a great rate about the newest gowns her grandmama had ordered for the impending trip to London, and had touched his arm several times before they came even with Carlesworth.

Charles, saying stiffly that if he had known Miss Ansley cared to drive, he would have taken her out himself, was met with a light laugh from the lady, who said that since he had shown himself so busy lately, she had had to look for other gentlemen companions.

Jack, startled to hear himself referred to in that way, kept his tongue as he watched the effect her words had on his brother. Carlesworth said almost savagely that he was pleased she was so well satisfied, and he would be on his way.

"Oh, yes," Miss Ansley had told Charles, waving one languid hand as with the other she twirled the mint green parasol she held over her left shoulder, "but of course! You have much to do, and I am sure the viscount does not care to keep his horses standing, so . . ."

Charles made a brief bow and applied his heels to his horse's side with more than usual force. Thunder, startled, sprinted away, and Jack could not help but notice that Miss Ansley was staring after his brother with an expression quite altered from the face she had shown Charles. In fact, she looked so sad, watching the lane even after Carlesworth had vanished from their sight, that Jack had been moved to say, most uncharacteristically, "I could tell you how to go on with him, you know."

Miss Ansley had started and flushed, and it was apparent that for a moment she had forgotten he was even there. The viscount, unused to finding himself so totally ignored by a lovely young lady, had suffered a slight start himself, but it had slipped away at her casual, "I don't know what you mean."

"Oh, I think you do," Jack had said, one hand going out to turn her face, which was averted from him at the moment, so that she would have to meet his eyes. She did so reluctantly, peeping up at him and then down with a sigh.

The viscount grinned. "Miss Ansley," he said, his voice mild, "I cannot but feel that you are using me."

Her eyes had flown to his face, but at the smile she found there she had smiled rather reluctantly herself, before disclaiming again that she did not know what he meant.

"Let me tell you," the viscount offered, settling himself more comfortably on the seat so he could better survey her. Miss Ansley shook her head.

"No," she said, looking away. "No. Please." She raised one hand as if in supplication, then dropped it into her lap and sighed again. She slanted a glance up at him. "Do you mind so very much?" she asked.

The viscount grinned. "Do I mind being used to make my own brother jealous? Do I mind that he looks daggers at me at the dinner table, and has offered to help me pack should I care to return to London? Do I mind that I live in mortal fear that Charles will enter my bedchamber one night and slit my throat under cover of darkness?"

"You do not!" Miss Ansley shook her head at him. "As if he would!"

The viscount grinned. "Plant me a flush hit, then," he substituted.

Miss Ansley eyed him speculatively. "Could he?"

Once again Jack grinned. "No, my dear, he could not," he informed her. "But that does not mean he wouldn't like to try."

"Really?" Miss Ansley looked so happy at the thought that Jack burst out laughing.

"I am so pleased, my dear Miss Ansley," he drawled, "to find you so concerned for my welfare."

Arabella frowned at him. "I suppose," she said, "that you would hit him back."

"If he hit me, certainly."

"You must not!"

"I beg your pardon?"

"He is your brother!"

"But if he hits me—"

Miss Ansley shook her head, a tad too regretfully for the viscount's taste. "He must not," she said.

"My sentiments exactly."

She was looking at him in that knowing way she had, and he raised an eyebrow. Miss Ansley immediately replied, "But you bait him to do so!"

The viscount grinned. "My dear, I have always done so."

"Well?"

His grin grew. "I cannot help it. But"—he raised a hand as she seemed inclined to interrupt—"never before has Charles

risen so readily to the bait. Not even when we were children.''
   ''Oh?''
   That, too, seemed to make her happy, emboldening Jack to
ask, ''What is your game, my dear? Do you mean to have him?''
   For a moment he had thought she might tell him, but just as
she appeared about to speak, Wooding and Blathersham had
come around the turn, pausing when they saw Jack's vehicle. He
had seen them look at each other, eyebrows raised, before they
approached the curricle to make their bows and inquire quite
offhandedly if Charles was, perhaps, under the weather?
   At Miss Ansley's look of surprise Jack had taken charge,
raising his eyebrow in a way that had squelched more sophisti-
cated pretensions than theirs, saying, ''No, why?'' in a manner
calculated to discourage a reply.
   Blathersham, blushing, had said, ''Well, no reason—just
thought . . .'' but Wooding, made of sterner stuff, had said
manfully that he rather believed it was Charles Miss Ansley
liked to go driving with.
   He had looked to Arabella for confirmation and she, surprised,
had said that yes, that was true, but Charles was so busy these
days, and his brother so obliging. . . .
   That made both Blathersham and Wooding frown.
   ''I,'' Wooding said, directing a look at the viscount that made
Jack grin in a way calculated to fan the flames of the young
man's disapproval, ''would be happy to oblige, should Charles
be busy in the future.'' He looked pointedly at the viscount.
''Friend of mine, is Charles.''
   ''Me, too,'' Blathersham had seconded, and when Miss
Ansley said in puzzlement that she understood his team to be
lame, so that he could not take her driving even if he wished it,
had said in a strangled way, ''True, but—friend, you know. Of
Charles.'' He, too, frowned at the viscount, who laughed and
gave his team the signal to start, leaving the two young
gentlemen behind them.
   ''Now, that is very odd,'' Miss Ansley said, gazing back at the
gentlemen before turning a questioning look toward her companion.
   ''Yes,'' the viscount agreed. ''Aren't they?''
   ''No, no!'' Miss Ansley said. ''That is not what I meant! They
have always spoken so glowingly of you, but today . . .''

She waited, but when Jack said nothing, continued, watching him, "Today, it was almost as if they were angry at you."

He grinned. "Yes, wasn't it?"

Arabella frowned. "But why?"

When he had told her he believed it to be because they thought he was trying to cut his brother out with her, she had turned bright red. "But they do not know—" she protested, then bit her lip. The viscount looked at her.

"Miss Ansley," he said, "I cannot help but feel that when Sir Rupert Omsley was here earlier this summer, he left the neighborhood with the distinct impression that you would not marry him because you and my brother were . . ." He paused, searching for the right word, and settled at last on, "involved."

"Oh!" If Arabella had been red before, she was cherry now. "That—that—" She had folded her umbrella with a snap and banged it against the rim of the curricle, to the surprise of his horses. The animals shied violently and might very well have bolted with a less skilled driver at the reins.

"I say!" He'd uttered the words indignantly, taking the parasol from her and settling it firmly to his left, out of her reach. Miss Ansley apologized, saying she had not meant to startle his team.

"But the infamy of it!" she said. "As if it is anyone's business but mine and Charles—if Charles cared to make it his business, which he does not seem to, since even your presence does not make him—"

She had bitten the words off then, looking mortified, and not even Jack's solemn and most persuasive assurances that she could trust him had led her to say more. In fact, she requested, in a stiff little voice that showed just how embarrassed she was, that he forget—she had not meant—perhaps they should not drive out together again. . . .

Jack, not wanting to be shut out, had called her attention to a bird on the hedge, and later to a brilliant growth of flowers, talking easily of things until she had regained her composure. By the time he set her down at Hedgwick Hall she was able to thank him for the drive and even, after a moment's hesitation, to agree to drive with him again sometime.

He thought of all that now, and so deep was his concentration that he did not see the assailant about to drop upon him until it was too late. He did not even have the opportunity to put his hands protectively over his chest before the full weight of his attacker hit him straight on, knocking the breath from him.

''What the devil?'' was Jack's first thought, followed closely by instant recognition, and a curse for letting himself be so distracted in enemy territory. Unable to rise, he could only lie there as his assailant grinned triumphantly down at him. He could feel the hot breath on his face, followed a moment later by a wet tongue that touched his chin and licked slurpily and comprehensively all the way up to his forehead.

''Confound you, Clorimonde,'' Jack said as he lay, arms spread. ''Get off me, you big lump.''

''Woof!'' said Clorimonde, pleased with this easy conquest of one he had never before been able to catch so totally unawares. ''Woof! Woof! Woof!''

Just for good measure, he licked the man again.

❧22❧

"You know," Jack said resignedly, struggling to free himself from the fifty-plus pounds of poodle sitting squarely on his chest, "I never have liked you, really."

"Woof!" said Clorimonde, obviously not impressed. Jack reached up to scratch the dog's head.

"You're too much like me, I think," the viscount informed him. "You always must take center stage, and you can be terribly rude to people, if the mood strikes you. You act on your slightest whim, without one thought for the consequences, and you're going to get your way, regardless—"

A soft giggle made him stop abruptly and he pushed the dog to one side, rising hastily as he looked around.

"Woof!" said Clorimonde again before racing toward a tall oak three trees over, where he stopped and wagged his tail invitingly. Miss Ansley stepped from the shadows, her eyes brimming with laughter.

"My lord," she said, making him a slight curtsy.

Jack shook his head in mock despair. "I suppose it would be too much to hope you didn't hear that, just now," he said.

A demure Miss Ansley informed him she had always had remarkably acute hearing.

"How wonderful for you," the viscount said, and then to Clorimonde, who had approached with a stick in his mouth and an obvious invitation to throw it, "No, it's too late for that now, you beast. Don't think you can make up with a little thing like a game of stick."

The dog almost seemed to shrug, as if he'd understood every word just said to him, and turned and trotted toward Miss Ansley, who accepted the stick and obligingly threw it for him. "I am sure Sir Rupert would be devastated were you to remain angry with him,'' she said, trying to make her face solemn, and failing abysmally.

"He hides it well.'' The viscount was watching the poodle return the stick to Miss Ansley's hand and wait expectantly for her to throw it again. When she did so he once again raced off in a happy chase. Arabella giggled.

"Perhaps in that, too, he is like you,'' she said, eyeing the viscount with a keenness that had disconcerted Jack more than once in their short acquaintance. "He does not want others to know those things that he feels quite deeply.''

"Oh?'' The viscount made her a polite bow. "Do you do character readings, then, Miss Ansley? With a deck of cards, perhaps? Or perhaps your speciality is tea leaves?''

It was a clear warning to drop the subject but Arabella ignored it, coming forward to put her hand on the tall tree Jack considered his own, and stare up the length of its trunk to the canopy of leaves above. "I imagine this is your tree, then,'' she said.

Jack started.

"I beg your pardon?''

She looked at him in surprise. "You needn't be embarrassed,'' she told him. "Everyone needs a place to go when the world is too much with them. That tree over there''—she pointed to the one by which she'd been standing when he'd first seen her—"that is mine. I found it within a week after coming to Grandmama's.''

"I don't know what you're talking about,'' Jack said, and there was a forbidding note in his voice that was known to make even the best of his friends think of an appointment that urgently required their presence elsewhere.

"Pooh!'' said Miss Ansley, unimpressed.

Jack frowned at her. "Pooh?''

Arabella nodded. "Pooh!'' she repeated, then said kindly, leaving him for a moment bereft of words, "But I won't tell anyone, if you like. I suppose, when I think about it, that having your own special contemplating comfort tree is hardly in keeping with the man-about-town, devil-may-care appearance you work so hard to maintain.''

That really was more than Jack could bear. He informed her somewhat roundly that it was not an appearance, it was who he was.

"Pooh!" Miss Ansley said again, and it occurred to the viscount that he was not nearly as enamored of the word as she.

"I wish you would stop saying that." The words came out more complaining that commanding, and when she continued to regard him in that calm way he was finding most disconcerting, Jack asked sarcastically if she thought she knew him so well, then, after only two short weeks of acquaintance?

Not at all, she said politely, it was just that she knew someone so very much like him.

"Oh?" Jack raised an eyebrow. "Well, if you mean Charles, I am sure neither of us would thank you for the comparison. We're not alike at all!"

"Don't be silly!" The viscount, unused to hearing himself characterized as silly by an attractive young lady—or anyone else, save his grandfather, Charles, and occasionally Lady Hedgwick—was momentarily taken aback.

Arabella continued. "You and Charles are nothing alike!" She thought a moment, then amended, "Well, hardly, anyway."

"Then who—" the viscount started. She looked at him in surprise.

"Who," Jack demanded, "do I remind you of, if not my brother?"

"Well," Arabella said, smiling at him in a way meant to rob the words of any sting, "if you must know, you remind me of my father."

"Your—*father??*" The viscount, used to hearing himself referred to as a rake, a rogue, a hot-blooded young buck, and several even less complimentary things, had never before had a young lady tell him he put her forcibly in mind of her father. Nor, he found, did he like it.

Arabella, misunderstanding, assured him she quite liked her father.

"Well!" He looked so affronted that it was several moments before she could determine why, and when she did, she went off into peals of laughter, affronting the viscount further.

"No, no!" she said, giggles gurgling up and around the words. "You misunderstand! My father, too, is a great rake! He is considered most dangerous where carefully raised ladies are concerned! I'm sure he wouldn't want you anywhere near me!"

That appeased the viscount greatly, and after scolding her for giving him such a turn, he said that that was something her father and Charles would have in common, then. Arabella's laughter diminished, and she looked at him wistfully.

"Do you think so?" she asked.

The viscount said he was sure of it, and Miss Ansley bit her lip. "Then my lord . . ." She took a step toward him, her hands clasping and unclasping in front of her, her eyes fixed searchingly on his face. "Will you help me?"

"Help you?" His experience with women had made the viscount nothing if not suspicious, and there was something in her anxiousness that communicated itself to him.

Miss Ansley nodded. "My lord," she said, watching him closely, "do you care for me?"

"What??" The viscount looked so appalled that if Arabella had not been so intent on her purpose, she would have laughed.

"Miss Ansley," he said, "I hold you in the highest regard, believe me! But my grandfather—Charles—"

Jack heard himself floundering and checked, running a harassed hand through his hair as he stared at the young lady in front of him. Where had this come from? he wondered. He had been so sure she was intent on attracting Charles's attention and now . . .

His eyes narrowed. There was something about her eyes, and the way she held her lips, as if she were secretly laughing at him. . . .

"You abominable girl!" Jack said. "You know very well I don't harbor any loverlike intentions toward you, don't you?"

Arabella tried to look stricken, failed, and burst out laughing. "You little minx!"

"You thought—" she choked. "You thought—" She was off again, and Jack could only stare at her. When she started to wipe her eyes at last, Jack handed her his handkerchief and waited.

"Miss Ansley," he said, "what is it you wish of me?"

"Well." Arabella took one more dab at her left eye and handed his handkerchief back to him, oblivious of the ginger way in which he received that crumpled article. "I am so very sorry. I knew you were just flirting with me to irritate Charles." At his demur she said brightly, "Oh, I quite understand, believe me! Sometimes the temptation is just too great! He can be such a stick, after all!"

She said it so fondly that the viscount felt no need to come to his brother's defense, only inclining his head attentively as he waited for her to continue. Miss Ansley gave him a reproachful look. "You might defend him, you know," she said.

"What?"

"I would not allow anyone to call Charles a stick if he were my brother," she informed him. "For a dearer, kinder, gentler, more responsible man never lived."

The viscount held up a hand as if to fend off her rebuke. "A paragon!" he assured her. "Yes, yes! It is true! Pray continue!"

Arabella frowned at him, but after several moments she did so. "As I was saying," she told him, "I felt I had to make sure you did not really care for me, because I quite realize that what I am about to ask you is outrageous enough without complicating it further—but you said—when we were out driving—that you could show me how to go on with Charles, so I believe you must want to help. . . ."

She realized the viscount was watching her with both uneasiness and suspicion, and took a deep breath.

"My lord," she said, "as long as you don't care for me—but you do, no matter how repugnant you may find hearing the words out loud, deeply love your brother—in that case—"

She took another deep breath, and as she did so, the viscount found he did the same thing.

"Viscount Chalmsy," Miss Ansley said, taking her fence straight on, "since you do not care for me at all—would you be so good as to run away with me?"

❧23❧

"What??"

Once, in his very callow youth, the viscount had been so enamored of a lady that he had suggested a flight to the border. She, several years older than he and, although he would not admit it at the time, much wiser in the ways of the world, had not swooned in tender and tremulous delight at the thought, as he had expected, but had laughed outright. Seeing his high dudgeon the lady had soothed his sensibilities and coaxed him from a heavy sulk brought on by chagrin. It would not do, she had told him; in several months he would thank her for refusing him.

In several months he had, and now, whenever the two met in public, it was with fondness and, on his part, a great appreciation for her far-greater wisdom.

Not since that time had the viscount considered such an ill-judged move as running away with anyone, the very thought of which made him shudder, nor had any young lady of his acquaintance been brazen enough to suggest it to him. Thank goodness!

"Miss Ansley, you forget yourself!" the viscount said, his back as stiff and his brow as dark as even Charles might wish. Had Jack known it, he looked and sounded for all the world like those overprotective, censoring fathers he was forever trying to outfox when he met their daughters in public.

Arabella giggled.

"And just what do you find so funny?" The sharp note was still in his voice, his stance still one of outrage.

Miss Ansley giggled again. "If you could see yourself!" she told him, then had another thought. "If Charles could see you!"

Peals of laughter burst forth at the thought, and Jack continued to frown at her.

"And what," he demanded, "would be so funny about that?"

Tears streamed down Arabella's cheeks again, and she had to breathe deeply several times before she could answer him. "It's just," she informed him, before laughter completely overtook her again, "that he would—*approve*—of you so!"

"Well, I should hope so!" Jack snapped. "Of all the—" He stopped, suddenly aware of her meaning, and began to grin in spite of himself. "You, on the other hand—" he said, pointing an accusing finger at her.

Miss Ansley nodded. "I know," she said.

"He would quite disapprove," he told her.

She nodded again. "He would say," she began, "he would say—"

"He would say it is not at all the thing to be asking gentlemen to run off with you," Jack supplied, "and you must never do it again."

The two of them exploded in laughter.

"That it would set up the backs of the Almack's patronesses—" Arabella began.

"—who would deny you vouchers to Almack's—" Jack supplied.

"—which would be *disastrous*!" Miss Ansley was laughing so hard she had to lean against Jack's tree to catch her breath.

"And all said just as seriously as you please, in his best effort to instruct."

Arabella nodded, straightening. "Is it any wonder," she asked, "that I love him so?!"

Jack's gaze was admiring. "You really do, don't you?"

Arabella nodded, and her smile began to fade.

"Then why don't you just tell him?"

The lady shook her head, this time quite serious. "Because," she told him, "I am not sure how he feels about me."

"Well, I am!" The viscount snorted, and she looked at him hopefully.

"You think—" she began, and her eyes finished the question.

Jack nodded. "He's not biting my nose off every time he sees me because he's indifferent to you, my dear!"

Arabella sighed. "I did think—" she said. "Sometimes—the way he acts . . . And then when I sent him Sir Rupert, I thought surely that would prompt him to recognize his own feelings, but . . ." She shook her head. "He said nothing. And then I was afraid I was wrong, and how could I ask him, when he might have to tell me he did not care for me, and then how could we go on, even as the friends we are now, for he would be so embarrassed, and he is so good, he would not want to hurt me—''

Her voice stopped on what sounded suspiciously like a sob, and she turned her head away as a surprised Jack once again reached for his handkerchief and handed it to her.

''Thank you,'' she sniffed in a small voice that made him smile.

''My dear,'' Jack said, ''whatever do you see in my dull dog of a brother?''

Arabella looked at him in surprise. ''What do you mean?''

''You are not at all like him, you know.''

''Oh, no!'' she agreed. ''I am much more like you than like Charles!''

The startled viscount agreed, after several moments thought, that that was true. ''Then why—'' he began.

Arabella appeared even more surprised. ''Surely,'' she said, ''you realize that one of the worst things you could do is marry someone just like you!''

Jack said rather stiffly that he could think of far worse things to do. Arabella assured him he was wrong.

''Don't you see?'' she asked him. ''People like you and me—sometimes we can't resist stirring the waters, just to see what will turn up. While someone like Charles—Charles is very good at calming waters. At least,'' she said wistfully, ''he is, when he is not arguing with me.'' She grinned half-apologetically at Jack. ''I fear it may sound maudlin to you, my lord, but he rests me. I feel safe with him, and cared for.'' Her grin grew even more apologetic. ''I have not had a very restful life, you see.''

Jack, who had heard something of her circumstances from their grandfather, nodded.

''Besides,'' Miss Ansley said, firing up, ''he is *not* a dull dog, and you are not to say so! Charles is a very interesting person, with a well-read mind, and a knowledge of Greek—''

Jack was grinning at her in clear disbelief. ''And you, of course, have always had an avid interest in Greek.''

''Well . . .'' Her dimple peeped out at him for a moment before it was firmly surpressed. ''And he is extremely kind, for I have tried him sorely these past few months.''

Jack's ''that I can believe!'' drew a quick frown as she continued.

"And still he helps me, and is concerned for my welfare, and wishes me—to go to London—and be a big success—" Tears sparkled in her eyes again, and she applied Jack's handkerchief to them before continuing, "All because he has promised Grandmama, and thinks it is what I want, but it isn't!"

With difficulty she regained her composure, and glared at her companion. "So you are not to call him a dull dog! Ever!"

The viscount's mild reply that he had heard her call his brother a stick more than once was rebuffed. It was, she said, her privilege. And if anyone were to call Charles a dull dog, it would be she, and not some brother not fit to polish his boots.

Jack demurred at once, saying that he had no intention of polishing his brother's boots, and he had known Charles much longer than she, and had been calling him a dull dog forever, and it was not a privilege he intended to have preempted by some small chit of a girl who thought she could give him direction just because she was to marry his brother!

Arabella looked at him with renewed hope. "You don't mind?" she asked.

The viscount said he did not; in fact, he thought the two of them deserved each other, and would do very well together.

"Well, I think so, too," Arabella confided, "but Charles is being so—"

"Idiotish?" supplied Charles's loving brother.

Arabella frowned at him. "Noble," she contended.

Jack shook his head in disgust. "It is just like him, you know," he said. "Once, when Charles was eight and I was thirteen, Charles took grandfather's charger out without a by-your-leave. It was most unlike him, so grandfather, of course, thought it had to be me. I was all ready to take the punishment—I was bigger than Charles, of course, and had more experience with being punished, for he was such a good-hearted boy he seldom provoked anyone, even me. But no, what must he do but step forward and tell grandfather it was he who took the horse. He was such a scrawny little runt, and you could see he was quaking in his boots, but there he stood, manfully admitting what he'd done wrong. . . ."

Arabella had the feeling the viscount was very far away as he continued. "I don't believe it ever occurs to Charles *not* to do the right thing, even if it is painfully hard. Seems as if every time

I've tried to protect him in my life, I've found he most needed protecting from himself.''

"Ahhh." It was a sound of sudden comprehension, and recalled the viscount sharply to the present. He looked at Arabella inquiringly, and she was watching him with new knowledge in her eyes. "That's it, isn't it?" she asked. "That is why you arrived here so unexpectedly two weeks ago! You'd come to save Charles from me!''

Jack's high color as he vehemently denied such a charge only confirmed her suspicion. "Why is it," she asked, "that everyone thinks you so bad, when you are really quite a nice man?''

Heartily offended, Jack gave her to understand that he was not a nice man at all. Just because he happened to care for his brother a bit, and didn't want the nodcock to fall into the snare of some pretty fortune hunter—

"Do you really think I am pretty?" Arabella interrupted, not minding at all that he had once thought her a fortune hunter.

Jack glared at her. "Of course you're pretty," he said, "and you know it, too, so don't go trying to play your tricks off on me. I'm not a green 'un, you know!''

Arabella giggled. "And you needn't try to play your tricks off on me," she returned, "for I am on to you. You want the world to think you're a care-for-nobody, but you care for your brother a great deal.''

"A little," the viscount protested.

"*And* your grandfather," Arabella continued.

Jack glared at her. "Oh, all right!" he snapped, picking up his hat, which sat at the foot of his contemplating tree. Cramming it on his head and offering her his arm, he continued, "I love my grandfather, and I love my brother. But not," he cautioned, one finger raised when she brightened and looked as if she would interrupt, "enough to run off with you!''

Miss Ansley's face fell. "Oh," she said. Accepting his arm, she allowed him to lead her several feet in the direction of the stream, where she'd left her horse tethered. "Well." She sighed, then straightened as another thought came to her.

"Tell me," she said, looking up hopefully to watch his face, "if you won't carry me off to Gretna Green, would you mind very much if I told Charles you wanted to do so?''

❧24❧

"Would I mind—" Jack dropped her hand from his arm as if he'd been burned, and took a few hasty steps away, staring down at her. Her hopeful gaze infuriated him.

"You really are the most outrageous chit I've ever met!" he told her roundly. "Of course I'd mind! Do you think I'd want my own brother to run me through?"

"Could he?"

Jack considered the interest she took in such a bloodthirsty event most unladylike, and said so. Miss Ansley continued to regard him with interest.

"No, of course he couldn't," Jack said testily, when he realized she was still waiting for an answer. "But he would certainly try, and there is danger in that, too."

"Yes." Miss Ansley sighed. "I would not wish Charles to be hurt."

It was on the tip of the viscount's tongue to thank her sardonically for her great concern for his health, too, but he refrained, contenting himself with wondering what outrageous thing she would say next. He did not have to wait long to find out.

"I do not know why you are so set against my plan," she complained, frowning up at him in a way Jack felt boded no good. "Your grandfather said he thought you might help, if I asked you."

"Oho!" the viscount said. "Now, that is too big a whisker, my dear, even for you! My grandfather would be the last to recommend that we run off to Gretna Green together, when earlier this week, after our last drive, he was suggesting that I might like to be back in London."

Arabella told him it was *not* a whisker; his grandfather had, too, said he thought Jack might help, if enlisted correctly.

Watching his face, she did not tell the viscount that the trip north had been her idea, and that it had taken a great deal of talking to get both her grandmama and his grandfather to say they would even consider it. It had been after more than three-quarters of a bottle of her grandmama's best port was consumed that they had allowed that it might answer, and the bottle was finished and another broached before they said that they might make the trip.

By then the earl and Lady Hedgwick had decided that it might be rather fun, Arabella's grandmother going so far as to say that she hadn't felt that young and foolish in years, and while she hoped dear Charles would forgive them all, perhaps it served the dear boy right for allowing his head to so thoroughly rule his heart, when they had all been doing their best to help his heart take charge ever since Arabella's arrival.

At that Arabella had fixed both the earl and her grandmama with a minatory eye and demanded to be told if arranging a marriage between Arabella and Charles had been their goal from the beginning. Both had looked so absurdly guilty that in the end she could only laugh and say that she would forgive them, because she must admit it seemed like a very good idea to her, too.

Her grandmother had beamed at that, assuring her that if the two had decided they would not suit, not a word would have been said; Lady Hedgwick and her granddaughter would have gone to London in search of another suitable young man, and Arabella and Charles would have gone their separate ways, neither knowing that their parting broke their respective grandparents' hearts.

"But," Arabella had objected, "if that is your goal, why don't you just *tell* Charles?"

"And have him think we've tricked him?" Lady Hedgwick had asked, much shocked.

"But you have," pointed out the fair-minded Arabella. The enormity of this truth hit her square in the face, and she frowned. "And you've tricked *me,* too!"

"But only with the purest of intentions!" the earl assured her, raising his glass toward her petite figure as he took a fortifying gulp of wine.

"Yes, but Charles thinks you wish me to go to London and be

a grand success, so he feels duty bound to forward that scheme," Arabella protested.

"Yes, plague take him," Lady Hedgwick said gloomily, also resorting to her wine. "It is very tiresome of the boy to be so loyal to us. Why can't he let his heart rule his head just once in his life?"

Arabella, who privately wondered the same thing, bit her lip. She, too, wanted the declaration of his affection to come from Charles. She wanted *him* to ask her to stay, so that she could know for certain that he was acting on his own accord, to please himself, and not to please his grandfather and her grandmama.

That was why, in desperation, she had concocted this mad scheme, and worked so hard to get her grandmother and the earl to agree they would make the trip north if the viscount would. That part she *did* tell Jack, adding that it wasn't as if they were really going all the way to Gretna Green; only north thirty miles to Greenthorpe.

"Greenthorpe?" Jack repeated blankly.

Arabella nodded. "One of your grandfather's estates," she said helpfully, when he seemed not to assimilate the name.

"I know what Greenthorpe is, you repellant girl!" Jack said testily, "but—my grandfather and your grandmama going along—"

"Oh." Arabella looked at him innocently. "Did I forget to mention that?"

Yes, Jack told her forcefully, she had left that little detail out!

Arabella grinned. "You didn't really think I'd travel north with only you for company, did you?" She hooted. "I would hope I am not such a green girl as that! Oh, no! My grandmama and your grandfather will be with us every mile of the way!"

Jack said he also would hope she wouldn't be such a green girl, but added acidly that he had no reason to believe their hopes would be fulfilled. Arabella stopped laughing.

"Well, I must say," she told him, "if you are going to be so ill-natured about it, I rather think I *won't* run off with you."

"Good!"

She took several steps away from him, pausing to stand where she could watch him out of the corner of her eye as she looked heavenward, saying, "Of course, if you *won't* help me, Charles and I may never work our way out of this muddle, and then I shall go off to London and marry someone else—perhaps a duke—and be miserably unhappy and no doubt die young, while Charles will wear the willow all his life and take to drink and some night fall from his horse and break his neck—"

"Enough!" Jack was laughing in spite of himself.

"Then you'll do it?" Arabella flew back to his side, her hands clasped together in anticipation, her face eager.

Jack held up one hand to ward her off. "Not just yet," he said, and watched her face drop. "If I am going to chance coming face to face with my brother's blade, I wish to know that every other means of untangling this knot has been tried."

A reasonable Arabella asked him what he had in mind.

Jack peered at her closely. "You wouldn't consider talking to him?" he asked. "Just telling him how you feel?"

An adamant headshake was her reply.

Jack sighed. "Then *I* will talk with him," he said. "Perhaps he will allow me to give him just a little nudge."

Arabella shrugged. She had found Charles remarkably un-nudgeable lately, but if the viscount cared to try . . .

"You must promise me one thing, however," she told Jack, one hand touching his forearm as she looked straight into his eyes. "You must promise me that you will not tell Charles of our talk."

Jack, who had been hoping it would not occur to her to ask such a thing, said austerely that he was surprised she would even think to make such a request.

"That," Arabella responded, her eyes narrowing, "is not a promise."

"I don't see why—" Jack began.

Her pressure on his arm increased. "Promise."

"I'm sure it won't come up—"

She gave his arm a sharp pinch. *"Promise!"*

"Ow!" Jack shook his arm from her grasp, frowning down at her. At last, in the tone of a man goaded almost beyond endurance, he gave an ungracious, "Oh, very well!" that seemed to satisfy her.

Drat the girl, he thought. It would have been so much easier to tell Charles the chit was mooning after him every bit as much as he was mooning after her. But no, she had to go and make it hard on him.

"You know," he said, striving for reason, "it would be much easier—"

❧25❧

Jack's efforts on his brother's behalf were not happy ones.

With the purest of motives he'd run Charles to earth in the library that very evening, where he'd found his brother sitting with a book open on one knee and a contented kitten on the other. Charles's forehead was furrowed, and his eyes were fixed on the opened book as with one finger he stroked the fur of the purring cat.

"Oh," Jack said, walking into the room and enjoying the tableau there, "having a bit of trouble with a translation, brother mine?"

Charles, starting, said, "What?" in a sharp tone that made the viscount raise his brows as he walked forward.

"The book," Jack explained, motioning toward it. "You were frowning so deeply I thought those old Greeks of yours must be giving you quite a go in trying to understand them."

"Oh." Charles snapped the book shut and rose, to Davida's evident consternation. Her meow was loud and accusing, and Charles bent to pick her up, cuddling her in his arms as he bid his brother a curt good night.

"Good night?" Jack's mobile eyebrows rose further. "Charles, it is not yet nine o'clock!"

"Oh." Charles looked toward the quietly ticking grandfather clock in the corner and frowned.

"If I'm interrupting—" Jack began, thinking that this might not be the best time to approach Charles, after all. The fellow seemed in a most abstracted mood.

"No." Charles was speaking in monosyllables tonight. "I wasn't translating."

"Oh." Jack was surprised. "Then what—"

He picked up the book and his surprise grew. "Shakespeare!" he exclaimed.

Charles flushed.

"Sonnets!"

Charles's color deepened. "I wasn't really reading them," he mumbled.

"Ahhhh."

It was an amused sound, and Charles snatched the book from his brother, jamming it back onto the library shelf from which it had come. "And what do you mean by that?" he demanded, his chin jutting out, his posture that of a man more than ready to fight.

Jack, thinking it might be good if he obliged him, just to let the poor fellow work out some of his frustration, remembered Miss Ansley's admonishment that he was not to hurt his brother, and sighed. He supposed she'd think a blackened eye and bruised nose were hurting, although he suspected they would be less painful that what Charles currently seemed to feel.

"So tell me," Jack said, settling himself comfortably on the corner of the large desk that was the centerpiece of the room, one leg swinging, "what were you doing in here, then, holding Shakespeare's sonnets which you were *not* reading?"

Charles's color had begun to fade, but at that his cheeks flamed again, and his eyes smoldered. "Well, if you *must* know," he said, at his most ungracious, "I was thinking."

Jack, fascinated, tried to think of the last time he had known his brother to be ungracious. Barring this visit home, it must have been when Charles was four—three?—and not at all pleased to share his new ball with his older brother.

"About?"

"None of your business!"

Davida, not sure what was causing the belligerent tone of her master, but knowing where her loyalties lay, hissed at Jack. The viscount laughed.

"That's a loyal little lady you have there, Charles!" he said.

"Yes, well . . ." Charles stroked the kitten's head protectively. "At least one lady of my acquaintance is loyal."

"Ahhhh."

It had never before occurred to Charles, but he quite hated the way his brother said ahhhh in that low voice, as if he knew more than anyone wished him to, and certainly more than he should.

"If you say ahhhh one more time, Jack," Carlesworth said, "I swear, I will hit you."

"My, my!" Jack tapped one fingertip gently on the top of the desk. "Such a violent character you've become, dear brother. You, who always advocated the peaceful way through, when possible."

"Oh—" Charles bent down to put the kitten on the floor and straightened, sighing.

It occurred to Jack that Charles was looking tired—had been for days—and some of his amusement left him.

"Have done, Jack," Carlesworth said, easing his long frame back into the large leather chair he'd so recently vacated. One hand went wearily to his head, and he ran his fingers through his hair. "I'm in no mood for your baiting tonight."

"Yes, well—" Jack straightened, suddenly determined to have this business done as quickly as possible. There was no reason for Charles to be looking as if he'd lost his best friend, and for Miss Ansley to be bursting into tears, each alone, when they could both be boringly blissful together. "I'm glad. Because I've not come to bait you."

"Oh?" Charles gave that crooked smiled that had been his since childhood, and ran his hand through his hair yet again. "Well. This must be the first time."

Jack grinned. "I suppose there must be a first time for everything."

"Yes." Charles nodded, leaning his head back and closing his eyes. He really did look dreadfully tired, Jack thought, prompting the viscount to ask if his brother was feeling quite the thing.

"What?" Charles opened his eyes.

"You're looking rather worn, dear boy. Are you well?"

"Well enough."

"A toothache, perhaps?"

Charles looked at his brother in surprise. "I've never had a toothache! You know that!"

"Stomachache, then?" Jack was looking suitably concerned, causing Carlesworth to say impatiently that it was no such thing, and what did his brother want?

The viscount eyed him consideringly. "Heartache, perhaps?" he asked at last. Charles started and frowned heavily.

"I would thank you, Jack, to mind your own business!" Carlesworth said.

The viscount grinned. "I must remember that," he said, "should I ever wish you to thank me!"

"I mean it, Jack! You are being foolish beyond permission."

No, the viscount interrupted, he was not. But even if he was, he couldn't remember it ever being said that he needed his brother's permission for being foolish. Or anything else.

The latter was said so meaningfully that Charles at once fired up, demanding to be told just what he meant by that.

Jack sighed. "Charles," he said, rushing his fences, "I have come to talk with you about Miss Ansley."

"Oh?"

There was a distinct menace in the word, and the viscount curbed with difficulty his inclination to tell his brother not to be such a nodcock. Instead he nodded. "What are your intentions toward her?"

"My—" Charles had gone from angry to surprised. "*My* intentions?" He gave a derisive laugh. "Oh, that's rich, coming from you!"

The viscount's eyebrow rose. "I am pleased to provide you with amusement, dear brother. But you have not answered my question."

"Completely honorable," Charles snapped. "And yours?"

The viscount grinned. It was one of his most devilish grins, and he was gratified to see it had the effect he had expected.

"Jack," Charles said, starting up, "if you so much as—as—" Words failed him, and he took a step toward his brother, his fists clenching and unclenching.

"Down, bantling!" Jack said, not moving from his position on the desk, although he did hold a hand out as if to stay his brother. "You misunderstand me."

"I do?" It was clear Charles did not believe him, and Jack smiled inwardly. If Arabella could see her beloved now, she would have her answer as to how much he cared for her.

"Yes." Jack transferred his attention from Charles's face to his own nails, and gave them his closest attention. "What I am asking you, if you will let me get the words out, is if you care for Miss Ansley."

"Well, of course I do!" Charles said.

Jack slanted him a quick glance. "Do you love her?"

"Love—" Charles took a step back as if he'd been slapped, and stared at his brother.

"Well?"

"No!"

"No?"

"I cannot!" It was clear the answer cost him dearly; the words were almost wrenched from Carlesworth's throat, and Jack's left eyebrow rose again.

"Cannot?" he questioned.

Charles shook his head. "I was asked to instruct her," he said, the words coming out low and rushed, "to help her prepare for London, for a brilliant match, for—for—"

"Well," Jack said, as if considering, "I don't know why that would mean you can't love her."

"Because!" Charles said. "She trusted me—to be her friend! And grandfather, and Lady Hedgwick—"

"But if Arabella loves you—" Jack started. Charles looked at him eagerly.

"Why do you say that?" Carlesworth demanded. "Has she said something to you—something that would lead you to think—"

Watching his brother's eager face, the viscount cursed himself for promising Arabella. "Well, not exactly," he hedged.

Charles's shoulders fell. "All she talks of is her trip to London."

"Maybe that is because she is hoping you will ask her to stay."

Charles eyes lit for a moment, then he shook his head. "No," he said. "That cannot be. It is not logical."

"Charles," the viscount began in exasperation, wondering how someone as intelligent as Charles could be so stupid. When had anyone ever said love was logical, for goodness' sake?? Wanting to put his brother straight, he stopped as Miss Ansley's face rose before his eyes. Drat the girl! If he could just tell his brother the truth, he could clear this up and go back to London. Frankly, young love was driving him to distraction!

"Charles," Jack began again. "Why don't you just ask the chit?"

"Ask her?" His brother was staring at him as if his wits had gone begging, and Jack sighed.

"Ask her if she cares for you. If she would like to marry you."

"Marry me?"

A hideous thought occurred to the viscount. "You do want to marry her, don't you?" he demanded. "You're not considering a carte blanche—" He saw Charles bolt from the chair and said hastily, "No, no! Of course you're not! It's just that—I was so sure—"

"So sure?" Carlesworth said, advancing on his brother purposefully. "So sure of what?"

"So sure you love the girl, of course! You're acting like an idiot, and if it's not love, you'd better call the doctor and have yourself dosed, because it's dashed unpleasant for the rest of us, believe me."

"Thank you," Charles said, hunching a shoulder. "Thank you very much."

Jack put a hand on that shoulder, only to have Charles pull away. "Now listen," the viscount demanded, "do you love the girl or not?"

"Of course not!" Carlesworth said, turning away so his brother could not read the opposite message, clear in his eyes. "She will do much better than me, believe me!"

"Oh. Well." Jack seemed to consider. "Do you mean a title?"

Charles looked up in surprise. "Well—I suppose—"

"And a fortune?"

"She is not a fortune hunter!"

"Of course not," Jack agreed. "But I suppose if one is going to marry for position, one might as well make sure that position carries money with it, don't you think?"

"I hadn't thought of that." The words were cold, and Carlesworth was frowning at his brother again.

"No, I don't suppose you would," the viscount said. "You were never one for such things, Charles. But I imagine Miss Ansley has."

"She is not so mercenary!"

"Charles!" The viscount opened his eyes wide, and held out his hands in protest. "I am not accusing her of being mercenary, merely wise! It is you who insists she wishes to go to London to marry well."

"I—I—" Charles took several hasty steps around the room. "She must," he said at last, the words heavy. "To please her grandmama. And to win the place in society she is born to, and has every right to occupy."

"Yes." The viscount nodded. "I am sure you are right." He watched his brother take his agreement to heart, then said in the blandest voice possible, "So tell me. Do you think she would care to be a countess?"

"A *countess?*" Carlesworth whirled, incredulous, and Jack appeared surprised.

"Yes." Jack nodded. "A countess. I shall be an earl one day, you know."

"*You?*" The disbelief behind that word told the viscount in what regard his brother held him as a potential husband, and caused him to grin crookedly. Charles's eyes narrowed. "You cannot mean it!"

"Why not?" Jack held his surprised look with difficulty.

"You do not wish to marry!"

"Well . . ." He let the word drift off.

"You would not suit!"

One mobile eyebrow rose, and Charles took a hasty step forward.

"She would not have you!"

The viscount grinned. "I do not care to boast, Charles," he said, "but more than one young lady has set her cap at me since I first appeared in town."

Charles waved that away impatiently. It was true, of course, he knew it. Had even admired that about his brother before, but now—when they were talking about *this* young lady . . .

"The two of you are too much alike," Charles said. "It would never work."

"Funny," the viscount mused, "that is what she said."

"*WHAT?*"

Too late Jack realized he had said the words aloud.

"You have discussed marriage with Miss Ansley??"

"Well . . ." The viscount thought. He had discussed Miss Ansley's marriage to Charles. Would that do? He nodded.

"And she sent you to the right-about!" Charles was looking satisfied, and a satisfied Charles would never do.

"Well, not exactly," the viscount said. "We were only discussing marriage in general. I wanted to know where you stood before I decided to have a go at fixing my interest. But if you are sure you do not love the chit—"

"You do not love her either!" Charles was staring at him in patent disbelief, and the viscount grinned.

"But I have the succession to think of, Charles!" he protested. His brother snorted. "You never have before!"

"No." The viscount's face was enigmatic. "But I had never before met Miss Ansley! And it occurs to me that a man might be wise to fix his interest with the girl before she's the toast of London, and all the young bucks are vying for her hand. You have the reputation of a wise man, Charles; tell me—what do *you* think?"

Charles, weighing the possibilities of planting his brother a facer, chose to frown heavily at him instead and quit the room, taking Davida with him.

❧26❧

Jack tried one more time to talk with his brother, but unfortunately it was just after Charles had returned from a ride with Miss Ansley, and Carlesworth was in no mood to listen to the viscount.

Charles had asked Arabella if she was enjoying her drives (which now occurred daily) with his brother, whereupon she brightened and said yes, she found the viscount most droll.

"Droll?" Charles repeated.

"Yes, you know!" Miss Ansley said. "So witty. I enjoy his company immensely!"

"Wit," Charles told her, keeping his tone neutral as he slanted a glance away from his horse and toward her, "is often said to run in our family."

"Oh?" Her head was tilted inquiringly. Charles nodded.

"People are always saying Jack and I—" he began.

Miss Ansley laughed. "Oh, Charles!" she told him. "You are nothing like your brother Jack!"

Mr. Carlesworth had the feeling that was not a compliment, and frowned.

"No," Miss Ansley continued, "if Jack reminds me of anyone, it is my father!"

Charles, knowing how much she valued her father, frowned further, and was—as Miss Ansley pointed out to him—quite uncommunicative for the rest of their ride.

Thus when he encountered his brother in the High Point Hall and Jack tried to talk with him one more time about Miss Ansley, the viscount was met with a curt, "When will you be leaving, Jack?"

Chalmsy opened his eyes wide. "If I were a thin-skinned

189

person, Charles, I would almost think you grow tired of my company,'' he purred.

A forbidding Carlesworth said he would be right.

Jack laughed. ''Then thank goodness I am not a thin-skinned person!''

Carlesworth said he saw no reason to thank goodness or anyone else for that.

Jack grinned, noting his brother's riding crop and jacket. ''Been riding with Miss Ansley, have you, Charles?''

Carlesworth muttered something rude and stomped down the hall, his mood not at all soothed by the sound of his brother's gentle laughter behind him.

Jack was not laughing now, however, as he rode beside the carriage that carried Miss Ansley, her grandmama and his grandfather toward Greenthorpe. The only reason Clorimonde wasn't with them was because Jack, upon learning that Miss Ansley actually intended to take the brute because, she said, the dog would feel badly if she did not, had bribed a footman most handsomely to take the poodle for a long walk in the opposite direction. Immediately.

Thus, when they were finally ready to start—after many delays occasioned by Lady Hedgwick and her granddaughter both disremembering what they had packed, and unpacking several bags to see if what they wanted was there, which Jack could not understand since they were only to be away for one night—Miss Ansley's Sir Rupert was nowhere to be found. She had, at last, been cajoled to leave without him, but only after Jack pointed out that if they weren't on the road soon, Charles was likely to ride up and find them, spoiling her whole plan.

The viscount had declined a seat in the carriage, telling them frankly that he intended to see them to Greenthorpe and then ride for London, having fulfilled his part in their scheme by leaving behind enough incriminating evidence to send Charles hotfooting after them when he returned from tenants' visits and found his brother gone, with his luggage and his manservant. The last two had left for London that morning.

Their grandfather's absence would be explained, should Charles think to ask, by a visit to Lady Southeby; the earl had informed his staff that he was invited for the day, and would not return until well past suppertime.

"But Jack," Lady Hedgwick had protested when she heard his plans, "don't you want to see Charles's face when he realizes it's all a hum?"

No, the viscount told her, he did not. Because before Charles discovered it was all a hum, he might have gone straight for his brother's throat, and his brother was very fond of that throat, thank you.

"Not afraid of a little turnup with Charles, are you, Jack?" his grandfather had joked jovially, causing the viscount to ask if he had paid much attention to his other grandson lately. The earl, thinking back on Carlesworth's demeanor for the past several weeks, pursed his lips and said he thought Jack might have a good idea, after all.

Miss Ansley, who did not want her rescue by Carlesworth to be marred by anything as terrible as fisticuffs, a bloody nose, or broken furniture, agreed.

"We shall not need you, Jack, once we are at Greenthorpe," she informed him airily. "After Charles charges through the door, having ridden *ventre à terre* to my rescue, I shall know he loves me, and I will tell him how you have helped us."

"Oh, yes," the viscount said, his tone dry. "Do that. I am sure he will be most impressed."

Arabella tilted her head to the right as if that position could help her better decipher his meaning. After a moment she smiled. "You shall dance at our wedding, Jack."

"If Charles doesn't break my legs first."

She giggled. "Charles is not a violent man!"

"No. He is an idiot in love."

"He is not an idiot!" Arabella cried. "And oh," she said wistfully, "I do so hope you are right about his being in love! Or I will have made such a cake of myself I shall never be able to face him again!"

"Making a cake of oneself seems to be in vogue these days," the viscount said, handing her into the carriage that would carry her and their respective grandparents to Greenthorpe. "We all seem to be taking part."

Now, as Jack rode beside the carriage, he eyed the clouds gathering menacingly on the horizon. It looked if they might be in for a rare storm, and he supposed it was too much to hope that it would hold off until he had delivered these partners in crime to their destination, and continued on his way.

He was right.

The first huge drops were falling as the carriage lumbered into the Greenthorpe carriage drive, and by the time the ladies had been helped down and hurried into the house, all four of the travelers were soaking wet.

"You can't leave now, Jack," the earl said, placing a hand on his grandson's shoulder as the viscount stood gazing gloomily out at the sheets of windblown rain. "You'd likely catch your death of pneumonia."

"Hmmmm." The viscount rubbed his chin. "Death by Charles, or death by pneumonia. I suppose the former would be quicker. . . ."

The earl chuckled. "Don't worry, lad. You can still be out of here before he arrives. If you can't travel in this weather, neither can he. Charles is the sensible one, remember? Come now, let's get out of these wet things and see what the cook has to offer us for supper. Even if Charles is hot on our trail by now, you can bet he's sitting out the storm in some snug little inn or farmhouse. I would be."

Jack, casting one last look at the rain before following his grandfather upstairs, sighed. A month ago he above everyone would have depended on Charles to be sensible. But now . . .

The viscount really would rather all this had been explained to Charles and all was forgiven before Jack ever saw his brother again.

The rain did not let up during the evening; in fact, it seemed to increase in intensity. Jack continued his restive pacing, so after supper Miss Ansley offered him a game of piquet in the library, while the earl and Lady Hedgwick enjoyed a sociable coze before the fire in the morning room. At first Jack was inclined to refuse, having little faith in the card skills of ladies, but Arabella amused him by putting up her chin and saying, "Afraid?" in a voice guaranteed to goad men of far less spirit than Jack. Acquiescing to her challenge, he soon found she was no inexperienced miss, as he'd expected, but an opponent who chose her cards well and could be depended upon to give him a run for his money. Settling down to the game, they soon were no longer aware of the pounding rain, or the crackling fire, or any other sounds in the house—until the door to the library banged open, causing Arabella to jump violently.

"Charles!" she said, starting up. Her cards fell from her hands as she stared at the tall, drenched, glowering figure in the doorway. A dripping streak flew by Carlesworth and bounded toward Miss Ansley.

"Sir Rupert!" she shrieked. The dog, pausing midway between Arabella and the viscount, gave himself a vigorous shake, liberally splashing them both with the water his coat had absorbed in several hours in the rain.

"Oh, Lord," said the viscount. He, too, laid down his cards, but did not rise.

"Charles, you are all wet!" Miss Ansley said, for once ignoring the poodle as she hurried forward. "You will catch your death, you foolish man! Come close to the fire at once!"

Mr. Carlesworth had endured a trying day. On his way back from a visit to his grandfather's farthest-outlying tenant he had encountered Mr. Wooding, who had asked in the airiest way possible just what required Miss Ansley to travel north with only Jack as her companion.

Charles had given his friend his most freezing stare and told him he was mistaken. Jack was on his way back to London having announced at breakfast that morning that it was a good day for traveling; Miss Ansley, as far as the viscount knew, was safe at home with her grandmama.

"Yes, well . . ." In light of that stare Wooding thought it wise to retract a bit. Perhaps he had been wrong about the face of the lady he saw peeping out from the carriage window. "But it's really hard to mistake Jack, you know, Charles. Especially when he is riding that roan of his, and waves a hand as he rides by!"

Charles's eyes had narrowed, and his face had hardened. "You're sure he wasn't on the London road, and you've mistaken his direction?"

"Not unless they've moved London to Scotland," Mr. Wooding insisted. "I tell you, he was riding north!"

Charles thought. Jack had not really said he was returning to London, just that it was a good day to travel. Charles had assumed . . .

Carlesworth frowned at Mr. Wooding again. "Probably going north to visit some friends before he returns to the city."

Mr. Wooding accepted that without a blink.

"And as to a lady being with him—you are mistaken."

There was such a threat behind the words that Mr. Wooding gulped. Never before had Charles seemed as willing to sport a man's cork as he had been in the past few weeks. Usually the most even-tempered of companions was Charles, but now . . . He nodded. "Sun got in my eyes," he suggested.

"Yes." Charles nodded. "Sun got in your eyes—thought you saw something you didn't."

Mr. Wooding nodded again. "Wouldn't be the first time. Seeing's just like my memory. Sometimes I remember things I didn't know before, either!"

Mr. Wooding had ridden gratefully on then, leaving Charles frowning after him. It was ridiculous, of course. Neither Jack nor Miss Ansley would be so impetuous—

He brought himself up short. Yes, he thought, they would. It was exactly what they would do. Jack knew their grandfather would disapprove. Well, Charles himself had heard the earl warn the viscount to leave Miss Ansley alone. Maybe Arabella, too, thought her grandmama might not quite like it. And during one conversation in the past week Charles had, if brusquely, assured his brother that were Jack to do something foolish, Carlesworth would, of course, in the end stand by him, so maybe Jack had taken that to mean—

Charles slapped his forehead forcefully. Sometimes he could be so stupid!

There was, of course, still the possibility that Wooding was wrong. Wooding was often wrong. Everyone knew that. But . . .

Perhaps, Charles thought, he would just look in at Hedgwick Hall, since he was closest to that establishment, to relieve his mind, and to see how Miss Ansley went on.

At Hedgwick Hall, of course, Carlesworth had been informed that Miss Ansley had driven out not two hours past. Charles had inhaled sharply, and his voice was harsh as he demanded to know if his brother, Viscount Chalmsy, had driven out with Miss Ansley.

Holmsley frowned at him. He was not used to hearing this tone from Mr. Carlesworth. "No," the butler told him precisely. Charles's evident relief was short-lived as the man continued.

"Viscount Chalmsy was on horseback. Miss Ansley was in the carriage."

"And you let her *go*?" Charles shouted.

A proper Holmsley said it was not his place to be stopping Miss Ansley. She had ridden out with the viscount many times before. Many times when—and here he looked down his nose at Charles—*someone else* was too busy to accompany her.

Charles, feeling the butler's words strike home, said, "Lady Hedgwick! I must see Lady Hedgwick."

"Lady Hedgwick," Holmsley said, "is also from home."

Had Mr. Carlesworth asked if Lady Hedgwick was with Miss Ansley, the butler would have told him. But Holmsley was perturbed with Mr. Carlesworth's manner, and saw no reason to be forthcoming.

Charles, who remembered his grandfather had said he was going visiting for the day, assumed their old neighbor was with him, and saw no reason to ask. Instead he swore roundly, shocking Holmsley further, and ran from the house, forgetting to take even his hat, which the butler still held.

He had raced home, exchanging his horse for his team and phaeton, and headed north, oblivious to the sky. He'd driven several miles before he realized he was being followed. Glancing back over his shoulder he'd seen Clorimonde, who'd returned to Hedgwick Hall with the footman by the time Charles arrived, and who'd taken off after this friend for lack of anything better to do. Now the dog labored after Carlesworth's phaeton, his tongue hanging out. It was apparent he was winded.

"Go home!" Charles shouted, and drove on.

He did not look back again until the first drops of rain began to fall. Then he'd seen the poodle, still chasing after him but falling farther and farther behind. The animal's sides were heaving, and Charles swore.

It was not, he thought, something he'd done often before meeting Miss Ansley.

It would be just like the dog to get lost, and just like Miss Ansley to blame him for it.

Swearing again, he hauled his team to a stop and climbed down, waiting for the spent Clorimonde to catch up with him.

"You're as bad as she is," Charles told the dog severely when he limped up. "Always getting into trouble."

A grateful Clorimonde licked his hand.

"Don't think that will make it right," Charles said, bending to lift the dog. He staggered slightly as Clorimonde, unused to such treatment, shifted in his arms, but in a moment the dog got the idea and scrabbled up onto the seat, where he sat grinning down at Charles.

"Oh, certainly," Charles said, springing back into the seat. "You're happy now, aren't you?"

"Woof!" said Clorimonde. He said it a lot. He said it to every carriage they passed, every cow, every tree. He said it every time Charles, who was not fond of the odor of wet dog, pushed him away. The more it rained, Charles found, the chummier the poodle became.

"Don't think I like you," Charles said, trying once again to move Clorimonde over to the opposite side of the seat.

"Woof!" said Clorimonde, snuggling closer.

"Oh, for goodness'—" Charles started, staring in disgust at the wet animal.

"Woof!" said Clorimonde.

Charles shook his head. "Pooh!" he told him. "Pooh! Pooh! Pooh!"

❧27❧

Now Charles stood dripping water onto his grandfather's carpet. He was cold, he was tired, and he was, as Miss Ansley had just pointed out, wet. He was very, very wet.

"Jack," he said, advancing purposefully upon his brother. At that the viscount did rise, and thoughtfully took his place behind the chair he'd been sitting in. Miss Ansley stepped between them, putting her hands on Mr. Carlesworth's chest as if to stop him. Clorimonde shook himself again, and sneezed.

"Charles—" Miss Ansley began. Mr. Carlesworth put her aside.

"Jack," he said again, taking another step forward.

"You really shouldn't have ridden through that rain, you know," his brother told him. "You've probably caught your death of cold."

"No!" Arabella was between them once again, looking beseechingly from one to the other. "Do not say so! It would be my fault!"

Once again Mr. Carlesworth put her firmly aside. "Jack," he said, and took another step. Clorimonde, taking an interest, growled.

The viscount sighed. "I know you would like to blacken my eyes for me, dear boy, but there really is an explanation."

Mr. Carlesworth swung; the viscount deflected the blow by putting out his left arm and backing. "Now, Charles—" Jack began.

Mr. Carlesworth swung again and the viscount, trying to back away, this time fell—over Clorimonde, who was behind him.

"Charles!" shrieked Arabella, getting between the brothers again. "Charles, stop this! If you do not stop this at once, I will not marry you! I will not! Even though I love you to distraction,

197

I will not! You must not knock Jack down just because of me!''

Well, Jack said, as for that—Charles had not knocked him down. It was that confounded dog. Charles could jolly well try, but they'd see just who got knocked down. . . .

The viscount stopped talking when he realized no one was listening to him—not even Clorimonde. Mr. Carlesworth had his eyes fastened on Arabella, who was looking right back at him with her eyes wide and her hands clasped around his arm as if she could prevent his swinging again. The poodle watched with interest.

''*What?*'' Charles said. One hand went to his forehead, as if to see if he had a fever.

Arabella blushed, and let go of his arm.

''What did she say?'' Charles demanded, glaring at Jack. The viscount grinned.

''You mean that nonsense about knocking me down, or the other part, about not marrying you if you did so?''

''Marrying—*me*?'' Charles repeated, as if the words were foreign to him. ''But—she ran off with you—''

''Only because you wouldn't run off with her, dear boy,'' the viscount assured him, as if that made any sense. Charles shook his head, then shook it again.

''I don't quite understand,'' he began, and sneezed.

Clorimonde sneezed in sympathy.

The viscount thoughtfully handed Charles the glass of brandy that recently had been at Jack's right hand, and Miss Ansley dragged him toward the fire.

''Honestly, Charles!'' Arabella scolded as she helped him out of his riding coat and set it to dry before the fire, then pushed Charles into a chair in front of the crackling flames. ''This is not at all like you! To have been riding through that rain—''

''—*ventre à terre*—'' said Jack, sotto voce. Miss Ansley frowned at him.

''—when there was no reason for it! You didn't *really* think I'd be foolish enough to run off with Jack, did you?'' She hooted at the idea. ''Jack!''

''Well,'' said the viscount, with some asperity, ''if you didn't expect him to believe it, you certainly went to a good deal of trouble to make him do so! And put me out no end, I might add!''

Charles was looking from one to the other as if they, or he, had lost their minds. He gulped the brandy and set the glass down with a long exhalation of breath.

"I think," Charles said, "that perhaps if you started at the beginning—" He was interrupted by the entrance of the earl and Lady Hedgwick, who had been drawn by the slamming of the library door, and the loud voices that followed it.

Noticing them, Charles absently rose and made Arabella's grandmama a bow, saying, "Lady Hedgwick," before he returned his attention to Jack.

A moment later Carlesworth really registered the newcomers' presence, and his jaw dropped as his eyes widened.

"Lady Hedgwick!" he said.

She smiled at him.

"Grandfather!"

The earl, too, grinned, and came forward. "I must say, lad," he told Charles proudly, putting a hand on his shoulder, "you made excellent time!"

"But—but—" Charles was stuttering and the viscount took pity on him, pushing him back into the chair by the fire before refilling his brandy glass and pressing that upon him again.

"Yes," Jack said, "as you can see, we are quite well chaperoned. In fact," he sighed, "it is quite a family party."

"But—" Charles said. His eyes focused on Arabella's, who was watching him anxiously.

"I think, Charles," she said, "that you should get out of those wet clothes at once. If your grandfather doesn't mind, I shall go find the housekeeper and see if she will have a room prepared for you."

Mr. Carlesworth delayed her departure by the simple expedient of catching her wrist and refusing to let go. "Arabella—" he said.

"But Charles—you are wet, and cold, and"—she placed one small hand worriedly on his forehead—"you might be coming down with fever."

Charles removed her hand from his forehead by rising. As he stood looking down at her, he was not aware of the amused glances exchanged by those around him; all he saw was Miss Ansley. "Arabella," he said, "when I came in—you said you would not marry me if I struck Jack—"

"As if you could!" said the viscount, then subsided. No one was listening.

"If you wished to marry me—" Carlesworth continued.

Miss Ansley whipped her hands behind her back, breaking his hold, and looked down at her feet.

"I did not say I wished to marry you!" she told him.

"But—" Charles's forehead was furrowed, and the viscount sighed.

"Oh, for goodness' sake, Charles," his brother said, "tell her you love her. That's what the silly chit has been waiting for all along!"

"Jack!" Miss Ansley's cheeks flamed with color, and her eyes shot daggers. The viscount shrugged and rolled his eyes.

"*What?*" It was Mr. Carlesworth again. His eyes, too, were fixed on his brother's face. Jack nodded.

"But of course I love you!" Charles said, tilting Arabella's chin up so he could better see her face. "But I thought—London—a brilliant match—"

"You did not think at all!" Arabella told him, pulling her chin away. "I never said I wanted to make a brilliant match! You just assumed it! And when I told you once that what I wanted most was to love as my mother and father had loved—" She glared at him accusingly. "You said nothing!"

Her eyes fell on her grandmother and the earl, giving her more ammunition. "And all along grandmama and your grandfather have been scheming to throw us together."

"*What?*" Charles's attention turned toward his grandfather and Lady Hedgwick, who had the grace to blush.

"Well, it was plain as a pikestaff, lad, that the two of you cared about each other, even when you were arguing so," the earl said.

"Especially then," Lady Hedgwick amended.

"Especially then." The earl nodded.

"But—" Charles was clearly dazed, and Miss Ansley frowned up at him.

"You still have not said it," she said.

"What?"

"Oh!" Arabella gave an angry flounce and walked away. Once again Charles looked toward his brother for guidance.

"That you love her, dear boy," Jack said. "Really. This grows most wearying of you."

"Oh! Well!" In two steps Charles stood behind Arabella.

When she did not turn he put his arms around her and pulled her against his chest, kissing her soundly, in front of everyone.

"Why—Charles!" Miss Ansley said, surprised.

"I love you, Arabella Ansley."

"Why—Charles!"

He kissed her again.

"Charles!"

And again.

"Charles!"

She became blushingly aware of the grinning faces in the room and pushed away from him. "Charles," she said, looking down at her light green gown that now showed generous patches of dark green, "you are getting me all wet!"

"I ought to toss you out into the rain, you little baggage!" said her love. He looked at his brother, and his brow darkened. "You, too!"

The viscount grinned.

"Charles!" Arabella looked at him reproachfully. "How can you say that, if you love me?"

"Did I say I love you?" Mr. Carlesworth demanded, catching her to him. "I was wrong. I don't." He kissed her soundly. "I dislike you excessively!"

Miss Ansley heard the viscount laugh, and tried to bring her future husband to his senses. "Charles," she whispered, peeping over his shoulder as he picked her up and hugged her to him. "We are not alone."

"I know," Mr. Carlesworth said. "I cannot imagine why they don't leave!"

"Charles!" Miss Ansley was much shocked. "That is no way to talk, when they have all tried so hard to help us."

"They might have helped us more," Mr. Carlesworth said, refusing to loose his hold but turning so that he could survey the others in the room, "if someone had just told me of your sentiments."

"Don't look at me," Jack begged, as he came under his brother's accusing glance. "I wanted to, but—" He shrugged.

"You see, lad," the earl began, "Miss Ansley—well, all of us—wanted to be sure that you loved her because—because—" His grandson's raised eyebrow was having an unnerving effect on the earl, who was never unnerved, and Lady Hedgwick came to the rescue.

"Because you did, Charles, and not because you were told to, or thought it was expected of you, or . . ."

"This," Mr. Carlesworth said, "is the greatest piece of nonsense I have ever heard."

The viscount nodded in agreement.

"But Charles!" Miss Ansley protested. "How can you say so?" She was distracted as he kissed her again, but only momentarily. "When you are so very good about doing what is expected of you! I did not want you to love me for that reason; I wanted you to love me for myself!"

"And is that why you love me, Arabella?" he demanded. "For myself?" He was looking at her sharply, but with such yearning that Miss Ansley thought the warmth within her would expand and fill the room.

"Love you, Charles?" she said, taking his face between her hands, and kissing him gently. "Love you? Whatever makes you think so? Do you say it because I was so desperate I sent the odious Sir Rupert to you in the hope you would speak, or because I study the constellations so we might talk of them, or because I run off with your brother so you will come after us? Are those the actions of a woman in love, Charles?" She kissed him again, seeing the uncertainty leave his face to be replaced by a joy seldom seen there. Watching him, she was able to totally ignore Jack's comment that they seemed to him more the actions of a total twit.

"No. No. They cannot be," she said, drawing back to smile up at her love. "I, too, must dislike you excessively!"

"Arabella!" Charles tightened his hold, and swung her about the room. "Arabella, Arabella, Arabella!"

"Woof!" said Clorimonde, getting into the spirit. "Woof! Woof! Woof!"

"Well," said the viscount, watching them. "Such transports weary me." He listened for a moment. "I believe that the rain is lessening, and I shall be on my way."

His grandfather protested, saying it was late and Jack must stay the night, but the viscount shook his head.

"Stay, Jack," Charles said, coming forward to take his brother's hand. The viscount gave a crooked grin.

"I do believe, Charles," he said, "that it is true what they say. You always have been the clever one."

"What?" Mr. Carlesworth was puzzled, but when the viscount met Miss Ansley's eyes it was clear she understood, for she smiled and raised on tiptoe to kiss Chalmsy's cheek.

"Thank you, Jack," she said.

He grinned. "Thank me for annoying my brother?" he said. "You needn't do that! I've been doing it for years! I am very good at it!"

"Thank you, Jack!" Charles seconded, shaking his brother's hand heartily. The viscount grinned again.

"I shall expect you to name your first son after me," he informed them, and put a careless finger to Miss Ansley's cheek. "And I shall dance at your wedding—whenever it is."

"Soon," Charles said, his eyes shining. Arabella smiled. "Soon."

*"A moving love story...the perfect
mix of tenderness and adventure."*
— Jill Marie Landis, bestselling author of *Jade*

SEA OF DREAMS

Elizabeth DeLancey

*Two hearts on a
journey of desire...*

Norah Paige must leave with her employer
on a six-month voyage across the Atlantic. Parting
with everything she holds dear, Norah boards the ship
and hesitantly embarks on her journey . . .
But the ship is captained by Rob McKenzie,
a man she once knew—and secretly loved. When
Norah steps back into his life, he's seduced by her tenderness and charm. Norah's life is transformed, until
a bitter truth threatens to tear them apart—and put an
end to their love forever . . .

___1-55773-681-2/$4.99

For Visa, MasterCard and American Express orders ($10 minimum) call: 1-800-631-8571

FOR MAIL ORDERS: CHECK BOOK(S). FILL
OUT COUPON. SEND TO:

BERKLEY PUBLISHING GROUP
390 Murray Hill Pkwy., Dept. B
East Rutherford, NJ 07073

NAME_____

ADDRESS_____

CITY_____

STATE_____ZIP_____

PLEASE ALLOW 6 WEEKS FOR DELIVERY.
PRICES ARE SUBJECT TO CHANGE WITHOUT NOTICE.

POSTAGE AND HANDLING:
$1.50 for one book, 50¢ for each ad-
ditional. Do not exceed $4.50.

BOOK TOTAL	$ ____
POSTAGE & HANDLING	$ ____
APPLICABLE SALES TAX (CA, NJ, NY, PA)	$ ____
TOTAL AMOUNT DUE	$ ____

PAYABLE IN US FUNDS.
(No cash orders accepted.)